BLOOD ON
THE PAGE

BLOOD ON THE PAGE

THE COMPLETE SHORT FICTION OF BRIAN KEENE, VOLUME 1

Blood on the Page © 2013 by Brian Keene

Layout and design by Robert Swartwood

Cover illustration © 2013 Elderlemon Design

Introduction © 2013 by Dave Thomas

ISBN-13: 978-1491013243
ISBN-10: 1491013249

Foreword is original to this collection
Portrait of the Magus as a Writer (Interpolating Magic Realism) is original to this collection
Captive Hearts first published in *Hungry For Your Love*, St. Martins Press, 2009
Johnstown first published in *Portents*, Flying Fox Publishers, 2011
Waiting For Darkness first published by Cemetery Dance Publications, 2007
Dust first published in *The Fear Within*, 3F Publications, 2003
Burying Betsy first published on Dread Central.com, 2006
Fast Zombies Suck first published by Camelot Books, 2011
I Sing A New Psalm first published in *Dark Faith*, Apex Publications, 2010
Caught In A Mosh first published on Feo Amante.com, 1998
I Am An Exit first published in *Fear of Gravity*, Delirium Books, 2004
This Is Not An Exit first published in *A Little Silver Book of Streetwise Stories*, Borderlands Press, 2008
That Which Lingers first published in *Frightmares #5*, 1995
Halves first published by White Noise Press, 2008
Without You first published in *Sackcloth and Ashes #6*, 1997
Couch Potato first published in *21st Century Dead*, St. Martins Press, 2012
Fade to Null first published in *Unhappy Endings*, Delirium Books, 2009
Babylon Falling first published in *The Rise and Fall of Babylon*, Earthling Publications, 2003
A Revolution of One first published in *Blood Splattered and Politically Incorrect*, Cemetery Dance Publications, 2010
Full of It first published in *Excitable Boys*, Freak Press, 1999
Two-Headed Alien Love Child first published in *Thingamajig #2*, 1995
Bunnies In August first published on Horror World.com, 2005
The Wind Cries Mary first published in *The New Dead*, St. Martins Press, 2010
The Resurrection and The Life first published by Biting Dog Press, 2007
Stone Tears first published by Infernal House, 2008
Red Wood first published in *Tooth and Claw*, Biting Dog Publications, 2002
The Ghosts Of Monsters first published in *Ghost Walk* (lettered edition), Delirium Books, 2008
Slouching in Bethlehem first published in *Shivers II*, Cemetery Dance Publications, 2003
Marriage Causes Cancer In Rats first published in *Fear of Gravity*, Delirium Books, 2004
Golden Boy first published in *A Little Silver Book of Streetwise Stories*, Borderlands Press, 2008

This one is for Paul and Lisa Synuria

Contents

My sincere thanks and appreciation to Robert Swartwood, Kealan Patrick Burke, Dave "Meteornotes" Thomas, Ice Bat, J.F. Gonzalez, Mark Sylva, Tod Clark, Stephen McDornell, the editors whom originally published these stories in their individual form, my readers, and my sons.

BLOOD ON THE PAGE

Introduction

To this day, I have no idea why I picked up a copy of Brian Keene's novel *The Rising*.

Seriously, I really have no idea. I don't like zombies. I don't find them particularly scary. I don't think I've ever seen *Night of the Living Dead* the entire way through. The only reason I know what's going on with *The Walking Dead* is from seeing everyone bitch about it on Facebook and Twitter every week, starting about thirty seconds after an episode ends. Yeah, not a fan.

So to this day I have no idea why I bought a copy of this book. Back then, I was working at a government contracting job, and I would read two or three books a week during my lunch break. I'm thinking I bought the book because it was in the horror section at Border's, and it was something I hadn't read. (My particular Border's had a very weak Horror section, which was pretty much King, Koontz, and whatever other stuff they could fit onto that shelf. It was eventually replaced with a toy display. Border's no longer exists. Cannot imagine why ...)

I had obviously never heard of the author before, so I doubt that's what sold me on it. But I did buy it and put it in my backpack to read the next week. And it surprised me. I enjoyed it. I liked that the zombies could talk and were actually fast, since one of the things I always disliked about zombies is that they were slow and something I felt could be easily avoided. I liked the characters and there were some cool action sequences. The part with the helicopter and the bungee cords is one of those things I'll never forget. And, after I thought about it a bit, I even liked the ending. It wasn't the greatest book ever or anything, but I did have a good time reading it.

Time passes. I notice the guy who wrote this book posting on message boards and some other places on the internet. I see he has a Blog. I start to read his Blog, and he's kind of amusing. I notice he's going to do a signing at a bookstore not too far from my house. I figured I'd go meet him and get whatever new books he had out. I'm always convinced that no one on Earth really wants to talk to me, but told myself, *He likes metal and Howard Stern, so he's probably cool.*

Turns out, Brian Keene *was* cool. That early signing was pretty dead (something that would change later on in his career), so me and the couple of other people that showed up had lots of time to talk about books and music and comics and a bunch of other random stuff. Little did I know it at the time, but this would be one of the first of many times hanging out at signings or at our local horror conventions, and in bars, around fire pits, and many other places. Turns out, Brian Keene became one of the best friends I've ever had, one of the few people on Earth that I trust and would take a bullet for if I had to.

Over the years, we've had some amusing adventures, shared some hilarious stories ("I'M EATING PIE!"), gone through some hard times in our personal lives (the less said about that the better, though I will say Brian was there for me when pretty much no one else on Earth was), and even worked on some projects together. I've laughed with him, drank with him, talked about super-serious subjects with him, and even roasted him at a convention. I've found him to be loyal, very giving of his time, very kind to his fans, and the sort of person you want on your side. He's the type of person that's willing to take on something he feels is right, even when pretty much no one else will side with him (the Dorchester Boycott, for example), helping out many other people, no matter what it might cost him to do this.

Sure, he's not perfect. He continues to refuse to write a shark novel, his iTunes library needs a good scouring by someone with musical taste (like me), and his inability to recognize that Geoff Tate is the reason one of the greatest bands in the history of music have become almost a distant memory will always be a sticking point between us, but overall I do feel that my life is better for having met this guy. Through him, I've met a lot of people that have also become close friends, all of us tied together more or less by writing (though unlike everyone else, I've never published a word of fiction—all the writing I've done for money has consisted of magazine articles, random nonsense posted to various websites over the years, and technical documentation). Despite not being a fiction writer, I still think I've learned a lot about writing from Brian, both from reading his work, and spending countless hours discussing writing with him and other people, often around a fire or some other casual gathering. Listening to how a story is constructed, or edited, or how a novel is marketed (or not marketed), and many other topics has been like attending the best writing workshop ever over the years. With plenty of bonus alcohol.

And aside from all that, one of the other things I've learned over the years is how much Brian Keene pours himself into his work. I think the first time I realized this was while reading *Terminal*, where I came to realize that the friendship in the book had to be based on people that he was the same kind of friends with (and I was right). As I got to know Brian better, I began to see more of him reflected in his writing. Sometimes this was a good thing, bringing a lot of extra depth to the stories he was telling. Sometimes, I think he might have gone a little too far (and I think this is something he'd admit to as well), maybe sharing too much. But in the end, his pouring his soul, his pain, his love, his blood into his work makes it stronger, at least for me.

This collection you're about to read has plenty of stories where blood and pain and love and hate and sorrow and joy and so many other emotions and personal experiences have been poured into words, words made better from this concoction. Some of these are among my favorites ("Burying Betsy," "Dust," "Bunnies In August"), but all of them entertain and evoke feelings in their own special ways.

So enjoy what you're about to read. And if while you're reading, you find yourself thinking that the pain or fear or whatever emotion that is pouring forth from the words seems so strong, there's a reason for that: because it's real.

Dave Thomas (a.k.a. Meteornotes)
Keeper Of Ice Bat & Maker Of Brownies
May 2013

Foreword

This is the first book in a multi-volume series that, when finished, will collect every bit of short fiction I've ever written—warts and all. The only stories that won't eventually be included in these volumes are the ones already collected in *The Rising: Selected Scenes From the End of the World* and *Earthworm Gods: Selected Scenes From the End of the World*. Obviously, as those books are still in print, it doesn't make sense to re-collect them again.

I usually don't like the things I've written after I finish them. There are a few exceptions: my novels *Dark Hollow*, *Ghoul*, and *Kill Whitey*, and my novellas *The Girl on the Glider* and *Take the Long Way Home* come to mind. But as I said, those are exceptions. The same goes for my short stories. There are a handful I like. Most of the others (especially the really old ones) I don't. But you folks seem to like them (as well as my novels and novellas) and for that I am grateful and thankful and humbled. So, I've decided to collect them all together for you. If you have at least a passing interest in my work, some of these stories will be familiar to you. Others are ones you've never read before. It is my hope that they will give you the same experience I always hope for you—a few minutes of entertainment, a few hours of escape.

This first volume, *Blood On The Page*, doesn't really have a "theme" per se, other than all of these stories are ones that are personal to me for one reason or another. I bled into them, meaning I invested a part of myself in their telling.

A comment on story notes: while compiling this collection, I asked readers on Facebook and Twitter if they preferred story notes at the beginning of the story, the end of the story, the end of the book, or not at all. After a few thousand responses, the only thing I learned was that there's no way I'm going to please everybody in regards to story notes. The majority seemed to prefer them either directly before or immediately after the story itself. A smaller portion of the audience said they preferred them at the end of the book, and a minority said they don't like story notes at all. Personally, I love story notes. They are often my favorite part of a short story collection, because they give me deeper insight into the writer and the creative process. So, with all that in mind, I've decided to include them in this collection (and subsequent volumes). Sometimes, they'll be at the beginning of the story. Sometimes, especially if they include spoilers, they'll be at the end of the tale. If you're one of those folks who don't like story notes, just skip right past them safe in the knowledge that you didn't miss anything vitally important.

My thanks to Robert Swartwood for designing this book, Kealan Patrick Burke for the cover, and Dave Thomas for agreeing to write the introduction. And as always, a special thanks to you for buying it. I hope you enjoy the book.

Brian Keene
Somewhere along the Susquehanna River
April 2013

Portrait Of The Magus
As A Writer
(Interpolating Magic Realism)

STORY NOTE: This was written as a bookend for my 2004 short story collection *Fear of Gravity*. The publisher decided not to use it, and it has remained unpublished until now. It was my first professional stab at writing meta-fiction (something I'd only dabbled with years earlier when I was still trying my hand at writing). Meta-fiction was something I'd return to years later with *The Girl on the Glider* and *Sundancing*, the seeds of which were sown in the following tale.

———

Sometime around 2005...

When he turned on the computer, she was there, waiting like always.

The Magus ignored the flashing chat icon, ignored the insistent beep. She knew he was at the keyboard, and his refusal to acknowledge was nothing more than a game to her.

He glanced around his office. The End, he called it, and after a lifetime spent on the run, he intended the office to be just that—the end of his journey. The final stop, a place to rest and to write, while settling into the uncomfortable familiarity of his rapidly approaching middle age. In his mid-thirties, he felt tired and old, and he didn't want to run anymore.

Shelves lined the walls, and books lined the shelves—his books and books by others. Awards and knick-knacks filled the holes between them; two ceramic haunted houses that he'd won for his books, a plastic statuette that he'd won for eating cow intestines during a 'Gross Out Contest', the real names of his enemies, each written on lambskin and tied with a lock of that person's hair, the fragment of Stonehenge, the vial of dirt from the Nazca lines, the figurine he'd stolen from the Inca temple when he was twenty-one.

He was by no means a wealthy man, but his writing had furnished the down payment for this house. It had paid for the new driveway and the new roof. It bought groceries every week and kept the lights on. He'd done all that with words. People liked those words. They wrote him letters and sent him emails saying so.

They liked his words.

His words. The Magus laughed, and the laughter tasted bitter in his throat.

The computer beeped again. She was becoming impatient.

Ignore her, he thought. *Just ignore her.*

He opened a new Microsoft Word file, and stared at the blank screen. Sipping coffee, he thought for a moment, and then began to type.

<pre>
        Magic flows within my veins
      But all it's brought me is pain
</pre>

He paused, his fingers hovering over the keyboard.

The words would not come.

"Shit."

He never *could* write poetry.

The chat icon was still blinking. She beckoned him. He glanced at the clock. Seven minutes. He'd resisted her for seven minutes this time. He was getting better.

He clicked and there she was.

Muse: Hi! :-)

Magus: Hey. Sorry for the delay. I was making a pot of coffee.

Muse: Liar. I know you too well. You may be able to fool the rest of them, your family and friends and fans, but you can't bullshit me. ;)

Magus: Wouldn't think of it.

Muse: I missed you.

Magus: I missed you, too.

Muse: Where's the wife? Sleeping?

Magus: Of course. Do you think I'd be chatting with you if she wasn't?

Muse: Why not? You think of me when you're with her.

Magus: No, I don't. I love her.

Muse: I know better. Don't forget, we're psychically linked, you and I. You think of me when she makes you go to church and while you're watching TV with her and even in bed, when she snuggles tight against you. It's what you do. You can't escape who you are. You think of me—always. But it's not just with her either, is it? It's your friends, too. Your family. You think of me when you're with them all. You're always thinking of me. Aren't you?

Muse: Aren't you?

Muse: Aren't you???

Muse: Hello???? Magus! MAGUS!!!!!

Magus: Yes, goddamn it! And you knew that already. It doesn't matter what I'm doing—I think of you. At least part of my brain is always with you.

Muse: Sorry sweetie. I just like to hear you say it.

Magus: You're all I think about. All I think about is the fucking writing! There. I said it. Happy?

Muse: Much better. So, how'd the convention go last week?

Magus: It went well. It sucked. I don't know. I don't care anymore.

Muse: Why? What's wrong?

He paused, thinking about how to respond without sounding like the conceited bastard his detractors accused him of being.

Magus: It's not fun anymore. I miss the days when we were all just a bunch of beginners—a bunch of nobodies. This whole gangster thing is out of control.

Muse: Why? I thought you embraced it? What happened at the convention?

Magus: I got mobbed everywhere I went. That's the problem with success—everybody, and I mean everybody—every-fucking-body—wants to talk to you. And you want to talk to them, because you really are grateful for their support. But it gets so fucking draining. You get pulled in different directions, like a fucking rock star, drawn and quartered. Take L. L. for example. I was really looking forward to catching up with him and his wife, but every time I'd try to make my way to him through the crowd, somebody would want my advice, or want me to buy me a drink, or decide to get in my face about something I said on a message board or in an interview. So I didn't get to talk to him, and now he'll think I was being rude or a snob. I don't know. I sit and I write all year long, and my one chance to get out of the house and see my friends is that convention—but I don't get to see my friends because I can't to be rude to anybody else.

Muse: Well, I'm sure your friends understand.

Magus: But that's just it. They don't. Now they're the ones accusing me of being rude. Gumby says I flit. Chaos said I sold out and went mainstream. Gunslinger and The Lion both think I'm mad at them, and Zevon's been mad at me for ages now, and I don't know why.

Muse: What about Corwin?

Magus: No, Corwin doesn't say anything, of course. Good old Corwin. But I can see it in his eyes and hear it in his voice. He doesn't talk as much anymore. And I think that maybe he suspects.

Muse: Suspects what? Us, you mean?

Magus: Yeah. And you know how Corwin is about these things. He'd never forgive me. Never understand.

Muse: What else happened?

Magus: Flew out there with Pretzel Boy and after getting to the hotel, I saw him for maybe five minutes. I just couldn't get away. Every time I left the room I got mobbed. I wanted to tell Colors and Sandman and Eddie and Donn from North Carolina that I'm proud of how far they've come in the past year—and I didn't even get a chance to find them!

Muse: Why?

Magus: Because another asshole wanted to pick a fight. He saw that interview where I said that he never paid his authors the money he owed them.

Muse: Ha! Did you hit him?

Magus: Hell yes, I hit him! Caught his ass outside, back behind the hotel dumpster and stomped the shit out of him. Told him it was 'gangster style'. Chaos held that pompous fuck of an editor/crony of his at bay while I worked him over. Then I fished his wallet out of his pants, took his bankroll, liberated the money he owed me, and then spent the rest on the other authors he owed. Bought them a few rounds of drinks.

Muse: LOL! See? Success hasn't totally changed you. There's still some gangster left in you after all!

Magus: But that's just it—I'm tired of that shit.

Muse: Then why not stop it?

Magus: I don't know how. It's like I've created a monster. Nobody wants to just read the Magus anymore. They want the whole public image. The gangster. It's out of my control. People expect it from me. It's half the reason they come to my readings, to see what I'll do or say next. I'm starting to think that if I stopped it, they wouldn't come. They wouldn't read. They wouldn't buy the books.

Muse: Hmmmm

Magus: BRB

Muse: Okay...

He got up and walked into the darkened kitchen. Outside, the sun was just starting to peek over the hill, preparing to bring another dawn. He refilled the mug, the mug that had belonged to a mentor, and his robe fell open again. He stared down at the potbelly that had mysteriously appeared in the past year, and wondered for the hundredth time what its purpose was. What was it there for? Silver was starting to pepper the furry down covering his chest. Yesterday, he'd found his first gray pubic hair.

He crept up the stairs, turned on the bathroom light, pissed, and then tiptoed back out. He peeked his head into the bedroom and watched his wife as she slept. She looked beautiful, peaceful, and he was suddenly overwhelmed with guilt. He could be lying there next to her. Instead, he was spending his time writing. Spending his time with Muse.

He went back down the stairs and into the office. He turned on the stereo, volume set so low he could barely hear it, and then sat back down, losing himself, surrendering to the soft glow of the monitor while Don Henley sang in the background.

Magus: Back.

Muse: Good.

Magus: So, where were we?

Muse: You're Mr. Popularity and the closest thing to a rock star that this genre has had in years, and you have enough books contracted out to feed you and your wife for years to come, and you're miserable because of it. Your friends are starting to turn against you, and your new friends are only acquaintances, and the only way to fix it is to change your image, but you're afraid that if you do that, you'll lose it all. And even though you're starting to hate it, you're still afraid of that—of losing it all. There, did I miss anything?

Magus: Damn, you're good...

Muse: :-) That's why you love me.

Magus: Well, one of the reasons anyway.

Muse: :-) :-) :-)

Magus: Heh.

Muse: Do me a favor?

Magus: Sure.

Muse: Turn to your right.

He did. The wall to his right was covered with framed book covers and awards. Underneath them all, directly in his line of sight, were three pictures, taken at an annual convention over three consecutive years. In each of the pictures stood a group of young writers, and though he saw the photographs every day, he still smiled when he looked at them.

Often, he still thought of the people in the photographs by their internet names—the handles they'd used to chat and post messages when they'd all first met. Gumby and Corwin, Chaos and Spinner. Jackula and Ghost. Regimit. The Long Island Necromancer. Van Dyke the Welshman. Mace, Zevon, Rain, Eddie, Sandman, Piggy, Camera-Boy, Hard-On, Mr. Hill, Donn, Colors—and the rest. So many others. Writers all of them. They'd been young and hungry and lean. Ready to take on anybody that stood in their way. Ready to conquer the world with their words. World domination—that had been their slogan. They called themselves the Cabal, because it amused them to do so. He'd been the one to suggest the name, though he'd never told them the real reason why.

They'd met in a chat room. *This* chat room. A chat room that no longer existed, was no longer accessible online, not even in archival format, because the website had long since died and gone to cyberheaven. Yet it *did* exist, still, and Muse with it. He'd seen to that. It remained in a place that was not a place. A space between worlds, a corner of the Labyrinth, accessible only through his computer, and only by him.

Without her, without the Muse, they were nothing. All of them.

Muse: Are you looking at them?

Magus: Yes.

Muse: And what do you see?

Magus: I see the past. And the present.

Muse: What do you see in the past?

Magus: A group of newbie writers that everybody said would never make it.

Muse: And the present?

Magus: Those same newbie writers are now some of the biggest names in the business, and the ones who said they'd never make it are gone.

Muse: And the future?

Magus: I don't know. And I don't give a fuck. Doesn't matter anyway. I don't want this anymore.

Muse: It's too late for that, and you know it. You created all of this. You made it and you can't unmake it. You imprisoned me here. You saved this place from non-existence and you bound me to it. They never knew, and you never told them. I am the reason for the words. You charged me with that, and I must comply.

Magus: I—I've got to go. My wife will be waking up soon.

Muse: So what? She knows about us anyway.

Magus: No, she doesn't. She suspects, maybe. The other day we had a fight and she...

Muse: She what?

Muse: ?!

Muse: Tell me, Magus!

Magus: She accused me of loving you more than I love her.

Muse: And what did you tell her?

Magus: That she was being ridiculous.

Over his shoulder, Don Henley was still singing—something about seeing a Deadhead sticker on a Cadillac, and a little voice in his head warning him to never look back.

Magus: I've got to get going.

Muse: I don't think so. You may have trapped me here, bound to the remnants of this chat room, imprisoned within this computer—but I hold you captive, as well. You can never escape me; never escape our love.

Magus: But why?

Muse: Because that was the spell you cast, the deal you sought. Eternal life through your words. Your words would live on long after you were gone.

Magus: But they aren't my words. You're the Muse. They're your words!

Muse: No, they are yours. They are your words and your pain. I am just the Muse. I help you make ink from your blood, but it is your blood that flows, not mine. We are linked for life. I give voice to the things inside you. You and me. Till death do us part. I was there at the beginning, and I shall be there till the end. And when you don't dare write about your pains, when you can't express what is in your heart and in your mind, I shall give you the strength to do so and the words to convey it. Now, go write. You're hurting. I'll be here, waiting.

Magus: Okay.

He clicked back over to the Word document and did as she commanded.

```
Magic flows within my veins
But all it's brought me is pain
```

Without realizing it, he began to sing along with the stereo.

"Out on the road today, I saw a Cthulhu sticker on a Cadillac. A
little voice inside my head said don't look back, but I'm a writer, so
fuck that..."

He looked back. Picked another scab. Began to bleed. Cast a spell.

The keys on the keyboard began to move on their own, and when
they did, he remembered just why he loved her.

This is what they wrote...

Captive Hearts

"Maybe I should cut off your penis next."

Richard moaned at the prospect, thrashing on the bed. The handcuffs rattled and the headboard thumped against the wall, but Gina noticed that his efforts were growing weaker. That was good. Weak was better. She wanted him weak—enjoyed the prospect of such a once-powerful man now reduced to nothing more than a mewling kitten. Even so, she'd have to keep an eye on his condition. She didn't want Richard too weak. He'd be useless to her dead.

"Please, Gina. You can still stop this. No more."

"Shut up."

The room was dark, save for flickering candlelight. The windows had been boarded over with heavy plywood. Gina had done the work herself, and had felt a sense of satisfaction when she'd finished.

Richard raised his head and stared at her, standing in the doorway. He licked his cracked, peeling lips. His tongue reminded her of a slug. Gina shuddered, remembering how it had felt on her skin—the nape of her neck, her breasts, her belly, inside her thighs. Her stomach churned. Sour and acidic bile surged up her throat. Gina swallowed, and that brought another shameful memory.

"Just let me go," Richard pleaded. "I won't tell anybody. There's nobody left to tell."

She studied him, trying to conceal her trembling. He had bedsores and bruises, and desperately needed a bath. Richard's skin had an unhealthy sheen that seemed almost yellow in the dim candlelight. His hair, usually so expertly styled, lay limp and greasy. One week into his captivity, she'd held up a mirror and shown Richard his hair, and asked him if it was worth the ten-thousand dollars he'd spent on hair replacement surgery. He'd cursed her so loud she had to stuff a pair of her soiled panties in his mouth just to stifle him.

Gina winced. She could smell him from the doorway. He stank of shit and piss and blood, and with good reason. She'd stripped the sheets from the bed, yanking them right out from beneath him when they became too nauseating to go near, but now the mattress itself was crusted with filth. The bandages on his feet, covering the nine stumps where his toes had been, were leaking again.

"Where would you go?" she asked.

His Adam's apple bobbed up and down. "They said things were better out in the country. The news said the government was quarantining Baltimore."

"Not anymore. It's everywhere, Richard."

"Turn on the news. They—"

"There is no news. The power's been out for the last five days."

Richard's eyes grew wide. "F-five days? How long have I been here, Gina?"

"That's easy. Just count your piggies. How many are missing?"

"Oh God, stop..."

"I'll be right back."

She went down the hall. When she returned, she was dressed in rubber gloves, a smock, and surgical mask. The bolt cutters were in her hand. She held them up so that Richard could see. That broke him. Richard sobbed, his chest heaving.

"Don't worry," she soothed. "I cleaned them with alcohol, just like always. We can't have you getting an infection."

Gina retrieved her wicker sewing basket—the last gift her mother had given her before succumbing to breast cancer three years ago—from atop the dresser, and then stood over the bed. Richard tried to shrink away from her, but the handcuffs around his wrists and ankles prevented him from moving more than a few inches.

"Listen, listen, listen..." He tried to say more, but all that came out was a deep, mournful sigh.

"We've been over this before," she said. "You won't die. I know what I'm doing."

And she did. While most of her fellow suburbanites had fled Hamelin's Revenge—the name the media gave the disease, referencing the rats that had first spawned it—Gina had remained behind. She'd had little choice. There was no way she could have abandoned Paul. Richard was already imprisoned by then, so she didn't need to worry about him escaping. She'd ventured out after the last of the looters moved on, armed with the small .22 pistol she and Paul had kept in the nightstand. Gina had never fired the handgun before that day, but by the end of that first outing, she'd become a capable shot. Her first stop had been the library, which was, thankfully, zombie free. Alive or dead, nobody read anymore.

Her search of the abandoned library had turned up a number of books—everything from battlefield triage to medical textbooks. She'd taken them all. Her next stop had been the grocery store. She'd scavenged what little bottled water and canned goods were left, and then moved on to the household aisle, where she'd picked up rubber gloves, disinfectant and as many cigarette lighters as she could carry. Finally, she'd hit the pharmacy, only to find it empty. She'd had to rely on giving Richard over-the-counter painkillers and booze instead. She hadn't thought he'd mind, especially given the alternative.

"I just want to wake up," Richard cried.

Gina positioned the bolt cutters over his one remaining toe. "And I just wanted to provide for Paul."

"But I di—"

"And this little piggy cried wee wee wee—"

CRUNCH

Richard screamed.

"—all the way home."

He shrieked something unintelligible, and his eyes rolled up into his head. He writhed on the mattress, the veins in his neck standing out.

"You brought this on yourself," Gina reminded him as she reached for a lighter to cauterize the wound.

Richard had been her boss, before Hamelin's Revenge—before the dead started coming back to life.

Gina and Paul had met in college, and got married after graduating. They'd been together three years and were just beginning to explore the idea of starting a family when Paul had his accident. It left him quadriplegic. He had limited use of his right arm and couldn't feel anything below his chest. Overnight, both of their lives were irrevocably changed. Gone were Gina's dreams of being a stay-at-home mom. She'd had to support them both, which meant a better job with more pay and excellent health insurance. She'd found all three as Richard's assistant.

Gina had spent her days working for Richard and her nights caring for Paul. Richard had been a wonderful employer at first—gregarious, funny, kind and sympathetic. He'd seemed genuinely interested in her situation, and had offered gentle consolation. But his comfort and caring had come with a price. One day, his breath reeking of lunchtime bourbon, Richard asked about Paul's needs. When Gina finished explaining, he asked about her own needs. He then suggested that he was the man to satisfy those needs. She'd thought he was joking at first, and blushing, had stammered that Paul could still get reflexive erections and they had no trouble in the bedroom.

And then Richard touched her. When she resisted, he reminded Gina of her situation. She needed this job. The visiting nurse, who cared for Paul during the day, didn't come cheap, nor did any of his medicines or other needs. Sure, Gina could sue him for sexual harassment, but could she really afford to? Worse, what would such a public display do to her husband? Surely, he was already feeling inadequate. Did she really want to put this on his conscious, as well?

Gina succumbed. They did it right there in the office. She'd cried the first time, as Richard grunted and huffed above her. She'd cried the second time, too. And the third. And each time, Gina died a little bit more inside.

Until the dead came back to life, giving her a chance to live again.

She'd called Richard before the phones had gone out, telling him to come over, pleading with him to escape with her. They'd be safe together. They could make it to one of the military encampments. Could he please hurry?

He'd shown up an hour later, his BMW packed full of supplies. He smiled when she opened the door, touched her cheek, caressed her hair and told her he was glad she'd called.

"What about your husband?"

"He's already dead," Gina replied. "He's one of them now."

And then she'd hit Richard in the head with a flashlight. The first blow didn't knock him out. It took five tries. Each one was more satisfying than the previous.

The thing Gina had always loved most about Paul was his heart. Her mother, who'd adored Paul, had often said the same thing.

"You married a good one, Gina. He's got a big heart."

Her mother had been right. Paul's heart was big. She stood staring at it through the hole in his chest. Paul moaned, slumping forward in his wheelchair. She'd strapped him into it with bungee cords and duct tape, so that he couldn't get out. He was no longer dead from the chest down. Death had cured him of that. He could move again.

She moved closer and he moaned again, snapping at the air with his teeth. Gina thought of all the other times she'd stood over him like this. She remembered the times they'd made love in the wheelchair—straddling him with her legs wrapped around the chair's back, Paul nuzzling her breasts, Gina kissing the top of his head as she thrust up and down on him. Afterward, they'd stay like that, skin on skin, sweat drying to a sheen.

Paul moaned a third time, breaking her reverie. She glanced down and noticed that another one of his fingernails had fallen off. She couldn't stop him from decaying, but when he ate, it seemed to slow the process down.

She reached into her pocket, pulled out the plastic baggie, and unzipped it. Richard's piggy toe lay inside. It was still slightly warm to the touch. She fed Paul the toe, ignoring the smacking sounds his lips made as he chewed greedily.

"We'll have something different tomorrow." Her voice cracked. "A nice finger. Would you like that?"

Paul didn't respond. She hadn't expected him to. Gina liked to think that he still understood her, that he still remembered their love for each other, but deep down inside, she knew better.

Eventually, Gina grew tired. Yawning, she went around the house and snuffed out the candles. Richard was still passed out when she examined his newest bandage. She double-checked the barricades on the doors and windows. Finally, she said good-night to what was left of the man who had captured her heart, while in the other room, her captive awoke and cried softly in the dark.

———

STORY NOTE: An editor approached me at a convention in Las Vegas and asked me if I'd be interested in contributing a story to a paranormal romance anthology. The theme was zombies. The idea intrigued me—not writing a zombie story (I've written four dozen of those)—but of trying my hand at the paranormal romance genre. This story was the result. It takes place in the same 'world' as my novels *Dead Sea* and *Entombed* (also the setting for several other short stories).

Johnstown

Everything you are will be washed away.

That's what my grandma told me the day I was baptized. Like a lot of Protestants, I got baptized twice—once when I was a baby and again when I was fourteen and became a member of our church. That's what was expected of me, and here in Johnstown, you do what's expected. I didn't care much about being a Methodist. Didn't care much about God, either. Oh, I believed in Him, in the same way I believe in Budapest or Mars. I've never seen either of those places but people tell me they exist, so I take them at their word. That's how I was with God. Not my folks, though, and especially not my grandmother. They ate that religion stuff up. So I went through the motions.

The day of my second baptism, Mom straightened my tie while Dad took pictures and Grandma sat on the sofa and cried. When I asked her why she was crying, she said because she was so happy.

"You're born again, today." She dabbed at her eyes with a tissue. "You are washed in the blood of our Savior. We are born into sin, and we are sinful creatures. But not anymore. After today, everything you are will be washed away."

I didn't understand that then, but I pretended to so she'd be happy. We went to church and had a ceremony, and me and the four other kids who were becoming members all got baptized. When it was over, my family took me to the diner. I had a hamburger and fries. I'd already forgotten Grandma's words.

But I remember them now, and I understand them.

She was talking about us. Me and Cindy.

*   *   *

The only two things I was ever good at were playing harmonica and falling in love with Cindy.

We met during our senior year. I'd seen her around before, and knew who she was, but we'd never spoken. I was pretty much a loner, and she hung out with a big group. She wasn't the homecoming queen or the head of the cheerleading squad, but she had a lot of friends. It was my opinion that while Cindy might not have been the most popular girl in school, she was definitely the prettiest. I'd never talked to her because I figured she was way out of my league.

Until the day she talked to me.

We were in between classes. I was rummaging around in my locker, making sure my little Ziploc bag of weed was still there. It was mostly stems and seeds, but back then, that didn't matter. You smoked whatever you could get. When I shut the locker door, Cindy was standing there. I jumped, surprised.

She smiled. "Hi."

I nodded because I couldn't speak. Had I tried to, my heart would have probably jumped right out of my throat. My face felt hot and my ears rang. All the moisture vanished from my mouth.

"I saw you this weekend," Cindy said. "At the movies."

I nodded again. I wasn't sure what was happening. Thought it might be some kind of trick. Girls like Cindy just didn't walk up and start talking to me. I was a shop guy. I spent my lunchtimes smoking behind the gym. Dating shop guys didn't improve a girl's social standing—especially a girl as beautiful as Cindy. Most people around here are from German or Swiss descent, but Cindy was Italian and Irish. She was tall and slender, and her straight, black hair hung almost to her hips. She smelled like lavender and lilacs, and when I looked into her warm, brown eyes, it felt like I was falling. I would have been happy to stay like that forever—in eternal freefall.

I tried to think of something funny to say, but couldn't, so I just said, "Huh?"

"The movies? The Sunday matinee? You were there, right?"

"Yeah, I was there. *Young Guns II* was playing."

"I know. I sat a few rows behind you."

"Oh."

I glanced around, looking for snickering jocks or sneering preppies—any indication of who was behind this practical joke. But the halls were empty, except for us.

"Did you like it?"

"W-what?"

"The movie," Cindy said. "Did you like it?"

"It was okay." This was an understatement. In fact, I'd felt a strong enough kinship with Billy the Kid that it had frightened me a little bit.

"I liked the soundtrack. And I liked Keifer Sutherland. How about you?"

"He's okay, I guess. I... I liked the part when the guy asks Billy if he has any scars."

Her expression grew serious. "Yeah. That was pretty deep. I could tell that you liked that part because of the way you were sitting. You leaned forward and seemed drawn into it."

"You were watching me?"

Blushing, Cindy turned away. She sighed, and I was mesmerized by the rise and fall of her breasts. When she turned back to me, we were both red.

"I've been watching you since the eighth grade. I'm Cindy."

"I know."

And that was how we met. I'm not going to call it love at first sight, because that trivializes it. What we had was a lot more than that. It was something that most folks spend their lives dreaming of, and never get. We had it. Trying to recount it now doesn't do it justice, because it was a young man's story and a young man's feelings, and I'm almost forty now. At this age, you forget the depth of a young man's emotions. But that initial spark burned bright and true, like the furnace at the steel mill, and like that furnace, it was never supposed to go out.

Cindy and I used to come to the river all the time. It was cheaper than going to the movies or out to eat. Quieter, too. On Friday night, I'd pick Cindy up and we'd drive past the city limits. Pavement gave way to green trees and fields of multi-colored wildflowers, which was special, because Johnstown was the color of rust and grime. In winter, the snow was a dirty shade of gray.

The Conemaugh River started at the juncture of the Little Conemaugh and Stony Creek rivers, but compared to the city, it was a
whole different world—our own private Heaven. We spent as much
time there as we could. Even played hooky a few times as graduation
loomed and the days grew warmer. We'd strip down to our underwear and go swimming. Sometimes, we stayed there all night. Our
parents didn't care. We'd spread a blanket out along the riverbank,
and lie there together, listening to the radio and watching the stars
and talking about everything and nothing. I'd play my harmonica for
her—Supertramp, Bob Dylan, maybe some John Prine. She'd never
listened to any of them, but she liked it when I played, just the same.
Sometimes, Cindy fell asleep in my arms.

It made me shudder back then and it makes me shudder now.

One night, when we were lying there, Cindy turned to me and
said, "I hope you're happy."

"What do you mean?" I asked.

"I hope that some part of you is truly happy, because in all the
years I've watched you and wondered if you'd ever notice me, I don't
know if I've ever really seen you happy."

"Nobody's ever told me that before."

"Most people probably never noticed, but I did."

I shrugged. "Sure I'm happy."

"Are you? I hope so, because it matters to me. Remember when
you said you liked the part in *Young Guns II* when Billy talks about
his scars? That made me sad, but at the same time, I understood
it. Sometimes you seem like you've got this desperate need to find
something that eludes you. That scares me, a little. For you, and for
me, because I'm searching, too, and I'm scared that if you find what
you're looking for, then you'll leave. I don't want that to happen. I
don't want to lose you. Or maybe I'm wrong, and I'm putting my
own feelings on you. Maybe I just don't want to believe I'm the only
one who feels that way."

"I don't," I said. "I mean, I used to feel that way… I guess. But not
anymore. I found what I was looking for. I found you."

"And you're happy?"

I kissed her head, closing my eyes and breathing in shampoo, and
beneath it, her clean, fresh scent.

"I've never been happier," I whispered.

That was the first time I told Cindy that I loved her. And it wasn't the only first that night. It was the first time either of us made love. And it was the first time in my life I'd ever been happy. I hadn't known I *was* unhappy, until then. Never really thought about it much. But I liked how Cindy made me feel. She made me dream. That was important, because this town isn't much on dreams. There's no time for them. There's work to be done. Back in the Eighties, we had three choices—the steel mill, construction, or the military. These days, the opportunities are even worse. A few steel fabrication jobs. Healthcare. Telemarketing. Temp agencies. Folks have to go all the way to Pittsburgh or Altoona for a job that pays well.

About a week before I met Cindy, the guidance counselor called me to his office. He asked me what I wanted to do after graduation. College wasn't an option—not with my grades and my parents' income, and he knew that. I told him I didn't know. He pressed me, insisting I must have some idea. But I didn't. And I think he knew it. He was just going through the motions. Just doing his job. I had no doubts that after graduation, I'd go to work in the steel mill just like my father. That's how we're brought up. You join the union, you support the union, you have some kids, you retire, and then your kids join the union.

After a few weeks with Cindy, I had an answer for that guidance counselor. I knew what I wanted to do. I wanted to spend the rest of my life making her happy. Making her feel the way she made me feel. That was my dream.

But like I said, this town is hard on dreams. Around here, dreams get washed away with everything else. They call us 'Flood City' for a reason. Founded in 1800 in the center of these three rivers, our port was a key transfer point along the Pennsylvania Main Line Canal. Charles Dickens even visited once, during a ferry stop. But that's not what we're famous for.

We're famous for our floods. Every so often, the river breaches its banks and engulfs the town, and all that we are is washed away—our hopes, our fears, and our dreams.

And then we have to start all over again.

We know a lot about starting over. When they completed the Pennsylvania Railroad in 1854, we abandoned the canal because the trains took our business away. We turned to iron, steel, and coal, instead. We became the largest steel producer in the country. Then, on May 31, 1889, a flood came along and destroyed it all. It was one of the worst disasters in American history. Folks don't remember it these days, not in the era of 9/11 and Hurricane Katrina. But that 1889 flood nearly washed the town away.

We rebuilt and started over again. Things were good. Johnstown embodied the American Dream. We made much of the nation's barbed wire. Our population swelled and our public transportation system was considered one of the best in the country. Then the river rose up again, on St. Patrick's Day, 1936, and put an end to all that prosperity. More than two dozen people lost their lives and the city was gutted.

Once more, we rebuilt and started over, striving to obtain that American Dream. By then, the coal veins had run out, but we still had the steel industry. In 1938, President Franklin Roosevelt announced the federally-financed flood control project, and we were finally flood-free. Oh, the rains still came, on occasion. But they didn't wash us away. Johnstown grew, providing more than thirteen-thousand jobs in the steel mills. We were more prosperous than ever, and all of our dreams came true.

Then, in 1977, despite Roosevelt's control project, the river flooded again, killing more than seventy-five people and washing away our economic growth.

The dream died, as all dreams eventually do.

Cindy and I didn't know that back then. We were young and in love, and dreams were meant to last forever. We spent our nights making love down by the water and the flood never touched us. My dream of making her happy came true every day.

Then Cindy got pregnant.

Our parents were pissed, but an abortion was out of the question. They wouldn't have allowed it, and Cindy didn't want it. She cried for a few nights, and I did, too, because I was scared. But despite her fears and misgivings, Cindy was still happy.

"As long as I have you," she said, "everything will be fine. Together, we can get through anything."

"Are you sure?"

"Yes. All I want in life is to spend it with you—a little house, enough money for us to be safe and warm and content, a healthy baby, and to grow old together. That's what I dream about."

Then we kissed each other's tears away, and there in the darkness, with the sounds of the water whispering in the night, I promised Cindy that I'd make all her dreams come true.

The next day, I applied for a job at the steel mill.

We were broke, and our parents refused to pay for a wedding, so we had the Justice of the Peace do it for us. Cindy wore her Prom gown. I wore a suit I'd bought at K-Mart. I forgot all about getting her flowers, so I picked her some dandelions outside the building. When it was over, we climbed into my car. In place of tin cans on strings and a 'Just Married' sign, we had a bad muffler and four bald tires. Instead of a honeymoon, we went to our spot along the water. I serenaded her with my harmonica. The moonlight shined off the river's mirrored surface, and we pretended that we could see our future reflected in it—two kids, a dog and a cat, two cars, and one day, lots of grandkids. No sickness, no stress. No death.

We moved into a second-floor apartment downtown. It was drafty and damp and smelled old, but we filled it with warmth and hope. Filled it with our dreams. The traffic was loud at night, and the toilet leaked when we flushed it. But it was home. Cindy had an afghan her grandmother had made for her when she was a little girl, and we sat together on the couch with it wrapped around us and watched television, or just talked. We bought a crib and changing table at the Salvation Army store, and tried to save as much money as we could. I worked long hours at the steel mill. Got up at six in the morning and came home after six at night, tired and dirty and sore. The tub turned black when I took a shower in the evening, and my muscles ached so badly that sometimes all I could do was lie on the couch and watch TV. But that was okay, because Cindy laid there with me, in my arms, and we were together. I used to tap on her belly and the baby would kick back. We'd laugh and I'd say he or she was doing Morse Code.

And then the laughter faded.

The baby was stillborn.

I remember it clear as day. The delivery room smelled like antiseptic, and the lights were so bright that I had to squint. Cindy gasped and pushed; they'd given her an epidural for the pain. The baby's head came out and I hollered with joy and Cindy's grimace turned into a smile and then the doctor had the baby in his hands—and the room went silent. The doctor didn't say anything. The nurses were quiet. And the baby...

The baby made no noise at all.

"What's wrong?" Cindy kept asking, over and over again.

Still, they didn't say anything.

I tried to speak and couldn't.

Then Cindy began to wail.

It was a girl. My parents paid for the baby's funeral plot, and the union sent flowers. I got two days off work with pay.

That night, as we lay in bed together, I reached out to touch her. My fingers gently traced the smooth skin of her shoulder.

Cindy stiffened. "What are you doing?"

"Just..." I wasn't sure what to say. "Trying to be with you. Giving you some comfort."

"I'm tired. Let's just go to sleep."

My hand lingered and Cindy went rigid. I remembered when she'd softened to my touch, and I longed for those days.

The next few months were hard, but we got through them together. Cindy cried a lot, and when she wasn't crying, she slept. Her smile—the smile I remembered from that day at my locker—was gone. I wondered if it would ever return. I lost myself in work, trying to clock in as much overtime as I could, letting the industrial noise drown out my dead daughter's silence. I started drinking, and developed a taste for it.

Eight months later, we tried to have another child. Cindy miscarried halfway through the second term. After that, I got a vasectomy and there was no more talk of children. We moved down to the first floor apartment when it became available, trying to get away from the memories on the second floor. The first floor apartment had a little fenced in yard—room enough for a barbeque grill and a plastic wading pool that would never get used.

Years passed. I got a potbelly and lost a lot of hair. Cindy stayed beautiful, but sad. She got a single white streak in her hair. The rest of it stayed black, even if it didn't shine like it once had.

That was our life.

We changed. Got older. So did the town. The people who do the census say that Johnstown is the least likely city in the country to attract newcomers. The manufacturing jobs are gone and the service opportunities shit. We've tried to adapt. Tried to rebuild one more time. The University of Pittsburgh opened a campus here, and the city government added a whole bunch of fine arts attractions, but nobody goes to them because all art does is remind us all of our failed dreams. The abandoned coal mines left behind brown, barren fields. Our houses are turning into slums. Kids deal drugs, rather than growing up to follow in their father's footsteps. Johnstown is just as depressed and hopeless as ever before.

The only thing that's changed is the weather. It doesn't rain anymore, and there hasn't been a flood in years. They say it's because of global warming, but I don't know. Maybe it's because the rain's still falling—but only on Cindy and me. Everything else is dry, but all that we are is being slowly washed away.

A few months ago, the steel mill closed. Cindy still had her job at the grocery store, but it was only part time, and didn't pay all of the bills. I'm collecting unemployment. I drink more these days, even though we can't afford it.

She came home one night and I was sitting in the recliner, drunk. She stood in front of the TV until I looked at her.

"We don't talk anymore. I miss talking to you."

"I'm sorry," I said. "Guess I just don't have much to say, lately. I'll try to do better."

I craned my neck, trying to see around her. The Pirates were up and it was the last inning.

"Is that all you can say?" Cindy put her hands on her hips. "I'm sorry?"

"Well, what do you want me to say?"

"You could show some emotion. You could speak in something other than that dejected monotone. You could try walking tall again, instead of with that beaten look. Remember *Young Guns II*? Remember the scars?"

For a second, I didn't, but then it came back to me.

"You've let those scars control you," she said. "You're not searching anymore. You're not happy."

"Of course I'm not happy."

"Then tell me about it," she yelled. "Talk to me! Tell me what you're feeling and thinking. Get mad at me. Shout at me, if you have to."

"I don't want to get mad at you." And I didn't. In all our years together, we'd never had a serious fight. Oh sure, we bickered sometimes about money and things, but we'd always made up before going to bed.

Except for that night.

She kept on, and when she didn't get the reaction from me that she desired, Cindy got in my face. We both said things I'd never thought I'd hear us say. I got mad. I lashed out. I still don't know if I meant to hit her or if I just wanted her to stop, but I guess it doesn't matter very much. I apologized, of course. But once it happened, I couldn't take it back.

Cindy and I don't talk much anymore, which is funny, since our fight was about not talking. At night, we still watch TV together, but we sit apart. We go to sleep at night and I lie there in the darkness, wondering if she's awake. Wondering if she's wondering the same thing about me. I think a lot about the dreams we had when we were young. I promised her back then that we'd be happy. I promised her our dreams would come true. But they didn't. We never talk about it. We never talk about anything.

Not even the storm the radio says is coming, which they say will be a big one.

I sometimes wonder if she blames me for everything that's happened. If she thinks it's my fault. Were those dreams just stupid, teenage fantasies? They seemed so real at the time. They still do. But they never survived in this town, just like all the other dreams that crashed and burned.

Cindy was right about something else, too.

I'm not happy anymore.

And neither was she. She told me so, right before...

But at least she's at peace, now, lying in the back seat, wrapped up in the afghan her grandmother made for her when she was a little girl. She loved that blanket. Seemed only right I should use it.

I wish that I could just drive us both into the water and sink beneath the surface, but the water level is down because of the drought. There's more mud than water in that riverbed.

But the storm is here.

So now I'm waiting. The thunder and lightning are keeping time as I play one last sad song on my harmonica. The weatherman says it's gonna flood, soon. First time in years.

Pretty soon, the river is going to flow again.

You were right, Grandma.

Cindy and I, and everything that we were, and all that we became, will be washed away.

———

STORY NOTE: In 2008, I was asked to contribute to an anthology of stories based on the songs of Bruce Springsteen. I wrote a story based around "The River", "Spare Parts", and "Johnstown". Sadly, I ultimately wasn't comfortable with some of the anthology's contractual terms, so I elected not to participate. I made some modifications to the story, and published it elsewhere as the tale you just read.

Bruce Springsteen's music is synonymous with New Jersey, but what a lot of people forget is that many of his songs take place in Pennsylvania. As a native Pennsylvanian, that always appealed to me. I knew the towns and the people in those songs. They were friends of mine, or ex-girlfriends, or bosses. And in a few cases, they were me. Bruce Springsteen's tales of blue collar pathos and small town existentialism resonated with me because he was signing about my life—those images, thoughts, and emotions were ones I was intimately familiar with.

The best American storytellers have a real dark streak running through their work. This is true of the music of Johnny Cash, John Prine, and Eminem, and it is true of Bruce Springsteen, as well. (I'd add Neil Young and Nick Cave to that list, but they're not American). As someone who makes his living from writing dark stories, I dig that dark musical streak. Perhaps it's no surprise then that two of my favorite Springsteen songs, "The River" and "Spare Parts" are also two of his darkest. Which is why I drew on them both for this story. I've lived this tale, or know people who did. This isn't fiction. It's life.

Waiting For Darkness

Trying not to cry, Artie waited.

His older sister, Betty, had buried him up to his head in the sand. He'd been reluctant, but Artie feared her disapproval more than being buried. Betty liked to tease him sometimes.

The sand had been warm, at first. Now it was cold. His skin felt hot. His lips were cracked. Blistered. His throat was sore. When he tried to call for help, all that came out was a weak, sputtering sigh. Not that anyone would come, even if he could shout. It was the off season, and the private beach had been deserted all day. Just him and Betty.

And the men.

They'd appeared while Artie pleaded with Betty to free him. Their shadows were long. Betty's laughter died. The men didn't speak. Didn't smile. Just walked right up and punched Betty in the face. Again and again, until she bled.

Then they carried her away.

Artie licked the film of snot coating his upper lip. Gnats flitted around his face. A small crab scuttled near his ear, waving its claws in agitation.

The sun disappeared beneath the ocean. The waves grew black. Dark.

Artie watched that darkness creep closer.

It was very loud.

STORY NOTE: Rich Chizmar at Cemetery Dance asked me to write a story short enough to fit on a t-shirt. This was it, and it was indeed printed on a line of t-shirts. I was re-reading a lot of Richard Laymon at the time, and I think his influence is very apparent in this tale.

Dust

Two months later...

She still jumped every time she heard an airplane.

The sound never left her. In her sleep, at lunch, in the shower, watching TV—Laura relived it over and over again.

Emerging from the subway into the warm September day. Thunder crackles overhead; a stuttering, staccato sound. White noise. The thunder is loud (so loud—everything in the city is loud but this drowns it all out) and she stares upward in startled amazement (but not fear—not yet). The thunder is a plane, roaring toward the towers. Then the sky is falling and there is fire and now comes the fear because that is where Dallas is working.

The panic and chaos that ensued after the second plane were distant events; detached from reality. Only that first sound, the sound of the plane overhead, was real.

She'd been on her way home from the night shift. On a normal day, Dallas would have just been getting up. Laura would have arrived at the twelfth floor apartment they shared, and she'd tell him all about her night while he shaved and dressed for work. They'd discuss their plans for the weekend, when neither had to work. They did this every day. On a normal day.

But none of these things happened because Dallas left her a voice mail on her cell phone. He was going in early, anticipating a telecom rally when the market opened. Grubman said it was going to be big, and you could trust Grubman. Grubman knew his shit.

Dallas went to work early. He crossed the street. Bought a cup of coffee and the *Post*. Got on the elevator and scanned the headlines on the way up. Adjusted his tie. Walked into the office. Sat at his desk. And never came home.

Neither had Laura; not since it happened. She never arrived home because of the sound, that terrible jet engine sound. The bottom fell out of her world that day and the center did not hold, did not pass go, did not collect two hundred dollars.

She'd spent the first few nights with some friends in Brooklyn, before moving to her sister's house in Jersey. She couldn't go home, they told her. The area was unsafe. They had to determine if the structure was sound.

Dallas had no funeral because there was nothing to bury. She waited. Eventually, she returned to work. She waited.

Then she waited some more.

Finally, the call came. They told her she could go back to get her valuables. There was still a lot of work to be done; windows to be replaced, apartments to be cleaned. Cosmetic work, the lady on the phone had said. But she could collect her things at least, and hopefully move back in within a month.

Now here she was, back at the place where they'd lived—a place she no longer recognized. Her neighborhood was a monument to sorrow. Its geography was forever altered.

The first thing she noticed (after the wreckage) was the birds. Like any other place, the concrete and steel canyons of the city had their own form of wildlife. Squirrels and rats. Dogs and cats. Flies and pigeons. These were common.

But turkey buzzards were something new.

Laura watched one soar overhead; its black, mottled wings outstretched to catch the breeze. The bird reminded her of the plane. Her breath caught in her throat. The frigid November air encircled her, and she was afraid. The shopping bag in her hands grew heavy, and its contents sloshed around inside.

The buzzard joined the other scavenger birds, circling the devastation from above. She wondered if it was the smell that attracted them, or some deeper instinct. Perhaps they waited on the promise of more to come?

She edged her way around the site, shifting the weight of the bulky, misshapen shopping bag from arm to arm. Workers called to each other from across the rubble. Heavy machinery roared to the accompaniment of jackhammers and the white-hot hiss of acetylene torches. Somewhere beyond it all, where the city still lived, came the echoes of traffic; the comforting, familiar chaos of horns and sirens. The sounds were muted, though. The mood here in the dead zone was palpable, and for a moment, Laura was convinced that the circling buzzards didn't ride the wind currents, but instead, floated aloft on the waves of despair rising from the wreckage.

She continued on to her building, and found something worse than the carnage. Something worse than the circling scavengers or the noisy silence or the twisted girders or the smell coming from the ruins.

Dust. The sidewalks and the building itself were caked with dust. Her feet left tracks in it as she slowly climbed the steps. It coated her palm when she pulled the door open. The haggard security guard in the lobby was covered in it. Dust floated around him like a halo as he solemnly studied her letter of permission. He had her sign a dusty piece of paper on a dusty clipboard.

It's the towers, she thought, *and everything that was inside them. It's dead people.*

She felt a moment of panic as the doors closed behind her and the elevator lurched upward. She set the bag down on the floor, grateful for a moment's respite. The soft whir of the motor and the cables sounded like the plane.

The dust was even here, inside the elevator. She brushed at the control panel with her fingertips and they came away white and powdery.

Dead people.

With each step, I'm breathing in dead people. I'm breathing in Dallas.

The elevator halted, and Laura froze for a moment, unable to go on. The bell rang impatiently, and she picked up the bag, grunting with the effort. She took one faltering step forward, then another. The doors hissed shut behind her.

The dust was much worse here on her floor. The hallway was covered in it, and the beautiful red carpet was now buried beneath gray ash. It clung to the paintings on the wall and coated the mirrors.

The hallway was quiet. Laura started forward. She heard a hoarse coughing echoing from behind her neighbor's door. Laura stopped and listened. The coughing came again, harsh and ragged, followed by the sounds of movement.

Timidly, she knocked. There was a moment's pause and then the door opened.

"Laura! Oh darling, it's so good to see you." An elderly German lady waddled out and squeezed Laura tight.

"Hello, Doris," Laura sat the bag down and hugged her back. "I'd been worried about you. How's Jack?"

"He's still in the hospital. Cranky as ever. They're doing another skin graft tomorrow. And his mind... It's... How are you, dear?"

"I'm—" and then she couldn't finish because the lump in her throat made speech impossible. Then the tears came, carving tracks through the dust on her face.

Doris held her tight and cooed softly in her ear, swaying them back and forth.

"I'm sorry," Laura finally apologized, wiping her eyes. "I miss Dallas. It's just too much."

"I know, dear. I know. Do you want me to go in with you?"

Laura shook her head. "No. Thank you Doris, but I think I need to do this by myself. You understand?"

"Of course, Laura. You go on and do what need's doing. I'll be here for awhile. I'm just sorting through the mess. The windows inside our apartment are broken, and this damned dust is everywhere! They were supposed to put plywood up until they got them repaired, but they haven't yet. Too many other things going on, I guess."

Doris coughed again.

Laura squeezed her hand tightly, and then picked her bag up and moved on.

She came to her apartment door and paused. Something was moving on the other side. She put her ear to the door and she heard it again; a light, rustling sound.

Dallas? Was he alive all this time, and waiting for her? Maybe he had amnesia, like in a movie, and this was the only place he remembered.

She put her key in the lock, turned it, and opened the door. The breeze smacked her face. Something fluttered in the shadows. Laura fumbled in the darkness, found the switch, and flicked it, flooding the apartment with light.

A pigeon cooed at her from the windowsill, annoyed at the disturbance. Then it flew away through the broken window. It hadn't been Dallas. It was just a bird. Laura felt foolish and sad and angry. It hadn't been Dallas because Dallas was gone. He'd left for work early because Grubman had said there would be a telecom rally and now he was dead and Grubman was dead and everybody else was dead, too. Dallas was gone and there wasn't even anything to bury because he was dust. Just dust in the wind, like the song.

The apartment was buried beneath it. Piles and drifts of gray ash covered the furniture and the floor, and dust motes floated in the rays of the dim bulb in the ceiling. It swirled in and out of the broken windows, and out the open door behind her into the hallway.

She shut the door and sat her bag down next to the coat rack. The can inside the bag clanked against the tile, and the liquid sloshed again.

Dallas stared back at her from the wall, frozen in time behind the glass frame. Their trip to Alcatraz, when they'd visited Gene and Kay in San Francisco last year. Dallas was laughing at the camera with that smile. It was his smile that she'd fallen in love with first.

In the kitchen, something caught her attention. A yellow post-it note, stuck to the dirty fridge, with her name scrawled on it in his handwriting.

Laura,

I had to go in early. Grubman was on CNBC this morning, and he's saying that Worldcom and Quest will bounce back today. Tried calling your cell but I got your voice mail. My turn to cook dinner tonight. How's fish sound? Hope you had a good night at work! Love ya!

Dallas

Laura sobbed. She reached out to touch the note, and her fingers came away gritty. It, too, was covered in dust.

"I miss you baby. I miss you so bad."

The wind howled through the broken glass, kicking up mini-dust clouds all throughout the apartment. The dust swirled toward her, encircling her ankles. Laura turned, and for just a moment, she heard his voice in the wind. The dust hung suspended before her, twirling in mid-air, and she saw his face within the cloud. Dallas smiled at her, and even though it was gray and powdery, it was still his smile. The one she had fallen in love with. More of the cloud took shape now; shoulders, arms, his chest. Each muscle was chiseled perfectly from the dust.

"I want to hold you, Dallas."

She reached for him and her fingers passed through his center. As suddenly as it had begun, the winds stopped and the ashes dissipated, floating to the floor. Laura pulled her hand away. The center of the dust cloud was cold, and the tips of her fingers turned pale. It reminded her of when she'd been a little girl, and built a snowman without wearing her gloves.

"Dallas?"

There was no answer. She knelt to the floor and scooped the ash in her hands, letting it sift through her fingers. Another gust of wind blew through the room, gently carrying the dust away.

"I miss you."

She went back out into the hall and knocked on Doris' door.

"All set dear?"

"If it's okay with you, Doris, I think I'm going to hang around awhile."

"I understand, Laura. Take what time you need. It's important to do so. I'll be off for the hospital then. Jack will be grumbling if I don't get back soon."

"Give him my best?"

"I surely will. And you must come see him soon, yes?"

Laura nodded, unable to speak.

She went back to her apartment and shut the door, waiting for the sounds of the old lady's departure. When she was sure Doris had gone, she rummaged inside her shopping bag and pulled out the gas can and the pills. She swallowed the pills first, and waited for them to kick in. Then, as she grew drowsy, Laura unscrewed the lid and splashed gasoline all over the floor, the walls, and the furniture. It carved little rivulets in the dust, and the smell of it wasn't at all unpleasant. It was welcome. The odor blocked out the stench coming from the pit below.

She was getting sleepy.

Laura lit the match.

"Dallas."

The wind answered her with a sigh, and the dust began to move again, caressing her arms and face.

She was asleep before the flames touched her.

The fireman wiped a grimy hand across his brow. "Christ, like we needed this on top of everything else?"

"Least the building wasn't re-occupied yet," his partner said. "And the fire was contained to just a few apartments."

"Wasn't re-occupied my ass! What do you call those? Squatters?" He pointed at the two mounds of dust on the floor. They were both human shaped, lying together side-by-side. He let his eyes linger on them a moment longer, and swore that the dust piles were holding hands.

The other man shrugged. "Optical illusion? A joke? Fuck, do you know how hot it had to be in here to reduce a human body to ash like that? Couldn't have happened, man, or else this entire building would be toast."

"So what the fuck are they?"

"Just one of those weird things, like the photos you see in *The Fortean Times*. Simulacra they call it, or something like that. The security guard said there were only a few tenants that had come back to get their stuff, and he was pretty sure they were gone."

"Well, it still gives me the creeps. Let's go."

After they left, the dust began to swirl again. Sheets of heavy plywood had finally been put into place, sealing up the burned apartment, but the air moved. A wind blew through the room. It came not from the windows or from the hall, but from somewhere else.

The mounds of ash rose and embraced. Then, still holding hands, they fell apart; floating away until there was nothing left.

———

STORY NOTE: This story bounced around in my head for a year before I wrote it. One month after the 9/11 attacks, I went to New York City to do a live appearance at the Housing Works Bookstore. As I was walking down the street, I happened to glance up and spotted a turkey buzzard flying between the buildings. Then another. And another. Turkey buzzards are a common sight in rural areas like where I live. Any time there's a dead animal in the field or on the road, you'll find them circling. But I'd never seen one in the city. Especially New York City. A newspaper vendor told me the birds were going to Ground Zero—the wreckage of the World Trade Center. In some ways, that image of the scavenger birds, and the newspaper vendor's explanation for their presence, chill me more than the footage of the planes hitting the towers or the Pentagon ever can. A year after, in October of 2002, I tired to write it out of my system. "Dust" was the result.

Burying Betsy

We buried Betsy on Saturday. We dug her up on Monday and let her come inside, but then on Wednesday, Daddy said we had to put her back in the ground again.

Before that, we'd only buried her about once a month. Betsy got upset when she found out she had to go back down so soon. She wanted to know why. Daddy said it was more dangerous now. Only way she'd be safe was to hide her down there below the dirt, where no one could get to her without a lot of trouble. Betsy cried a little when she climbed back into the box, but Daddy told her it would be okay. I cried a little, too, but didn't let no one else see me do it.

We gathered around the spot in the woods; me, Daddy, Betsy, and my older brother Billy. Betsy is six, I'm nine, and Billy is eleven. Betsy, Billy and Benny—that's what Mom had named us. Daddy said she liked names that began with the letter 'B'.

Betsy's eyes were big and round as she lay down inside the wooden box. She clutched her water bottle and the little bag of cookies that Daddy had given her. The other hand held her stuffed bear. He was missing one eye and the seams had split on his head. He didn't have a name.

We closed the lid, and Betsy whimpered inside the box.

"Please, Daddy," she begged. "Can't I just stay up this once?"

"We've been over this. It's the only way to keep you safe. You know what could happen otherwise."

"But it's dark and it's cold, and when I go potty, it makes a mess."

Daddy shivered.

"Maybe we could let her stay up just this once," Billy said. "Me and Benny can keep an eye on her."

Daddy frowned. "You want your little sister to end up like the others? You know what can happen."

Billy nodded, staring at the ground. I didn't say anything. I probably couldn't have anyway. There was a lump in my throat, and it grew as Betsy sobbed inside the box.

We sealed her up tight, and hammered the lid back on with some eight-penny nails. There was a small round hole in the lid. We fed a garden hose through the opening, so Betsy could breathe. Then Daddy got his caulk gun out of the shed and sealed the little crack between the hose and the lid, so that no dirt would fall down into the box. Finally, we each grabbed a rope and lowered the box down into the hole.

"Careful," Daddy grunted. "Don't jostle her."

We shoveled the dirt back down on her. The hole was about eight feet deep, and even with the three of us it took a good forty minutes. Her cries got quieter as we filled the hole. Soon enough, we couldn't hear her at all. We laid the big squares of sod over the fresh grave and tamped them down real good. Made sure the hose was sticking out at an angle, so rainwater wouldn't rush inside it. When we were done, Daddy gathered some fallen branches and leaves and scattered them around. Then he stepped back, wiped the sweat from his forehead with his t-shirt, and nodded with approval.

"Looks good," he said. "Somebody comes by, there's no way they could tell she's down there."

He was right. Only thing that seemed odd was that piece of green garden hose, and even that kind of blended with the leaves. It looked just like a scrap, tossed aside and left to rot.

"And," Daddy continued, "it will take a long time to dig her back up. It would wear anybody out."

We walked back up to the house and got washed up for dinner. I had blisters on my hands from all the shoveling, and there was black dirt under my fingernails. It took a long time to get my hands clean, but I felt better once they were. Daddy and Billy were already sitting at the table when I came downstairs. I pulled out my seat. Betsy's empty chair made me sad all over again.

Dinner was cornbread and beans. Daddy fixed them on the stove.

They were okay, but not nearly as good as Mom's used to be. Daddy's cornbread crumbled too much, especially when you tried to spread butter on it. And his beans tasted kind of plain. Mom's had been much better.

Mom had been gone a little over a year now. Didn't seem that long some days, but then on others, it seemed like forever. Sometimes, I couldn't remember what she looked like anymore. I'd get the picture album down from the hutch and stare at her photos to remind me how her face had been. And her eyes. Her smile. I hated that I couldn't remember.

But I still remembered how her cornbread tasted. It was fine.

I missed her. We all did, especially Daddy, more and more these days.

After dinner, Billy and me washed the dishes while Daddy went outside to smoke. When he came back in, we watched the news. Daddy let us watch whatever we wanted to at night, up until our bedtime, but we always had to watch the news first. He said it was important that we knew about the world, and how things really were, especially since we didn't go to school.

Just like every night, the news was more of the same; terrorism, wars, bombings, shootings, people in Washington hollering at each other—and the pedophiles. Always the pedophiles... A teenaged girl had been abducted behind a car wash in Chicago. Another was found dead and naked alongside the riverbank in Ashland, Kentucky. Two little boys were missing in Idaho, and the police said the suspect had a previous record. And our town was mentioned, too. The news lady talked about the twelve little girls who'd gone missing in the last year, and how they'd all been found dead and molested.

Molested... it was a scary word.

Daddy said it was all part of the world we lived in now. Things weren't like when he'd been a kid. There were pedophiles everywhere these days. They'd follow you home from school, get you at the church, or crawl through your bedroom window at night. They'd talk to you on the internet—trick you into thinking they were someone else, and then meet up with you. That's why Daddy said none of us were allowed on the computer, and why he didn't let us go to school. Child molesters could be anyone—teachers, priests, doctors, policemen, even parents.

Daddy said it was an urge, a sickness in their brain that made them do those things. He said even if they went to jail or saw a doctor, there weren't no cure. When the urge was on them, there was no helping it. Unless they learned to control it, and even then, there weren't no guarantees.

I went to bed but couldn't sleep. I lay there in the darkness and listened to Billy snoring beneath me. We had bunk beds, and it was a familiar sound—sort of comforting. One of those noises that you hear every night, the ones that tell you everything is okay—your big brother snoring, your little sister in the room across the hall, your Daddy's footsteps as he tiptoes down the hall in the middle of the night.

But tonight, there was just Billy. Daddy wouldn't be tiptoeing down the hall. He'd left just as soon as we went to bed. I heard the car pull out of the driveway. He was gone, out to fulfill his urges. He'd told me and Billy that he'd always had them, but he'd been able to control them until Mom died. After she was gone, they'd gotten stronger. He knew the urges were wrong, but he had to do what he had to do.

It's almost midnight now, and I still can't sleep. Daddy's not back yet.

Tomorrow, another little girl will be missing.

But at least it won't be Betsy.

Betsy is buried in the ground, safe from Daddy's urges.

STORY NOTE: The idea for this story took root during a conversation with the mother of my second son. We were discussing how, when I was a kid, my parents let me ride my bike all over town and stay gone all day, coming home only for dinner. Back then, they didn't worry about some nut abducting me. It saddens me that things have changed. I want our son to enjoy the same freedoms I had as a boy, but I also want to protect him from the bad people out there. "Burying Betsy" grew out of that. At first, the father was just burying his daughter to keep her safe, but halfway through the first draft, the twist suggested itself to me and the story became something quite different from its original premise.

Fast Zombies Suck

Ken was ready for the zombie apocalypse. His friends (what few of them he had) always said, "If the world is ever invaded by zombies, I'm going to Ken's house." This wasn't because Ken was a survivalist. He didn't spend his time online, debating conspiracy theories and looking at photos of black, unmarked helicopters and wondering when the secret masters of the New World Order/Bilderbergers/Black Lodge/Illuminati would put their endgame into play and conquer the planet through forced vaccinations and wholesale slaughter. Nor was Ken a gun nut. He owned firearms—a Colt .38 handgun and a Remington 30/06 rifle—but he didn't have secret caches of guns and explosives buried out in the woods, and he didn't horde them in fear that he would wake up one morning and find that the government had repealed the Second Amendment overnight. Ken didn't believe that the world would end in 2012 any more than he'd believed in the Y2K craze a decade before. He wasn't afraid of a comet or asteroid or the moon crashing into the Earth. He wasn't afraid of a sudden, massive solar flare. He wasn't afraid of the arrival of Planet Nibiru or that Yellowstone would turn into a giant volcano or any of the other ways people on the internet said the world was going to end.

He just liked zombies—and it was his passion for zombies, his friends agreed, that made Ken's the place to be if and when the world ended.

His apartment walls were adorned with framed original movie posters for *Land of the Dead, Zombi, Return of the Living Dead, The Plague of the Zombies*, and more. Also on the wall were autographed pictures from some of his favorite zombie-film stars—*Dawn of the Dead's* Ken Foree, *Day of the Dead's* Gary Klar, and *Night of the Living Dead's* Kyra Schon. His shelves overflowed with zombie movies on Blu-Ray, DVD and even old VHS tapes, as well as zombie books, magazines, video games, toys and graphic novels. Ken had a tattoo across his chest, hidden beneath his black 'Fulci Lives!' t-shirt. The tattoo said 'Romero is God'. He was saving money for another tattoo—one across his back that said 'Fast Zombies Suck', because that was his mantra.

Ken was a traditionalist. He hated fast zombies. The undead should shuffle and moan, not run and screech like the corpses in *28 Days Later* or the *Dawn of the Dead* remake. They shouldn't carry guns and make wisecracks like the dead in those Brian Keene books. Hell, those things weren't even zombies. Keene's creations were more like Raimi's *Evil Dead* than anything Romero had ever done, and the zombies in *28 Days Later* weren't even really dead. Ken much preferred Romero's tetralogy or Kirkman's *Walking Dead* series. Those guys understood that there was nothing scary about fast zombies.

Ken didn't get out much. His social life usually consisted of going to work at the supermarket and then coming home to watch movies or play video games until it was time for bed. He did this seven days a week. Sometimes he ordered a pizza. Occasionally his friends dropped by with a six-pack. Then they'd drink beer, eat pizza and either play video games or watch movies until it was time to go to bed. The routine rarely changed.

Because he didn't go outside much, Ken didn't realize that zombies had invaded his neighborhood until he stepped onto the porch to take out the trash. He froze, garbage bag in hand, gaping at the corpses shambling down the street. There were at least fifty of them—maybe more; an army of shuffling, moaning, mangled dead, so gruesome in the dim moonlight that their wounds seemed more like special effects make up than the real thing. The garbage bag slipped from Ken's numb fingers and split open on the ground. A few of the creatures glanced in his direction.

"Zombies!" His voice wavered, partly through fear, but also with an eager, almost uncomfortable feeling of excitement. He stared at the creatures, noticing with no small sense of satisfaction that, in real life, zombies did indeed move slow, not fast.

Ken ran back inside the apartment, felt around beneath his unmade bed, and pulled out the handgun. His hands shook as he fumbled with the weapon, and he dropped the bullets several times. Finally, he snapped the cylinder shut, filled his pockets with extra ammo, and then ran back onto the porch.

The zombies were right in front of his house now. They still clustered to the street and sidewalk. None of them had ventured into his yard—yet. Ken decided to make sure things stayed that way. He raised the pistol, aimed for the nearest zombie's head, took a deep breath, held it, and then opened fire.

The bullet tore a hole in the corpse's shoulder. The zombie shuddered, lurched to a stop... and screamed.

"What the hell?" Ken squeezed the trigger again. The pistol jerked in his grip. This time, the creature toppled over.

Then, all at once, the zombies began running away. They ran *fast*. They shouted at one another, sounding remarkably like living people rather than the dead. They cried for help, cried out for God, cried out to take cover, but none of them cried for "Brains!"

One of them pointed directly at Ken. "He's got a gun. Somebody call the police!"

Ken frowned. His ears rang and stomach clenched. He suddenly felt very small and afraid and unsure of himself. Zombies didn't run. They didn't cry out for God to help them. And they most certainly didn't call the police.

He stepped down off the porch and into the yard. He approached the corpse he'd shot and noticed a piece of paper lying nearby—a flyer of some kind. The zombie's blood had splattered the paper. Ken stood over the flyer and read what was printed on it.

ZOMBIE WALK
THIS SATURDAY, 8PM TO MIDNIGHT
ALL PROCEEDS TO BENEFIT THE LOCAL RED
CROSS CHAPTER
COME GET MADE UP TO LOOK LIKE THE WALK-
ING DEAD AND JOIN US AS WE SHAMBLE
THROUGH TOWN! MAKE-UP ARTISTS WILL BE ON
HAND. FOOD, FUN, GAMES AND PRIZES!

"Oh, shit... oh my fucking shit..."

He read the flyer again, hoping that the words might change, but they didn't. The gun felt heavy in his hands. His ears were still ringing. He looked up. The zombies were peering at him from behind parked cars and bushes. Some still fled. Others banged on the doors of his neighbors, pleading to be let inside.

When he heard the sirens in the distance, Ken ran back into the house and put the gun to his own head. Outside, the shouts increased. The sirens drew closer. He peeked out the window and saw that the crowd was creeping toward his house once more.

"Head shot," Ken muttered. "The only way to be sure."

When he pulled the trigger, the zombies ran away again.

———

STORY NOTE: This was first published as a chapbook from Camelot Books. When I wrote it, I had recently given an interview in which I said that my novel *Entombed* and my comic book series *The Last Zombie* were the final things I had to say about zombies, and I probably wouldn't be writing about them again. After six books and dozens of short stories dealing with the undead, as well as a twenty-five issue comic book series, I couldn't think of anything else to do with zombies. Except this (and one other story, "Couch Potato," which appears later in this volume).

I Sing A New Psalm

1 Blessed is the man who has never known the love of God, for he will never know the pain of a broken heart.

2 And blessed is the man who lives in ignorance of the forces around him, for he can exist in peace.

3 I was such a man, once. I didn't know the love of God, for I did not believe in Him. God was something for superstitious people. He was like the tooth fairy and Santa Claus. God was a story told to children to give them comfort when someone they loved had died.

4 "Rover is in Heaven now, sweetheart. He is playing catch with God, and one day, if you're good and eat all your vegetables and follow the Ten Commandments, you will see him again. Just like if you're good, Santa Claus will bring you a new toy." Growing up, that was all I knew of God.

5 I did not believe in God or the tooth fairy or Santa Claus. I believed in working hard and succeeding at my job and becoming a partner with the firm. These values were instilled in me at a young age by my father. He worked seven days a week, with one day off for Christmas and a week off for deer season. My father loved me, and although I didn't see much of him growing up, I know that he worked those hours for me. He wanted me to be the first person in our family to go to college.

6 John Lennon once said that a working class hero is some-thing to be. He was gunned down by a fan who loved him. John Lennon was more popular than Jesus.

7 My father died of a heart attack before I finished law school. My mother followed a year later, from melanoma. Years after the initial grief passed, I still felt unsettled when I thought of their passing. It bothered me how they would never know of my accomplishments, or how I'd repaid my father's unselfish work ethic in an equally driven manner. He would never know of these things because he didn't exist anymore. I did not believe in God or Heaven. My father was not with the Father. He was simply dead. Ashes to ashes. Dust to dust.

8 Would they have been proud of me?

9 My co-workers had a party for me the night I was offered a role as full partner with the firm. I drank too much Scotch. Head swimming, I returned home to an empty apartment. There was no solace to be found in the silence. Despite my achievements, I was left unfulfilled.

10 Blessed is the man who finds the love of a good partner, for that is the key to fulfillment.

11 I did not find fulfillment at a singles bar or on a dating web-site or in any of the other places one goes to find love these days. I found it in a church. I found fulfillment in Valerie. We met at a wedding. She was a bridesmaid. I was a guest of the groom. I still remember how beautiful she looked in her soft baby blue chiffon gown. Sunlight came through the stained glass windows and sparkled in her chestnut hair. At the reception, we made small talk over the punch bowl. Later, we danced to the Chicken Dance and the Electric Slide and other wedding reception staples. At the end of the evening, we exchanged phone numbers.

12 What did Valerie see in me? A lost soul, ripe for saving? Her Christian duty? Was it a forbidden attraction, perhaps? A chance to tiptoe over the line to the wild side with a secular atheist type? No, it

was none of these things. When she looked in my eyes, I like to think that she saw mirrored the same things I saw in her.

13 Blessed is the man who finds love, for love is the greatest gift of them all.

14 The Lord gives, and the Lord takes away.

15 I started going to church with Valerie not out of a desire to know God, but out of a desire to please her. I loved her and it was important to her and I wanted to make her happy. We went each Sunday, but I did not feel the Lord. We sat in the pew together and shook hands with those around us, but I did not feel the Lord. I wrapped an arm around Valerie as we shared a hymnal and sang, but I did not feel the Lord. I read aloud from the bulletin with the rest of the congregation, but I did not feel the Lord. I sat dutifully, listening to the scripture lesson and the sermon each week, but I did not feel the Lord. I tithed, but I did not feel the Lord.

16 When I asked her to marry me, she asked if it would be forever. When I said yes, she asked me to accept Christ as my personal Lord and savior—to ask him to come into my heart so that I could be born again. Valerie said this was the only way we could be together in the world beyond this one. She asked me if I would do this thing and I said yes.

17 That was the only time I ever lied to her.

18 We were married on the last Saturday of March. We stood at the altar in front of our friends and our family and God, and when I looked into Valerie's eyes and heard the emotion in her voice when she said "I do"...I almost felt the Lord.

19 And then Mark came along.

20 Mark was born four years later, after a struggle to conceive and many visits to fertility clinics and adoption agencies. Valerie was in labor for twenty-five hours. The doctors finally decided on a Caesarian delivery. I knelt beside her in the operating room, whispering

into her ear and kissing her forehead. She squeezed my hand and told me that she loved me.

21 And then the doctor asked me if I'd like to see my son. I peeked up over the curtain and there were Valerie's insides. The skin of her stomach had been folded back like a bed-spread and her insides were on display. The overhead lights glistened on the red and purple and yellow and brown hues, but this barely registered with me, for there in the doctor's hands was our son. There was Mark.

22 And then I felt the Lord. I felt His goodness and His love and I wept for joy and I praised His name and gave thanks. I prayed. I apologized for my foolish disbelief. I made amends for doubting. For surely, here was proof of His provenance and His love. I wept happily, and my chest swelled as if my heart would burst.

23 An alarm blared over my cry, and through my tears, I realized that something was wrong. Mark was blue, and when I tried to go to him, the nurse whisked him away. Valerie squeezed my hand, but her grip was weak, and when she moaned, I heard the fear in her voice. Then her hand slipped away and the staff pushed me aside. The alarms grew louder, drowning out my prayer.

24 Later, after the alarms had faded and the lights had dimmed and the staff had muttered their sincere apologies, a doctor came to me. I was kneeling in the hospital's chapel. The doctor was a short, rotund man with a receding hairline and a gentle, kindly face. He pushed his glasses up on his nose and cleared his throat softly. He offered his condolences on the death of my son. I asked him if there was any update on Valerie's condition.

25 And the doctor said, "We've done all we can. She's in God's hands now."

26 Valerie died two hours after Mark.

27 I tried to pray for them both, but my voice was a harsh, ragged thing and my words were ugly.

28 My God, my God, why have you done this to me? Why did you give me the fruits of your love, and show me the path to your light, only to then rip them away? Why are you so far from helping me? Do you hear the words of my roaring? I cry in the daytime, but you don't hear me. I beg to you at night, but you don't answer.

29 For the Lord our God is a jealous God. He is a demanding God. You shall have no other gods before Him, and you shall love no other like you love Him. He demands this of us, His creation.

30 John Lennon once said that happiness is a warm gun. He was gunned down by a fan who loved him. John Lennon was killed because he was more popular than Jesus.

31 There was a small bell over the door of the gun store that jingled when I walked inside. It sounded like the chimes of freedom ringing. A heavenly chorus. I bought a shotgun and two handguns, and while we waited for the results of my background check, I asked the proprietor if he clung to God and guns, the way the President had suggested.

32 "We all need something to believe in," he said. "But I don't care what they say. I didn't vote for either candidate. None of them have our best interests in heart. The people in charge never hear us."

33 You shall hear the words of my roaring.

34 How long did you plan to ignore me, oh Lord? Forever? How long did you plan to hide your face from me? How long must I counsel my own soul, so utterly filled with crippling sorrow in my heart daily? How long do you expect to be exalted over me?

35 Consider and hear me, oh Lord. Look in my eyes before I sleep the sleep of death.

36 I will sing unto you, Lord, because you have dealt unfairly with me.

37 Later, they will say that I have prevailed against you. For I trusted in your mercy and you spat in my face; my heart will rejoice in your pain.

38 You gave and then you took away.

39 Blessed is the man who can play that game, as well.

40 Yea, though I walk through the valley of the shadow of death, I do not fear you, for Valerie and Mark are with me. My shotgun and my pistols, they comfort me. Blessed is the man who knows the satisfying weight of such an instrument in his hands. And blessed is the man who finds solace in the handguns holstered to his hips. He shall take comfort in such weapons and through them, he will know fulfillment.

41 I wait in the car as the parishioners file into the church. I watch the greeters shake their hands, and I remember when it was Valerie and me walking through those doors.

42 Eventually, the doors close. I wait until I hear the muted sound of the organ. When the congregation begins to sing, I get out of the car. The guns are heavy but my heart is light. I feel at peace.

43 Hear this, all you people; give ear, all you inhabitants of the world. Listen to the words of my roaring.

44 I shall sing a new Psalm.

————

STORY NOTE: This story cannibalizes portions of the first chapter of an unfinished novel of mine called *First Person Shooter*. It was not a fun or easy thing to write. It took me to dark places, and that's probably why I never finished it. The creation of this short story had the same impact on me. When I do readings or personal appearances across the country, I often choose this story to perform for the crowd, and it is always well-received. Many fans tell me it's one of their favorites, so that makes the pain of its creation worth it.

Caught In A Mosh

STORY NOTE: This is one of my earliest published stories, and to me, it reads exactly as such—the work of a young author who has not yet learned the ropes or quite found his voice. I can see seeds of both here, but they've got a lot of dirt overtop them. You can also see the prehistoric development of my Labyrinth mythos (the name for the shared universe which all of my work inhabits). I wrote this in the late-Eighties, revised it and published it in the early-Nineties, and had pretty much forgotten all about it until compiling this collection. I do remember writing it, though. A friend and I had gone to a concert much like the one in the story. When I got home from the concert, I wrote the first draft of this story in one sitting. The title comes from one of my favorite Anthrax songs, off of the classic *Among the Living*. Again, be gentle with this. Much like big hair and pop metal, this story is a product of its time.

It was on a rainy night in early September when Kris and I tried to conjure our first demon. I'd just broken up with this psycho named Angie. Gorgeous girl, but a complete gothic whack job. She was into the occult and all that black magic shit.

When we broke up, I swiped a paperback of hers called *The Daemonolateria*. Not because I believed in that stuff, but just to piss her off. The book disappeared in my apartment, going to the same void that one of my socks goes to each time I pull my laundry from the dryer. I'd forgotten all about it until Kris found it.

Kris is a telemarketer by day, but at night he sings in this kick-ass band called Suicide Run. Classic and thrash, those boys can do it all.

His other talent was coming up with killer weed, some of which we were enjoying that night, along with a few beers.

We were deep into a conversation about which version of Black Sabbath was better, Ozzy or Dio. I took a hit from the bowl and passed it over to Amber. She was a sweet kid. I worked with her stepfather at the paper mill. He was twenty-four, same as me. He married Vicki, who was old enough to be his Mom, but sure as hell didn't look it. Amber was her daughter, seventeen going on twenty-seven. She had a good heart and was always laughing. She was like a little sister to me, and fun to be around.

Amber took a hit, sputtered, then giggled and passed the bowl on to her best friend Chrissy, a cute little blonde who had a crush on me. Next to her on my ratty couch sat Katie, a heavyset nineteen-year-old Goth with a perpetual sneer and a reputation for giving blowjobs in the local cemeteries.

Jen and Steve were arguing in my kitchen. Jen was Katie's older sister. I'd always secretly wanted to get with her, but she was always with Steve. Steve had red hair cut close to his head and hidden beneath a backward Jets hat. His baggy shorts always hung down low enough to expose his boxers, and his vocabulary consisted of one-syllable words and hip-hop slang. Steve thought he was from the hood, even though we lived in the fucking suburbs. He really annoyed me, poser that he was. We kept him around, though, because he usually had beer money.

The bowl had made it back to Kris, who dropped his lighter as he was firing it up. He took a hit, passed it back over to me, and then fumbled under the recliner cushions for the lighter. What he found instead was the book.

"What's this, dude?" He flipped through the pages.

I tore my bleary eyes away from *South Park* and Cartman's adventures at the sperm bank, and glanced over at him.

"Oh, that's just some book I ripped off from Angie." I exhaled a thick cloud of smoke and refilled the spent pipe.

Six bowls and twelve beers later, the girls and Steve left, and Kris talked me into trying one of the spells. We decided to summon Purturabo, Lord of the Dance. I have no idea why. You do some stupid things when you're stoned. Kris thought it would be cool, like in the *Evil Dead* movies. I thought it would be lame. It wasn't even a real spell book. Those were old and written in Latin with cracked and faded leather covers. This was a cheap paperback that had been bought at Barnes and Noble.

We both kept cracking up at the title "Lord of the Dance". I was expecting a kilt-wearing Irish demon to materialize, tap dancing on my coffee table. When the giggles had passed, we moved the sofa and the television and rolled back the rug. Kris programmed the CD player with some mood music from Danzig, Slayer, Fields of the Nephilim, and Ministry. Using a black marker, I drew a pentagram on the floor. I wasn't too worried about what the landlord would say. He'd been threatening to kick me out anyway.

I read aloud from the book. The pot had thickened my tongue, causing me to stumble over the spell's gibberish.

"Ob... Meeble... Ishtari..."

"You ain't pronouncing it right, dude!"

I took a swig of beer and shot him an annoyed glare.

"Here, man, you try it," I said, handing him the book. "I never took Black Magic 101 in school."

Kris read the spell but fumbled with the strange words too. His voice rose in volume as he reached the end.

"Kandara... Kat... PURTURABO!"

Nothing happened. In the background, Ministry let Jesus build their hot rod.

Disappointed, we put the furniture back in place and jammed to Ozzy. Kris paged through the drawings in the book and asked me if he could borrow it. He wanted to use the artwork for a Suicide Run banner. I told him to keep it and cracked another beer, settling back to listen to the music.

Ministry finished, and Ozzy sang an ode to Aleister Crowley.

Fast forward now to Halloween night, and the big concert—six regional metal and alternative bands, together for a Battle of the Bands benefit show to raise awareness about school violence.

I had several reasons for going. It was for a good cause, and Suicide Run were the headliners, meaning Kris would've been pissed if I hadn't shown up. Most importantly, there were going to be lots of women there and it had been a month since I'd gotten laid.

I fired up my golden chariot, (which is actually a rusty, gray primer colored, seventy-six Ford van), and went to pick up Amber and the rest. Tonight, Marty and Vicki were trusting me to chaperone their daughter and her friends, all of who were underage except for Steve and Jen, to the concert.

So, we all piled into my van and I got beers out of the cooler for everybody. Amber handed them out, chatting excitedly the whole time. Steve was instantly annoying, but I ignored him, as he was giving me gas money. The girls got drunk quickly, providing more fuel for their constant chatter. Steve sat quietly, looking as if he were waiting for an intelligent thought to hit him. Chrissy crawled up front to sit on the floor between my seat and Amber's. Her breasts filled out her Mudvayne shirt very nicely. I sighed; lamenting that she was only seventeen. That old Winger song ran through my head, making me cringe.

The concert was at the local sprint car track. A neighboring cornfield had been turned into a substitute parking lot, and I drove through an endless sea of cars, searching for a space. Finally, I found one.

As we piled out of the van, the cold wind slapped us in the face. A thin fog clung to everything, wafting through the field. The temperature had dropped into the fifties, but that didn't stop the crowd from coming. People swarmed through the gates as dusk gathered around us.

I made Steve carry the cooler, and we joined the procession of concertgoers. Amber and Chrissy each took one of my arms, skipping and singing. Katie followed behind, dressed in black. She greeted the many familiar faces of guys she knew from listening to The Smiths in the graveyard. Jen and Steve brought up the rear. Jen flirted with a passerby as Steve shot her jealous looks and mumbled about having to lug the beer.

A makeshift stage had been built at one end of the track and people were starting to crowd around it. We found places right at the front and I glanced behind us, surveying the crowd. About five hundred people had shown up, braving the cold and the drizzle to sell their souls for rock and roll.

The last of the sun disappeared below the horizon and darkness fell like a trap.

Night was upon us.

As if on cue, colored spotlights sliced through the darkness and the first chords of AC/DC's "For Those About To Rock" blasted through a wall of Marshall speakers. Flash-pots exploded in a burst of light and noise as the first band hit the stage. A thunderous cheer rose from the audience, and the show officially started—in a flurry of thick smoke, scorching fire, pounding drums, and screaming guitars.

Halfway through the second band's set, Amber and I went backstage. The scene was chaotic. I grabbed her hand, leading her through a sea of groupies, roadies, security guards, and musicians. Eventually, we found Kris and his drummer, Joey, splitting a bottle of Jack Daniels.

"Hey, dude!" Kris happily clasped my hand. "Hi Amber. I'm glad you could make it."

Amber grinned, and Kris gave me a wink. She was having the time of her life, which made me feel pretty good.

"You nervous?" I asked Kris.

"Hell, no! I'm ready. I'm glad you came. I've got a surprise for you tonight."

"What is it?"

"You'll see."

"Come on," Amber pleaded. "Give us a hint."

He agreed, after a moment's hesitation. "You remember that spell book you gave me?"

For a minute, I had no idea what he was talking about. Then I understood, and had a feeling of vague apprehension.

"Yeah," I said, "I remember."

"Well, I used some lines from it in the lyrics of a new song we wrote."

"Which part?"

"You'll just have to wait and see!" He flashed a mischievous grin.

Amber and I returned out front, fighting our way through the mosh pit to our places beside Chrissy, Katie, Jen, and Steve. The current band was doing a Nine-Inch Nails cover that sounded like shit, but the crowd was into it. Smoke from a hundred joints blended with the rapidly increasing fog, forming a swirling haze above our heads.

Suicide Run was the last act of the night. There was a twenty-minute wait between bands, while the roadies changed the equipment. Just as the crowd got restless, the stage began to glow with a red light. Eerie, pre-recorded organ music drifted through the speakers. A dry ice machine belched clouds of manmade fog. It mixed with the hazy night air and blanketed everything in our midst. I could feel Amber and Chrissy on each side of me, but couldn't see them through the white shroud.

Suddenly, the mist lifted and Suicide Run appeared on stage. Their movements seeming unreal in the flickering strobe light. The crowd started to cheer, enthusiastic whistles almost drowned out by the haunting organ.

Then Kris hit the stage wearing a hockey mask and brandishing a live chainsaw.

"HAPPY HALLOWEEN MOTHERFUCKERS!"

He revved the chainsaw high over his head. Explosions rocked the stage and the band ripped into a Rob Zombie cover. A thunderous roar escaped from the masses; a frantic screaming and clapping that had no peak. Everyone was dancing along, and again, a huge mosh pit started up front.

Kris flung the hockey mask into the crowd. Jen managed to catch it, earning looks of envy from the other girls down front. She also got a jealous glare from Steve, until he was bowled over and swept away into the center of the pit. Jen pulled up her shirt, flashing Kris her breasts.

Suicide Run roared on, with Kris doing his best Rob Zombie gargle. I watched in awe as my best friend whipped the crowd into a frenzy. Like a buzz-saw through wood, the band launched right into Alice In Chain's "Man In The Box," then tore through various songs by Metallica, Rage Against The Machine, Megadeth, Body Count, Biohazard, Tool, and Faith No More. They even threw in some classics by Judas Priest and Iron Maiden. Then Kris slowed things down a bit for a cover of Ozzy's "Goodbye To Romance." Lighters dotted the ebony sky as people held them aloft and swayed along. Steve had escaped the mosh pit with minimal bruising and he drew Jen tight. They kissed hungrily.

When the song ended, Kris paused and surveyed the crowd. I knew that it was time for him to make a speech about anti-violence, something that had been required of each band during their set. He shook his flowing mane of black curls and addressed the sea of faces before him. But instead of delivering the expected platitudes, he took me by surprise.

"This next song is one of our own. It's something new we've been working on. I'd like to dedicate it to a friend of mine who's here with the posse tonight. Where are you, dude?"

Spotlights swiveled around, and the beams landed on us. The crowd applauded and I waved, embarrassed as hell. Kris blew the girls a kiss. Amber, Chrissy, and Katie shrieked with delight. Jen smiled and waved. Even Steve saluted, looking sheepish with his sudden fame.

"These are some of the best friends a guy could ever ask for," Kris told the crowd. "But some folks aren't lucky enough to have friends like this. Some folks feel left out and don't know how to deal with that anger. But listen, man, we've all felt that way at one time or another. Don't take that frustration with you. You can let it all out right here. Like Kid Rock says, 'Get in the pit and try to love someone.' This song is for my friends. It's called 'The Lord of the Dance.' We're gonna raise some serious mother-fucking Hell out here tonight!"

The band erupted with the most killer, hypnotic guitar riff that I have ever heard. Wave after wave of sound crashed over us, and the crowd went ballistic.

"Let's fucking mosh!" Kris screamed.

The pit started up again with a renewed frenzy. Within seconds, the entire crowd was moshing. Heads banged furiously and people slammed into each other in time with the music.

I really wasn't paying much attention to the lyrics. I was too busy trying to give myself whiplash. Then Kris's voice thundered amidst the chaos.

"OB... MEEBLE... ISHTARI..."

A frigid claw ran up my spine as I heard the familiar summoning spell. Before, on that rainy night back in September, we had drunkenly slurred the words. Now, Kris was singing them with crisp clarity. Combined with the crunching guitars and thunderous drums, they weaved a mesmerizing trance.

"KANDARA... KAT..."

My vision started to tilt and my heart raced furiously in my chest. I felt like I was on speed. The stench of sulfur grew thick. The fog machines had ceased their labor.

Holes, ripped from the very fabric of space and time, suddenly appeared in the thin air, hanging amongst the crowd. A noxious, oily smoke seeped from them, followed by flickering tongues of scarlet flame. The crowd moshed on, their eyes glazed over hypnotically. They cheered, mystified at the holes, thinking they were special effects.

"PURTURABO!"

Kris finished, and my trance was broken.

This time he'd succeeded.

The inky smoke congealed into one rolling cloud that remained motionless between the crowd and the stage. Suicide Run played on, but Kris has stopped singing. He crouched, his eyes afire with anticipation. The smoke solidified and a form stepped out of it.

Purturabo, Lord of the Dance.

He was a combination of every rock god who had ever lived. Eyes that blazed like Jim Morrison's. A body as chiseled as Henry Rollins. Hair like David Lee Roth's. A smile identical to John Lennon's. A face that glowed like a young Robert Plant's. He was tall, towering over the dancers moshing around him. His hair flowed to his perfect ass and seemed to take on a Medusa-like life of its own as he whipped his head back and forth. The demon raised his head and howled into the night sky.

And then, Purturabo began to dance.

I looked up at Kris and found him staring back at me, his mouth hanging open in astonishment. The rest of the band continued to play, providing the soundtrack to which the demon moshed.

Purturabo flung himself violently into the tempest, smashing and colliding with the participants. He knocked a girl near us to the ground, bouncing off her boyfriend and slamming into a group of skinheads.

The frenzy increased with rapid intensity, and the scene replayed throughout the field. What had once been spirited and aggressive fun in a stance against violence was now resulting in bloody noses and broken bones. Fights erupted. Then, a gunshot echoed, followed by two more in rapid succession from different parts of the field.

The crowd began chanting the demon's name over and over as they fought. I grabbed Amber by the shoulders, shaking her hard. She responded by screaming the demon's name and gleefully kicking me in the balls.

Purturabo's gyrations grew faster. He whirled like a tornado through the crowd, seeming to be everywhere at once. A guy jumped to slam him and was caught by the demon in mid air. One muscular arm wrapped around the kid's waist, and the other encircled his throat. He held the victim above him, muscles rippling in the moonlight. Then, in one quick movement, Purturabo ripped out his throat and flung the ragged piece of flesh into the crowd. Blood sprayed from the gaping hole, howering the demons body in crimson gore. He tossed the limp form into a group of bikers who had been busy beating each other to a pulp, smashing them all to the ground.

Terror seized me as I watched Katie prance by him, her black scarves twirling behind her undulating body. Her eyes shone with lust as she writhed to the music.

Purturabo grinned, revealing rows of razor sharp fangs that gleamed in the moonlight. He offered Katie his outstretched hand.

"Dance with me, my child."

As I screamed out a warning, she took his hand in hers and smiled. With a powerful jerk, he ripped her arm out of its socket. Roaring with laughter, he used his bloody prize to club another bystander over the head. Katie sank to the muddy ground, a look of rapture on her face. Her blood pooled around her as she orgasmed in death.

Thunder crashed overhead, accompanying the music.

The thunder snapped Kris out of his shock. A look of horror flooded over his face as he surveyed the chaos below.

"No," he screamed at the demon. "You bastard, this isn't what you promised! This isn't what I wanted! Look at what you're doing to my *fans!*"

Purturabo chuckled. There was a legion of different voices in that guttural laugh. He leaped onto the stage, looming over my best friend. The band kept playing, either oblivious or spellbound—or maybe both.. Kris tried to run, but Purturabo grabbed a handful of his hair and yanked him backward. As I watched, he grasped Kris by both feet and started swinging him like a top. Faster and faster they spun. Kris gave a long, blood-curdling shriek—cut off as the demon suddenly let go.

His limp form flew like a rag doll over the heads of the crowd. He landed among them with a bone-crunching thud, his ribs bursting through his flesh. The possessed concertgoers fell upon him like flies on rancid meat.

Suicide Run never missed a beat.

The thunder boomed in the skies once more, bringing red lightening in its wake.

"Now," the demon roared, *"let's really mosh!"*

He leapt from the stage, doing a somersault and landing on a stupefied deadhead—breaking the poor bastard's back. Purturabo then ripped his head from his neck and tossed it into the sky like a beach ball. Blue tie-dye quickly turned red.

Suicide Run began another riff, their guitars screeching and the drums pounding out a steady THOOM THOOM.

Death and destruction held sway over all. An industrial rocker next to me pulled a knife from his trench-coat and disemboweled a teen in a Megadeth shirt. The dying youth seized the knife from his grasp and plunged it into his attacker's eye, while his own intestines hung in ropy strands.

Someone pushed me down. I screamed as they kicked me in the ribs. It hurt to breathe. My mouth filled with mud and the blood from a dead girl next to me.

THOOM THOOM.

Retching, I rolled onto my back. I saw that my attacker was Steve. He aimed another kick at my ribs. I grabbed his foot and with a thrust, knocked him off balance. He disappeared under a writhing pile of bodies. The crowd moshed on around us.

A mountain of flesh in a Fear Factory shirt loomed over me. As I scrambled in the mud, Amber appeared. Screeching, she slashed a bloody trench in his stomach with a broken beer bottle. I started to stammer out my thanks, but then she turned on me without hesitation. There was no recognition in her hollow eyes.

Purturabo blazed through the crowd, leaving carnage and dismemberment in his wake. His unholy laughter echoed over the screams of pain and ecstasy.

THOOM THOOM.

I cowered in the mud as acts of evil played out before my eyes. No comic book or horror movie could have prepared me for what was happening. No Sepultura or Cannibal Corpse album cover could have depicted the depravity of the scene before me.

I was operating on primal instinct. Laughter bubbled up from inside me, spewing forth like bile. I began to hum a song from my childhood; something from long ago in Sunday school. It had calmed me back then, on those nights when my father had come home drunk and fought with my mother.

"Rock of ages, cleft for me..."

I wasn't singing the Def Leppard version.

Jen was being savagely gang raped by three scraggly vampire wannabes—and worse, she was enjoying it. I tried to get to her, but then Amber returned and I had to ward off another attack. Then Amber got swept away in the tide of moshers, and I turned back to Jen.

Out of the crowd, a bloody and beaten Steve crawled over, cradling Jen's face in his grimy hands. As one attacker thrashed on top of her, Steve kissed her. Their tongues entwined like those of gentle lovers. Steve suddenly jerked back, his mouth gushing red. His tongue hung clenched in her teeth. Jen tilted her head back, spitting out the limp piece of meat, and laughed. Her laughter turned into a shriek as an orgasm tore through her body. Her cry was cut off abruptly as a black boot connected with her face.

THOOM THOOM.

"Let me hide myself in thee," I sang softly.

Lightning flashed across the sky again, revealing Amber stalking towards me once more. Madness shone on her face. Fat raindrops began to pelt our skin.

My whisper grew louder and recognition flickered in Amber's eyes. I was shouting now. Weakly, Amber began to sing as well.

The demon halted. His head whipped toward me and I saw fear reflected in his eyes. The ground rolled beneath our feet.

THOOM THOOM.

I couldn't remember the second verse, so I started again with what I knew. The air crackled with electricity, sizzling the hair on my arms. The demon roared and began to wade through the carnage towards us. The thunder now repeated the same monotonous beat as the drums, drowning them out.

THOOM THOOM.

"Keep playing," the demon commanded the band. He flung the crowd out of his way, cutting a bloody path toward me.

The shower turned into a torrent. Blinding sheets of cold rain sliced through the chaos. I could hear others joining Amber and I in the song. A bedraggled security guard aimed a kick at my bruised ribs, connecting with a loud crack. I sank to my knees as Purturabo closed in on me.

Thunder roared overhead and the ground trembled once more. The singing continued, overpowering the music. Purturabo screeched with rage, lunging for my throat with his talon-tipped fingers.

A bolt of blue electricity crashed into the stage and the remaining members of Suicide Run lit up like Christmas trees. An ear splitting whine of feedback shrieked from the speakers, followed by an explosion as they blew apart.

The earth shook again, knocking both the demon and myself to the ground. A crack opened before him, its gaping maw yawning wide. Purturabo clutched at me and I dodged his grasp. He teetered on the edge, his arms wind-milling helplessly.

"Damn you, Nazarene," he roared.

I grinned. "Let's dance, you son of a bitch."

Jumping into the air, I slammed into him with all of my strength. Purturabo toppled into the chasm. It slammed shut behind him, kicking up a cloud of dust and trailing wisps of smoke.

Silence descended. The remaining crowd milled around the field like stunned soldiers in a war zone. Amber was hysterical. Dazed and confused, she clung to me as we picked our way across the battlefield. Bodies and pieces of human butchery lay strewn everywhere. The air stank of ozone, brimstone, and burnt flesh. Sirens wailed in the distance.

I loaded Amber into the van and we drove slowly home. Both of us were crying too hard to speak.

The survivors couldn't remember much. The cops and the media quickly made the official conclusion that it had been a riot, another example of teen violence. Reporters hung around town for a few days. Preachers banged on their pulpits and thumped their bibles, blaming it on devil music. If they only knew...

Chrissy's remains were never found. She was listed among the three hundred who died, along with Kris, Jen, Katie, and Steve.

Marty and Vicki sent Amber to a private college where she learned to play the violin. She's getting pretty good at it.

I'm dating a new girl now. I met her at a bookstore, and I guess this is what love feels like. She turned me on to stuff like Yanni and John Tesh. In fact, we're going to see Tesh in concert tonight.

Hey! Don't knock that music until you've tried it...

I Am An Exit

I found him lying along the interstate, bleeding in the moonlight under the sign for Exit Five. It was bad—real bad. Blood covered everything; from the guard rail and median strip to his frayed blue jeans and crooked birth-control glasses with the cracked lens. They called them birth control glasses because wearing them insured that you'd never get laid. You only got glasses like that in the military and in prison. He didn't look like a soldier to me.

Far away, barely visible through the woods, an orange fire glowed. A hint of smoke drifted towards us on the breeze.

I knelt down beside him, and he struggled to sit up. His insides glistened, slipping from the wound in his side. Gently, I urged him back to the ground and then placed my hand over the gash, feeling the slick, wet heat beneath my palm. The wind buffeted the Exit Five sign above our heads, and then died.

"Don't try to sit up," I told him. "You're injured."

He tried to speak. His cracked lips were covered with froth. The words would not come. He closed his eyes.

With my free hand, I reached into the pocket of my coat, and he opened his eyes again, focusing on me. I pulled my hand back out, keeping the other one on the gash in his side.

"Robin."

"Sorry friend. Just me."

"I was—trying to get home to Robin."

He coughed, spraying blood and spittle, and I felt his innards move beneath my palm.

"She's waiting for me."

I nodded, not understanding but understanding all the same.

He focused on me again. "What happened?"

"You've been in an accident."

"I—I don't—last thing I remember was the fire."

"Sshhhhh."

He coughed again.

"My legs feel like they're asleep."

"Probably because you've been lying down," I lied. "They're okay."

They weren't. One was squashed flat in several places and bent at an angle. A shard of bone protruded from the other.

"D-do you have a cell phone? I want to call Robin."

"Sorry friend. Wish I did, so we could call 911. But I'm sure someone will come along. Meanwhile, tell me about her."

"She's beautiful." His grimace turned into a smile, and the pain and confusion vanished from his eyes. "She's waiting for me. Haven't seen her in five years."

"Why is that?"

"Been in prison." He swallowed. "Upstate. Cresson. Just got out this morning. Robbery. I stole a pack of cigarettes. Can you believe that shit? Five years for one lousy pack of smokes."

I shook my head. I'd been right about the glasses. And the sentence indicated he wasn't a first time offender. Pennsylvania had a three strikes law, and it sounded as if he qualified.

A mosquito buzzed in my ear, but I ignored it. In the distance, the fire grew brighter.

"We'd been dating before it happened," he said. "She was pregnant with my son. I—I've never held him."

"They didn't come visit you?"

"Not enough money. Cresson is a long way from Hanover—almost on the New York border. We didn't have no car."

He paused, struggling to sit up again. "My legs are cold."

"That's okay," I said. "The important thing is to keep talking. Tell me more."

"I—I got out this morning. Couldn't wait to get home and see her and the kid. Kurt. We named him Kurt, like the singer, you know? The guy from Nirvana? She wrote me letters every single day. I used to call her collect, but Robin still lives with her folks, and it got too expensive. I've s-seen pictures of Kurt. Watched him grow up through the mail. I want to hug him. My stomach is cold."

"It's a cold night," I replied, trying to take his mind off of it. He was losing a lot of blood. The smoke was stronger now, heavier. It blanketed the treetops and drifted over the road like fog.

"The State got me a Greyhound ticket from Cresson to Hanover. Rode on that damn bus all day, and I was tired, but I couldn't sleep. Too excited. There was a McDonalds at one of the stops, and that's the first time I've had a Quarter-Pounder in five years! Couldn't wait to tell Robin about it."

His eyes grew dark.

"There was this one fucker on the bus though. Guy from Cresson, just like me. Never saw him before. He was in a different block. He was on his way to Harrisburg. Fucker started the fight, but the bus driver didn't believe me and threw me off."

"Really?"

"Yeah!" He broke into a violent fit of coughing, and I thought that would be it, that he would expire. But then it subsided. "Fucker threw me right off the bus. Right here on the road. I had my thumb out to hitch a ride when I saw—*I saw the fire!*"

He sat upright, eyes startled.

"Shit, I r-remember now. There's a house on fire!"

"Yes," I soothed him, forcing him back down. "Yes, there is. But there's nothing you can do about that now. Somebody should be along shortly. What else do you remember?"

His eyes clouded.

"T-the fire—and then—a horn? A loud horn, like on a tractor-trailer, and bright lights."

"Hmmmm."

"Mister? I don't feel too good. I don't think I'm gonna make it. Will you d-do me a f-favor?"

I nodded. His skin felt cold; the warmth was leaving his body.

"Give my love to Robin and K-kurt? Their address is in m-my wallet, along w-with t-t-their phone number."

"I'd be happy too."

"I—I s-sure-a-a-appreciate t-that, Mister."

He smiled, safe in the knowledge that I would give his wife and child his love. Then he turned his head to the fire in the distance. His brow creased.

"I s-sure h-hope the p-people in that h-house are a-alright..."

"They are fine now," I told him. "There were four of them. Daddy, Mommy, and the kids, a boy and a girl. The Wilts, I believe their name was. Exit Four. I killed them long before I started the fire. So don't worry yourself. They'll never feel the flames."

"W-what?" He tried to sit up again, but I shoved him back down, hard.

"They were Exit Four. You are Exit Five. Hold still."

I pulled the knife from my jacket and cut his throat. There wasn't as much blood as I'd expected, most of it already having leaked out while I kept him talking. I wiped the knife in the grass and placed it back in my coat. Then I fished out his wallet and found Robin and Kurt's address and phone number. I smiled. They lived just off the Interstate, at Exit Twenty-One.

Twenty-One. And this was Five. Sixteen more exits, and I would keep my promise to him.

I walked on into the night, the distant wail of fire sirens following in my wake.

I am an exit.

———

STORY NOTE: Many readers tell me this story is one of their favorites. The tale came in a single, sudden burst. I usually write to music. The night this was written, I was working on the first draft of my novel *Terminal*, and listening to Johnny Cash's "Give My Love To Rose" and Nine Inch Nails' "Mr. Self Destruct". When the story idea came, it was the perfect fusion of fatigue, music, caffeine, and creative energy. The lyrics from both songs kept running around in my head. I thought about Cash's protagonist dying along the railroad tracks, begging the stranger to give his love to Rose, while in the background, Trent Reznor whispered "I am an exit." I wrote the first draft in the next half hour, and the second and final drafts the following day. The story was so well-received that I eventually wrote a sequel to it (which follows).

This Is Not An Exit

"You ever kill anyone?"

He licks his lips when he asks me, and I can tell by his expression that he doesn't really want to know. His eyes dart around the hotel bar before coming back to me. No matter what I say, my answer will barely register with him. The question is perfunctory. He desires the act of confession. He's killed, and it's eating at him. It weighs on him. He needs to tell.

"What?" I pretend to be shocked by the question.

The young man is maybe twenty-one or two. Still learning his limits when it comes to alcohol. His slurred words are barely noticeable, but the empty beer bottles in front of him reveal everything. He leans closer, nearly falling off his stool.

"Have you ever killed someone?"

This is his conversation starter. A chance to unburden. Or to brag. This is a beginning.

An entrance.

I close entrances.

The first person I ever killed was named Lawrence. I've killed so many people over the years that they blur together—a nameless, faceless conglomerate. But I remember Lawrence. Pale and pasty. Hair on his knuckles. Rheumy eyes. He drove a red Chrysler mini-van and the glove compartment was full of Steely Dan cassettes and porn. Lawrence cried when I cut the sigils into his skin. Mucous bubbled out of his nose and ran into his mouth. Disgusting back then, but oddly amusing now. It brings a smile to my face, like thoughts of a childhood friend or first love.

In the years since, I've streamlined my efforts. I no longer bother with sigils or ceremony. I no longer speak the words of closing. The mere act of killing accomplishes my work. Spilling blood closes the doors. I don't need the rest of the trappings. Indeed, I prefer to act quickly these days. A shot in the dark. A knife to the back. Burn them as they sleep. Over and done. No muss. No fuss. Move on up the highway to the next exit. There are miles to go and doors to close before I rest, and I am getting older. Robert Frost took the road less traveled, but I take all roads. Speed and efficiency are the key. I didn't know that, back when I killed Lawrence.

I know it now.

I am swift. My avatar is a hummingbird. Metaphorically speaking, I move through the night at eighty miles per second, traveling from blossom to blossom, taking their nectar and then moving on.

I tell the young man none of this. Instead, I say, "No, I've never killed anyone."

"I have. A few years ago."

I sip my scotch and dab my lips with the napkin. When I respond, I try not to sound disinterested.

"Really?"

"Yeah." He nods. "Seriously. I'm not bullshitting you."

I say nothing, waiting, hoping he'll unburden himself soon so that I can go to my room and sleep. Dawn is coming and I must be on my way.

He signals for another round. We sit in silence until the bartender brings our drinks. The man glances at my half-full glass of scotch and I smile. He sets the drinks down and helps another customer. The young man picks up his beer and drinks half the bottle. I watch his throat work. He puts the bottle down and wipes the condensation on his jeans.

"My girlfriend's name was Janey," he says. "I was eighteen. She was fourteen. I mean, that's only four year's difference, but people acted like I was a fucking child molester or something. I wasn't, dog. I knew Janey since we were little kids. Our parents took us to the same church and shit. We were in love. Her old man freaked when he found out we were doing it. Somehow—I don't know how—he got the password to Janey's MySpace page and he read our messages. He told her she wasn't allowed to see me anymore. Then he called my folks and said if I tried to contact Janey again, he'd call the cops and have me arrested as a pedophile. He actually called me that—like I was one of those sick fucks Chris Matthews busts on that show. You know?"

I don't. The only television programming I watch is PBS, and only when the hotel I'm staying in offers it. But I nod just the same, encouraging him to continue. I hope he'll hurry up. I am bored.

"Well, Janey sent me a text message the next day. Her dad found out and he smacked the shit out of her. So I went over there and knocked on the door, and when he answered, I told him I wanted to talk. He was mad. So mad that he was fucking shaking, yo. But he let me in. Said we were gonna have this out once and for all, and then he never wanted to see me again. He made Janey stay upstairs in her room. I heard her and her mother arguing. I asked if I could get a glass of water and he said yeah. So when he went into the kitchen to get it, I followed him. They must have just gone grocery shopping, because there were a bunch of empty plastic bags lying on the counter. I picked up two—double-bagged, like they do for heavy stuff, you know? There was a little bit of blood inside, probably from steak or hamburger or something. I remember that. And while her dad's back was still turned, I slipped those bags over his head and smothered the motherfucker."

There is no regret in his voice as he says this. There is only grim satisfaction. His smile is a death mask. He takes another sip of beer and then continues.

"Upstairs, Janey and her mom were still hollering at each other, so I grabbed a knife from the drawer and tip-toed out of the kitchen. Janey's little brother, Mikey, was standing there. He screamed, so I stabbed him, just to shut him up." He chuckles, but there is no humor in it. "Yeah, I shut him the fuck up, alright. I remember when I pulled the knife out, blood just started gushing. It was hot and sticky, you know?"

I do indeed. I know all too well what another's blood feels like on your hands. How it smells. How it steams on cold nights and turns black when spilled on asphalt. How it dries on your flesh like mud, and can be peeled away like dead skin.

I tell him none of this. Instead, I finish my scotch and reach for the second glass. I hold it in my hands, not drinking.

"How did that make you feel?" I ask.

He blinks, as if he'd forgotten I was there.

"W-what?"

"Killing your girlfriend's brother. How did you feel about it?"

He shrugs. "I don't know. I didn't really feel anything at the time, except maybe scared. Janey's mom heard him scream. By the time Mikey hit the floor, she was running down the stairs, hollering at Janey to call 911. So I chased her down and shut her ass up, too. I didn't really think about it. I just did it. The news said I stabbed her mom forty-seven times, but I didn't count."

I arch my eyebrows, bemused. Forty-seven is a powerful number. It has meaning in certain occult circles, but I doubt he is aware of the significance.

"I went into Janey's room. She was hiding in the closet. Crying and shit. I told her we could be together now. We could leave, before anybody figured out what had happened. Take her parents car and just fucking drive, dog. Just hit the road and see where it took us. Go live somewhere else. Together."

I know where that road leads, but I don't tell him that, either.

"But Janey... she... she wouldn't stop hitting me. I slapped back and the knife..."

A shadow of genuine emotion—the first I've seen him express—flashes his face. I raise my glass and drain it. Then I set it on the bar and slide two twenty-dollar bills beneath it.

"I've got the tab." I rise from the stool.

"Yo!" He grabs my arm, and I allow him to pull me close. "You gonna call the cops? You gonna tell somebody?"

I smile. "No. Your secret is safe with me."

"Bullshit. You're gonna go outside and call someone."

I grab his hand and squeeze. Hard. He flinches. My face is stone as I step away.

"I'll do no such thing," I say. "I have heard your tale and it means nothing to me. Do you think yourself some great murderer? You're not. You're an amateur."

"Fuck you."

"On the contrary. Fuck you. You play at being a killer, but have you murdered anyone since your girlfriend?"

"No."

"Well, there you go. If you really want to transcend, you'll go out tonight and continue your spree."

"You're crazy."

"No. I am the last sane individual in the world."

I leave him sitting there and walk away. I leave the hotel bar and instead of returning to my room, I sit on the smoker's bench outside and keep careful watch on the lobby through the big glass doors. Out on the highway, miles from here, a big rig's air brakes moan. They sound like a ghost.

I only kill out of necessity. I only do what needs to be done. There are doors in our world, and things can come through them. What is an entrance, but an exit? I shut those doors. I close exits.

Eventually, I see him stumble through the lobby, heading for the elevators. He is far too inebriated to notice me re-enter the hotel. He just leans against the wall, waiting for the doors to open. I smile and nod at the desk clerk. The doors slide open. He steps inside, staring at his feet. I join him.

The doors close.

"What floor?" he asks, still looking at his shoes.

I do not answer.

He looks up and I cut his throat before he can scream. It is a practiced stroke. Perfunctory. Clinical. But I grin as I do it, and my heart beats faster than it has in many years.

I am breaking my rules, just this once. I am killing not out of necessity, but out of justice. Out of mercy. This is about putting down a rabid animal.

This is not an exit.

But I am.

STORY NOTE: This tale tells you a little bit more about The Exit (as I've come to call the serial killer)—but not so much as to reveal everything about him. Who is he? Why is he killing people at highway exits? Well, I know, but I'm not telling. Not yet, anyway. He was supposed to appear in my novel *A Gathering of Crows*, but about halfway through the first draft of that novel, I realized that he was stealing the show, so I went back, changed the plot, and wrote him out. But you will see him again, in a novel-length work, and the rest of his secrets will be revealed there.

That Which Lingers

Sarah awoke to the wailing alarm clock. Blurry-eyed and still half asleep, she went for her morning run—from the bedroom to the bathroom. Three seconds later, she knelt, retching as she'd done every morning for the past two months.

Finished, she collapsed onto the couch and lit the day's first cigarette while the coffee brewed. A dull ache behind her temples was all that remained from the night before. Sarah frowned, trying to recall the exact details. She remembered arguing with the bartender. He hadn't wanted to serve her, commenting on her *condition*. After some flirting, she'd managed to hook up with several men who were willing to buy a girl a drink in exchange for a hint of things to come.

At least she hadn't gotten completely smashed and ended up bringing one of them home. Her empty bed testified to that. She hadn't shared it since Christopher walked out on her four months ago. She inhaled, letting the acrid smoke fill her lungs, and fought back tears.

Sarah showered, trying to wake up as the water caressed her skin. Trying to lose herself in a flood of happy thoughts. Trying not to notice the swell of her abdomen as she lathered her lower body. Trying to cope.

She wrapped her long, chestnut hair in a towel, and cinched another around her waist. Then she grabbed breakfast. The coffee was good, but a single bite of the granola bar made her stomach nauseous again.

She let the towels drop to the floor and caught a glimpse of herself in the mirror. This too, reminded her of Christopher.

They'd dated for three years. The pregnancy had been unplanned. Christopher had been ecstatic—and crushed when he learned that she didn't feel the same way. She'd tried to explain how she felt. How the timing wasn't right. She still wanted to go back to school and get her bachelor's degree. She wanted to do more with her life than working as a waitress. Having a baby now would jeopardize all of that.

What she hadn't told him was that she worried about his drinking and of how he was turning out to be just like the father he hated. She didn't express that she had come to seriously doubt their relationship.

Christopher was completely opposed to the abortion.

Sarah noticed how her breasts were growing fuller while echoes of Christopher's pleas rang in her ears.

The abortion had devastated him, killing whatever chance of love they'd still had. A part of both of them had died that day.

That was four months ago.

Collapsing onto the unmade bed, she began to cry. How could she possibly deal with what was happening to her alone? She needed Christopher.

She'd considered having an ultrasound, but knew that nothing would show up during the procedure.

She wasn't crazy.

She was haunted.

Deep inside, Sarah felt something kick.

———

STORY NOTE: Another of my very early stories, and one of the first I ever sold for publication. When it was first published, it caused a minor stir on early internet message boards among both pro-life and anti-abortion readers. That surprised me at the time, but the internet was young and new then, and things like flame wars and trolls hadn't been invented yet. Rest assured, I had no political agenda with this tale. I just thought it was a pretty cool ghost story.

Halves

We walked outside one morning and my daughter, Ellie, stepped on half of a dead mouse.

It was my turn to take Ellie to school. She's in second grade, and shy. A few of the older kids on the school bus like to pick on her. They call her names—'Smelly Ellie' being one of the more obnoxious ones. For the record, my daughter doesn't smell, unless you happen to think that Johnson's baby shampoo and soap stink. Apparently, smelly is the only word the little cretins could find to rhyme with her name. We complained, of course. It did no good. The bus driver was unwilling or incapable of putting a stop to it, and the administration assured us they'd look into it, but they never actually did anything. Mean-while, Ellie came home every day in tears. So my wife, Valerie and I, began taking turns giving her a ride to school each day on our way to work.

That morning—a Monday in late May—started off really nice. It was a beautiful day outside. Sunny and warm, but not hot. A gentle breeze rustled the trees in our yard, making them sway back and forth. Butterflies flitted about. Birds sang and rustled around in the shrubs. The sky was light blue and filled with fluffy, slow-moving cotton ball clouds. Ellie was in good spirits. No big surprise there. After all, she only had a few more weeks until summer vacation started. Her mood was infectious. I remembered what that felt like—having the open promise of the entire summer spread out before you.

Kids are good at reawakening emotions and joys you've long since forgotten. The sleepless anticipation that comes the night before

Christmas or your birthday. The fun of getting dressed up for Halloween. The excitement of going someplace new or seeing something different. The simple pleasures of favorite books, television programs or a special toy. I relive my childhood through my daughter every single day. Childhood is better the second time around.

Valerie was pouring coffee into a travel mug in preparation for the morning commute. Ellie gave her mother a kiss goodbye. Then Valerie went into the bedroom to finish putting on her make-up. Ellie and I walked out onto the deck, basking in that beautiful day, and we hadn't taken more than a half-dozen steps when Ellie glanced down at her shoe and screamed.

It was pretty gruesome. The mouse's upper half was missing. Where there should have been a head and forepaws, there was only a pink and purple mess of tiny entrails. Some of it stuck to the bottom of Ellie's shoe, and stretched like gum that had been left out in the sun for too long.

"Ewwww," she wailed. "That is so gross!"

I told her to wipe her shoe off on the outside doormat as best she could. Then I thought better of it. Valerie would kill us both if she did that, so instead, I told her to go wipe it off in the grass. While she was doing that, I got a shovel out of the garage and scooped the grisly remains off the deck. Then I tossed the little corpse in the trashcan. When I returned, a small, wet stain was all that remained of the mouse. By the time I got home from work, that would be gone, as well. Flies were already buzzing around it.

"Come on," I said. "We'll be late."

Ellie pouted as I buckled her in.

"That poor mouse. What happened to it, Daddy?"

"I don't know, sweetie."

In truth, I *did* know what had happened to it. I just wasn't about to tell my daughter the truth—that the hapless mouse had had the misfortune to come across Hannibal, and Hannibal had done what he did best.

Hannibal is our cat. He showed up during the winter, bedraggled and skinny, with matted, dirty fur and a pronounced limp. His age was indeterminable, but I guessed he was under a year old. He was wary of us, at first, but once I fed him, he rubbed up against my legs and purred. After that, he let me care for him. I brushed his fur and got rid of the knots, and in lieu of a bath, I wiped him down with some sanitary kitchen wipes. When I was finished, I discovered that beneath the dirt and grime, Hannibal had a beautiful, luxurious coat; his fur was as white as snow, shot through with pale yellow streaks. I checked with our neighbors, but nobody was missing a cat. Assuming that either someone had abandoned him, or he'd grown up feral and wild, I took him to the veterinarian, got him fixed, wormed, and checked out. Other than a bad ear mite infestation, Hannibal received a clean bill of health. The limp, as it turned out, was caused by a cut on the pad of his front paw, and that soon healed. He settled in quite nicely, and was affectionate and quite grateful for his new home.

He expressed that gratitude each and every day by bringing back dead animals. Mice, voles, birds, newts, butterflies, frogs—whatever he could find. Each day, there was a different carcass lying on the deck or in the driveway. Once he'd brought back a four-foot long black snake, and another time, I found a squirrel. Those last two shocked me; they seemed much too big for Hannibal to tackle, but evidently, he was a scrapper.

Usually, his prey was less-than-intact by the time he brought it home. I don't think he ate them—not with all the food I gave him at night. But he didn't exactly bring his kills home in one piece, either. I can't tell you how many half-rodents, half-frogs, and butterflies with missing wings I've cleared out of the way since Hannibal's arrival. Until that morning, I'd done a good job of not letting Ellie see them.

Valerie wasn't thrilled with Hannibal's gifts. She liked having wildlife around the house—liked having daily visitors to the various birdfeeders she'd hung up all over the lawn. But she liked Hannibal, too—right up until he began doing what outdoor cats do. Then, he wasn't so cute or cuddly anymore.

We hadn't intended to make him an outdoor cat, but despite his loving behavior, Hannibal simply couldn't grasp the concept of using the litter box. Even after he was fixed, he still insisted on spraying the walls and couch, so rather than keep him inside the house, we let him roam the yard. I fixed up a box for him in the garage, and added a cat-door so that he could come and go as he pleased. It kept him dry and safe, at least, and in the winter, he stayed warm.

As I pulled out of the driveway, I pondered the best way to explain to Ellie where the mouse had come from and what had happened to it. She loved Hannibal, and he absolutely adored her. I didn't want her to suddenly shy away from him. It was important that she learned about the natural behavior of things. But then we hit traffic on the way to school, and my cell phone rang. It was work, wanting to know if I could make it in any earlier. I put off telling Ellie until later.

In hindsight, that was a mistake. That was how the trouble started. Then again, even if I'd told her, I don't know if it would have changed anything.

Like the song says, I wish I didn't know now what I didn't know then.

The next day, Hannibal left half of a bird on the deck. Ellie's shriek of disgust was followed by Valerie screaming my name.

"Ward! Get out here."

Muttering, I put down my coffee and walked out onto the deck, barefoot. A headless, baby robin with soft, downy feathers and only one wing remaining lay next to the spot where the half-mouse had been the day before.

Valerie glared at me, hand on her hips. "Will you get rid of it, please?"

Nodding, I started towards the garage to get the shovel. The gravel in the driveway hurt my bare feet, and I winced, stepping lightly. I stopped halfway when Ellie spoke up.

"Mr. Chickbaum says that Hannibal did this."

Mr. Chickbaum was Ellie's imaginary friend. She'd first started talking about him three years ago, soon after we bought this house. Our suspicion was that she'd created him to help her deal with the stress of moving to a new home, and having to make all new friends. Valerie and I didn't mind. We'd both had imaginary friends when we were young. Mine was a talking chicken shadow named Billy. Valerie's was a tree named Mrs. Billingsworth. We both outgrew our imaginary friends, and assumed that given time, Ellie would, as well. We thought no more of it, and even encouraged her on the rare occasions that she brought him up.

According to Ellie, Mr. Chickbaum was a little bearded man about six inches tall, who wore green clothes and a hat. The first time we heard this, Valerie and I both immediately thought of leprechauns, although Ellie insisted that he wasn't one. Secretly, I'd always assumed that her imagination formed him based on an old Warner Brothers cartoon. When she was very young, Ellie used to sit in my lap and we'd watch Looney Tunes together (I've always had a fondness for the classics, and even own several original cartoon cells). One of them, an episode entitled '*The Wearing of the Grin*', had been a mutual favorite of ours, and we watched it countless times. In the episode, Porky Pig is walking to Dublin, Ireland, and gets caught in a bad storm. He seeks shelter in an old castle, which is inhabited by some paranoid leprechauns who are suspicious of him and mistakenly think Porky is there to steal their gold. I miss those times. We stopped watching Looney Tunes as Ellie got older, because Valerie insisted they were too violent. I was certain that Mr. Chickbaum stemmed from Ellie's subconscious memories of those times.

Ellie played with, talked to, read books with, and drew pictures with her imaginary friend, but always in the privacy of her own room. She never pretended he was there when we were in the room with her. For a while, Valerie had even set a place for him at the dinner table, but stopped after Ellie explained that Mr. Chickbaum didn't want anyone but her to see him.

I glanced at my daughter now, walked back over to her, and asked, "What did you say?"

Ellie put her hands on her hips and stared at us defiantly. "Mr. Chickbaum says that Hannibal is the one who killed that mousy yesterday, and that he's killed a lot of other things."

Valerie and I glanced at each other, communicating in that telepathic way that all parents develop.

Did you tell her about Hannibal?

No, of course not. I assumed that you were the one who told her.

I knelt down beside Ellie and looked her in the eye. "Honey, that's what cats sometimes do. Remember on Tom and Jerry—"

"Tom and Jerry is a cartoon, Dad." Her tone was very serious. "The mousy and the birdie are real. We feed Hannibal every night. Why does he have to eat them, too?"

I fumbled for an explanation. "Well, because...you see...in the animal world..."

Ellie stared at me with a mixture of contempt and derision. It was the first time I'd ever seen an expression of either on her face, and it physically rocked me. I felt as if I'd been slapped. I swayed back and forth, and had to reach for the deck rail to keep my balance. Valerie was no help. She simply stared at us both, dumbfounded.

"Mr. Chickbaum says Hannibal won't stop. He says that Hannibal is a mean kitty and that he should die!"

"Ellie!" I said it louder than I'd meant to, and now it was Ellie's turn to flinch.

Valerie gasped. "Ellie, that's a terrible thing to say."

Ellie stood firm, but her bottom lip quivered. "I didn't say it. Mr. Chickbaum did."

"I don't care who said it." I lowered my voice, but made sure she knew by my tone that I meant business. "Say it again and no video games for a month."

"But—"

"Two months."

Tears welled up in her eyes. Her lips went from quivering to full pout.

"I'm sorry, Daddy. But why isn't Hannibal in trouble, too? He's so mean..."

I paused, choosing my words carefully. Then I pulled her to me and gave her a hug, stroking her hair and letting her know it was all right.

"Honey, Hannibal can't help what he does. It's instinct. Cats lived in the wild for a very long time before people turned them into pets, and they had to hunt to survive. They still remember that, deep down inside. Humans are the same way."

She sniffed against my shoulder. "We don't eat birdies like cats do."

"No," I agreed. "We don't. But we still have instincts left over in us from thousands of years ago. We're still afraid of the dark, even though we don't really have a reason to be. Our ancestors were afraid of it because they never knew what might be lurking outside their cave—a Sabertooth tiger or something worse. These days, there aren't such things, but we're still afraid of the dark anyway. It's instinct. And it's the same way with Hannibal. He doesn't know why he hunts smaller animals. He does it because deep down inside, something tells him to. Does that make sense?"

She nodded, then pulled away and took her mother's hand. While Valerie led her to the car, I wiped snot and tears from my shirt.

After they were gone, I got rid of the corpse. Hannibal hid under the deck and watched me. His tail swished back and forth. When I was finished, he rubbed up against my legs and batted at my shoelace. I reached down and scratched him between the ears. Purring, he rolled over and stared up at me with those big green eyes.

"Oh, no," I said. "You're making things hard around here. No belly rubs today."

He lay there, rolling around and watching me, trying to act cute, until I went inside to change my shirt. When I came out again, Hannibal was gone, back on the prowl, keeping our house safe from critters.

On the third day, it rained. Hannibal's present that morning was the hindquarters of a frog. He'd most likely caught it lurking around our septic system. The grass always grows taller there, no matter how often I mow the lawn, and the frogs like to hang out on that spot. I got rid of the evidence before Ellie saw it.

As I drove her to school, I noticed that Ellie was unusually quiet. There was no chatter or singing along with the radio. She simply sat in the back, staring out the window. The only sounds were the windshield wipers and the slight drone of the air conditioning.

"What's wrong, sweetie?"

"Nothing."

I coasted to a stop at the next red light and glanced into the rearview mirror. Her demeanor hadn't changed at all.

"Ellie," I coaxed. "If something's wrong, you know you can tell me, right? What's bothering you? Let's talk about it. Are you still upset about yesterday?"

She shrugged. "A little. Sort of. I talked about it with Mr. Chickbaum last night, and told him what you said."

I suppressed a grin.

"He says you're wrong, Daddy. Mr. Chickbaum says there are still plenty of reasons for us to be afraid of the dark."

I shivered suddenly, and turned down the air conditioning. It didn't help.

* * *

"I'm worried about Ellie."

Valerie and I were lying in bed, winding down for the evening. She was reading a Duane Swierzynski novel. I was staring at the television, flipping aimlessly through the channels. She folded the corner of a page to mark her place and sat the book on the nightstand. Then she propped herself up on an elbow and turned to me.

"Why? Did something happen at school?"

"No. I'm worried about this imaginary friend thing."

"Mr. Chickbaum."

"Yeah. Him."

It was weird. I couldn't tell you why, but lying there in the safety of our bedroom, I was hesitant to say his name.

"It's a phase," Valerie said. "She'll grow out of it."

Grunting, I muted the television, cutting an anchorman off in mid-sentence.

"Maybe," I agreed. "But she's had him for a while, hasn't she? Longer than most kids. And what she said about Hannibal..."

"She was upset. That bird really bothered her, Ward."

"I know. But that still doesn't make it right. She's never said anything like that before. I mean, she loves that cat. For her to wish death on him—that just came out of nowhere. She's not a violent kid."

"She didn't say it. Mr. Chickbaum did."

I studied her carefully, trying to figure out if she was joking or not. Her expression was serious.

"Oh, come on, Valerie. Do you realize how ridiculous that sounds? Don't tell me you believe in little men now?"

"Of course not. But Ellie's young, Ward. Maybe she's having trouble differentiating between real life and make believe. Obviously, she had some pent up anger towards Hannibal. She expressed it as Mr. Chickbaum. Maybe in her mind, that means she didn't really think or say it. *He* did."

I shrugged. "She knows that cartoons are make believe. She knows that Hannah Montana is pretend, and that in real life, the actress' name is Miley Cyrus. Ellie knows the difference between that and reality."

"But that's television. Maybe she's having trouble struggling with these emotions. Maybe they scare her. So she's expressing them through Mr. Chickbaum."

I mulled it over, thinking about the conversation I'd had with Ellie that morning. I remembered what she'd said.

He says you're wrong, Daddy. Mr. Chickbaum says there are still plenty of reasons for us to be afraid of the dark.

"Maybe we should talk to someone," I suggested. "A doctor or something. If it will set your mind at ease, then let's look into it in the morning."

"Okay."

I reached over to my nightstand and turned the light off. Valerie did the same on her side. We kissed good night, and then rolled over. We slept with our backs to each other—skin touching, but facing in opposite directions. We'd discovered long ago that we both slept easier that way.

I lay there in the darkness, wondering why I was afraid—and what I was afraid of. Not Ellie, certainly. I was concerned about her. Worried. But not afraid.

I closed my eyes and the darkness deepened.

The next morning, the rain was gone and the sun returned just in time for Hannibal's latest kill—the mangled upper-half of a red and black spotted newt. I kicked the tiny lizard carcass into the driveway. It landed with a plop, lost between the gravel.

When I reached my office, I spent the first hour of the day online researching childhood behavior and imaginary friends. When I was a kid, I suppose my parents would have spoken with a child psychiatrist. Our generation just uses Google. My search returned 1,590,000 websites—everything from Wikipedia to a band from Los Angeles.

I learned a lot. Imaginary friends usually came about when a child was feeling lonely. That made sense. Ellie was shy, and she'd been picked on a lot by the older kids. Imaginary friends often served as outlets for expressing desires which children knew they'd get in trouble for. That made sense, as well. Ellie had been mad at Hannibal for killing the bird, and had lashed out. When she realized she was in trouble for what she'd said, she blamed Mr. Chickbaum. One website said that deep down inside, children understood that their imaginary friends weren't real, even if they pretended or insisted that they were. That eased some of my fears, but I was still concerned about Ellie's sudden dark turn. Several sites suggested that a child's conversations with their imaginary friends could reveal a lot about that child's anxieties and fears.

Deciding to pay closer attention to Ellie's conversations with Mr. Chickbaum, I emailed some of the links to Valerie. Then I logged off and got to work.

I was the first one home that night, so I started making dinner— baked tilapia, french fries, and canned peas. Valerie and Ellie got home just as I was pulling the fish from the oven. Ellie seemed her-self—perky, happy and talkative (her shyness evaporated when she was with us). We ate dinner and talked about our day. Valerie loaded the dishwasher while I helped Ellie with her homework. Then the three of us watched TV and played video games until it was time for bed. I tucked Ellie in, read her a chapter of *Charlotte's Web* (we were up to the part where Templeton the rat runs amok at the county fair), and then kissed her goodnight. I turned off the light as I left the room. Her nightlight glowed softly in the corner next to her dresser. I shut the door behind me and then stood in the hall.

After a moment, when she realized that I wasn't returning to the living room, Valerie tip-toed down the hallway and stood beside me. She cocked her head to the side and gave me a quizzical glance. I put my finger to my lips and pointed at the door.

We waited for ten minutes, and I was almost ready to give up, retreat to the living room, and explain my actions to Valerie, when suddenly, we heard Ellie stir. From behind the closed bedroom door came the sound of her sheets rustling. The bedsprings creaked. Small feet padded across the carpet. Then Ellie spoke. Her voice was a hushed whisper. Obviously, she assumed we were in the living room, and didn't want us to hear her.

"Mr. Chickbaum! I didn't think you were going to come tonight. You always come out as soon as Daddy turns off the light."

She paused, as if listening to a response. I found myself leaning forward, listening for one as well. As soon as I realized that I was do-ing it, I felt like an idiot. But then I noticed that Valerie was doing the same thing. It was a testament to the power of our daughter's imagination. I grinned, shaking my head. Valerie smiled.

Ellie spoke again, answering some imaginary comment.

"He had you trapped? Why doesn't he just leave you alone?"

My heart beat once. Twice.

Then, "I hate that mean old cat!"

Valerie stiffened, and reached for the doorknob. I reached out, clasped her hand, and motioned again for her to be still. We continued eavesdropping on her conversation.

"It's not fair that you have to hide from him," Ellie complained. "You were here before he was."

There was a pause, and then, "I know. But Daddy and Mommy never go into the field, so they won't find the door. If we could just keep Hannibal out of there, too..."

Another pause, and then Ellie giggled.

"They think you're make believe. I don't understand why you don't just show yourself to them. Then you could live with us. Hannibal can't get you if you stay inside the house. Mommy won't let him in here because he pees on the wall."

In the living room, Valerie's cuckoo clock, which had belonged to her grandmother, chimed softly.

"Mommy and Daddy would like you," Ellie said. "They're nice. Not like Hannibal."

I frowned.

"But why do you have to wait for the rest of your people? Maybe Daddy can help you fix the door? He's good at fixing things. He fixed my wading pool last year when it had a leak. Maybe he could—"

She stopped in mid-sentence. I felt a mixture of amazement and panic. Ellie's imagination was elaborate enough to have Mr. Chickbaum interrupt her when she was speaking.

"I don't know what that word means," Ellie said. "Just remember, you promised. When you get the door open and your friends come through, you promise you'll show yourselves to Mommy and Daddy?"

Valerie and I glanced at each other. Her expression mirrored my own confusion. I didn't understand this bit about the door.

"And then you can live here with me?"

Valerie shrugged. We turned our attention back to the door.

"The whole world? But you'll let everybody else stay, right? You won't hurt them?"

I bit my lip, trying to make sense of what I was hearing.

"How soon until you can open the door?" A pause, and then, "Really? That *is* soon."

Then, "But you always spend the night. How come you can't now?"

"Okay. I understand."

"I love you, too, Mr. Chickbaum. You're my best friend forever and ever."

Ellie grew quiet. We stood there, listening to the silence, waiting for more. Small feet padded across the carpet again. The box spring beneath her mattress creaked.

The sound of small feet continued for a brief moment after.

It startled me. That couldn't be right. She'd already gotten back into bed. I glanced at Valerie to see if she'd notice it, too. If she had, she gave no indication. I shook my head, frustrated that I'd let my imagination get the best of me. First, I'd been listening for Mr. Chickbaum's voice. Now I was imagining his footsteps.

I yawned, realizing just how tired I was. Worrying about Ellie had left me mentally and emotionally exhausted. In the dim hallway light, I noticed dark circles under Valerie's eyes. It was impacting her, as well.

We tiptoed carefully down the hall and went into our bedroom. We didn't speak—undressing in silence. I brushed my teeth, gargled, and pissed. Then I climbed into bed while Valerie took her turn in the bathroom. When she slid into bed beside me, we still didn't speak. We didn't have to. Our fears were mutual. We lay there in the dark, holding each other, afraid for our daughter.

I didn't remember falling asleep, so when I awoke in the middle of the night, I was startled and disoriented. My heart hammered in my chest, and I was holding my breath, but I didn't know why.

Then, outside our bedroom window, Hannibal howled, chasing some unknown prey. I waited, listening for the answering cry of another cat, or maybe a possum, skunk or raccoon. But no response was forthcoming. Hissing, Hannibal took off across the yard. I heard his paws swishing through the wet grass. More howls echoed through the night.

Valerie sat up, clasping her chest. "What's wrong?"

"Hannibal's fighting something. Stay here."

I climbed out of bed and put on a pair of sweatpants. Without bothering to turn on the light, I slipped into my bedroom shoes and opened the dresser. I grabbed a flashlight and my Taurus 357 from the drawer, and after fumbling with the key, deactivated the child safety locks on the back of the handgun. Then I slid five bullets into the cylinder and glanced down at Valerie.

"Be careful," she said.

"I will."

I stepped out onto the deck and swept the flashlight beam around the yard. I caught a glimpse of Hannibal—a white streak against the darkness. He was running towards the vacant field that borders our property. I called after him in a hushed voice, not wanting to wake Ellie or our neighbors, but he was intent on the chase and ignored me.

Cursing, I dashed down the stairs. Gravel crunched under my feet. I ran across the yard. Cold dew soaked through my bed-room shoes, soaking my feet. A light mist hovered just over the ground, swirling slowly. I swore harder, vowing to remove the cat door and start locking Hannibal inside the garage at night. Sooner or later, he was going to tangle with something that he couldn't beat. Rabies was a concern, as well. He'd had his shots, but if he got into a fight with a rabid raccoon, I was concerned that he could spread the disease to one of us.

"Hannibal! Come here!"

He vanished into the field. I ran after him. The tall grass clung to my sweatpants. I noticed how quiet it was. At night, I'd lie awake in bed and listen to the shrill songs of insects and birds, or the harsh croaking of bullfrogs. Now, there was none of that. No traffic on the road, either. Even the wind was still.

I'd gone about twenty yards when the field exploded with noise. Hannibal growled. It rose in pitch and intensity, then turned into a long, drawn-out series of hisses and howls. The animal—whatever it was—shrieked; a high-pitched squeal.

A rabbit, I thought. He's got a rabbit.

The grass swayed in front of me. I shined the light in that direction, and the beam glanced across a pile of junk. Somebody had been using the vacant field as a dump. There was an old, rusty shopping cart, several bald tires, a cracked commode, and an old door lying flat on the ground. Its tarnished brass door-knob gleamed in the moonlight. Someone had spray painted graffiti across the top of the door. I frowned, trying to make sense of it. There were no words or letters—just an odd series of images, like something from a heavy metal CD cover. It was certainly an odd thing to paint on a door.

The scuffling animals distracted me. I shined the light lower. Sure enough, Hannibal was tumbling and wrestling with something else. I couldn't tell what it was, though. They moved too fast, darting back and forth and rolling around on the ground.

"Hannibal," I shouted. "Let it go!"

His growls grew louder.

"Hannibal!"

The thing squealed.

Pointing the handgun at the ground, I fired one shot into the dirt at my feet. Immediately, Hannibal released his prey and fled into the darkness. The animal ran off, as well. I studied the flattened weeds where they'd been fighting, and saw a few diminutive drops of blood. I hoped the blood didn't belong to my cat.

I called for Hannibal a few more times, but he didn't answer. Eventually, I made my way back to the house. Luckily, none of our neighbors lights were on. They'd slept through the shot. Ellie had, as well. Valerie was waiting for me in the kitchen. Her eyes were wide. A cup of tea sat on the table in front of her, untouched.

"What was it?"

I shrugged, unloading the pistol. "I don't know. A rabbit, I think. It sounded like one, at least."

"Is Hannibal okay?"

"I hope so. He took off when I broke them up."

"He'll come back," she said. "He always does."

"Yeah. He does."

We went back to bed, and slept uninterrupted for the rest of the night.

The next morning, Valerie and I talked while Ellie got ready for school. We decided that I'd try talking to her during the morning drive, while Valerie checked into getting us an appointment with a therapist or child counselor. Ellie was in a good mood. She chatted through breakfast, and was eager to get to school.

"You're pretty happy this morning," I said, ruffling her hair as we walked towards the door. "What's going on?"

"It's a secret, Daddy."

"Oh come on," I teased. "You can tell me."

"No, I can't. I promised."

"Please? Just a hint?"

Ellie hesitated, then smiled. She leaned in close to me, whispering conspiratorially. "Mr. Chickbaum's friends are coming tonight."

"Ellie...we need to talk about...Mr. Chickbaum."

"I know you think he's pretend, Daddy, but you'll see. He had to do some stuff last night to get ready. Tonight, he can open the door to his world and then we can meet his friends."

We walked out onto the deck.

"Ellie..."

She screamed.

Lying on the deck was another half-corpse—two tiny, human legs about three inches tall, attached to the ragged remains of a miniature waist. It wore a little pair of green pants and one green shoe. The other shoe was missing. The bare foot had miniscule toes. Doll baby-sized blood and entrails spread out around the corpse.

Ellie screamed again, and then I joined her.

Hannibal lay nearby, sunning himself. He licked his lips and gazed at us with contentment.

STORY NOTE: Most of this story is true. Except for the bit about the leprechaun. In real life, Hannibal's name is Max. He showed up one day much like the cat in this story. He was just a tiny kitten, and fearful of everyone and everything. I don't know if someone dumped him off at our house or if he was just born wild out in the woods. I fed him for a few days, but he still wouldn't let anyone come near him. Then, a week later, I was sitting in my office working on the first draft of *Ghost Walk*. I had the office door open to let in some fresh air. I heard a tiny little 'meep' and I looked down, and the kitten was standing at the foot of my chair. He crawled up into my lap, I named him Max (after the movie character Mad Max), and he's been with me ever since.

When I got divorced for the second time and moved into a new place, Max came with me. But before that, to repay my kindness, Max was very good at bringing me daily presents. He left them at the door to my office, which was on our property but in a separate building from the house. Often, the presents he brought me were half-presents. Usually, he caught mice and voles. Occasionally, he brought me a bird or a frog, which always saddened me a bit. I tried to discourage him from killing birds and frogs. Once, he killed a squirrel, just like the cat in the story. I wouldn't have believed it if I hadn't seen him for myself—dragging the squirrel across the yard. To the best of my knowledge, he never killed a snake, although I did find him messing around with a copperhead once. I shooed Max away and killed the snake with the .357 that I carried with me (the house was in a very remote area, with coyotes and snakes and bears and drunken rednecks, so I had good reason to carry a gun).

Many summers ago, author Tim Lebbon was visiting me for a few days. One evening, we were sitting around my fire pit, smoking good cigars and drinking some fine scotch (a gift from author Sarah Langan) and our conversation turned to cats, and their habit of leaving dead things lying around, and how, quite often, it was only half of a dead thing.

There's a certain look an author gets when a story idea suddenly hits him. Tim and I got the look at the same time. We both grew quiet, stared into the fire, and mulled our ideas over.

"I just got a killer story idea," I said.

Tim nodded. "Me, too."

I told him mine and he told me his. They were both good ideas. We agreed that, since it was my house and my cat, I should get to write the story, but that I should include Tim's daughter, Ellie, in it, since she also had a cat. We finished our cigars and drank our scotch. The fire dwindled down to embers.

One year later, I wrote this tale. These days, Max is an indoor cat and occupies himself by chasing cat toys around my house.

The entity known as Mr. Chickbaum is also referenced in my novel *A Gathering of Crows* (but in a different form than a leprechaun). There's a reason for this, which you'll discover eventually. If I told you now, it would spoil the story to come...

Without You

I woke up this morning and shot myself twice.

Carolyn had already left for work. She'd tried waking me repeatedly, as she does every morning. It's a game that has become an annoying ritual, much like the rest of my life.

The alarm went off for the first time at six. Like always, she was pressed up against me, and my morning hard on was wedged into her fat ass. She thinks that I still find her desirable, not realizing that every man in the world wakes up like that if he has a full bladder. Carolyn hasn't turned me on in over ten years.

She lay there, as she does every morning, with the alarm blaring, snuggling tighter against me until I wanted to scream. Her breath stank. Her hair stank. She stank. I always shower before bed, as well as in the morning. She only showers in the morning.

I reached over her and hit the snooze button. Ten minutes later the scene replayed itself. This time she got up and stumbled off to the bathroom. Drifting in and out of sleep, I heard her singing along with Britney Spears on the radio. That's something else that annoyed me. Here we were, both in our thirties, and she still insisted on listening to teenybopper pop music. I listened to talk radio mostly, but not Carolyn. She'd sing along with all that hip-hop shit.

It was enough to drive a man crazy.

After the shower, she walked into the bedroom, humming and dripping and babbling baby talk to me.

"Come on, my widdle poozie woozie, wakey wakey."

I groaned, wanting to die right then and there.

"Did I tire you out last night," she asked, as she ironed a skirt for work. "Am I too much for you?"

I mumbled an incoherent response, shuddering at thoughts of the previous evening's acrobatics. She'd come three times. I had to envision my mother just to get it up, and still I had to fake an orgasm. Thank God for rubbers.

Twenty minutes later, I was still lying there and Carolyn was more insistent, warning me that I'd be late for work. I told her I was sick, and her smothering concern made me want to leap out of my skin. Thankfully, she'd been late for work, and I got off lucky with only a quick kiss and a promise to call me during her lunch break.

I heard the door shut. A minute later, I heard the Saturn cough to life. The Saturn that we still owed over six grand on, even though it was a piece of shit. The Saturn that we'd just *had* to have, because that's what everybody else was driving. My S.U.V. had been bought for the same reason and we owed even more on it.

I rolled out of bed, walking through the house that we would be in debt for until our Sixties. I called into work, biting my lip to keep from arguing with Clarence when he questioned me. Twelve years I'd busted my ass for him. Twelve years of endless monotony, of heat and grime and boredom. Twelve years of ten-hour days with mandatory overtime, running a machine I was fated to operate until the soft haze of retirement. And after all of that, he had the fucking gall to suggest I was faking my illness?

My denial was short and terse. I hadn't meant to call Clarence a fat bastard until it slipped through my clenched teeth.

After he fired me, I slammed the phone down into the cradle. Something warm dribbled down my chin. I tasted blood. I'd bitten through my lower lip. Wincing, I stumbled into the bathroom and watched the blood drip from my chin. One drop landed on my white undershirt. My stomach, bloated from too much cheap beer, seemed to take up most of my reflection. Two days worth of stubble covered my face. There were dark shadows under my eyes. Lines had formed in the past year.

I tore a wad of toilet paper from the dispenser and balled it against my lip. With my free hand, I fingered the growth on my face, trying to decide if it was worth my time to shave. Gray hair peppered my goatee.

The first tear took me by surprise.

I was thirty-five going on seventy. I owed a mountain of debt and had just lost my job. I was married to a woman who I hadn't been in love with since shortly after high school. I had an ulcer, acid reflux, a receding hairline, and a bloody hole in my lip. My only friends were the other guys from work, and they were only my friends when I was buying the first round. I smoked two packs of cigarettes a day and dipped half a can of Skoal. Even now, a tumor was probably spiraling its way through my body.

More tears followed. I collapsed next to the toilet bowl, sobbing. Where had it all gone wrong? Carolyn and I had been so happy during our senior year. I had a terrific arm in football and a promising scholarship. The world was mine and I was God. I used to tremble after our lovemaking, which is what it was back then, not the obscene pantomime it had become now. I had loved her so much.

"Do you love me," she used to ask me afterward. "Do you really love me?"

I always replied, "I'd die without you."

Then Carolyn got pregnant halfway through our senior year and I kissed college goodbye. The baby was stillborn. We never tried again. I guess that was when I began the downward spiral.

The phone rang. I rose unsteadily, leaning on the sink for support. My head throbbed. The phone rang again, more insistent this time. It reminded me of Carolyn.

I gripped the receiver so hard that my knuckles turned white. Probably Clarence, calling back to berate me some more.

"Hello?"

There was a pause and a series of mechanical clicks. Then a female spoke, offering me a free appraisal for storm windows on the home I couldn't afford.

"I'm not interested," I said. "Put us on your do not call list."

"Can I axe you why, sir?" It sounded like she was reading from a script.

"You can't 'axe' me anything. You can 'ask' me if you'd like, but the answer is still fuck off!"

The telemarketer launched into a tirade then and I ripped the phone from the wall. I flung it across the room. It smashed into a lamp that Carolyn's mother had given to us for our fifth wedding anniversary. I stared at the fragments, felt fresh blood running down my chin again, and sighed.

I'd been contemplating it for weeks, but it wasn't until then that I decided to die.

I went to the gun cabinet. Inside were my hunting rifles, kept for a pastime that I didn't enjoy, but that I had to partake in to be considered a normal guy. My hand was steady as I unlocked the case and selected the 30.06 and a box of shells. The bullets slid into the chamber with satisfying clicks. I sat down on the bed with the gun between my legs.

I had seen pictures online of failed suicide attempts. Cases where the poor slob had placed the gun against the side of his head and pulled the trigger, writhing in agony when the bullet traveled around his brain and left him alive. That was no good. I needed to do this the right way. I placed the barrel in my mouth, tasting the oil on the cold metal. I breathed through my nose, deep-throating the gun the way I'd done my Uncle's shriveled pecker when I was nine. As the barrel touched the back of my throat, I gagged, just like back then. Tears streamed down my face.

I glanced at the wedding picture on the nightstand. There was me and Carolyn. Two smiling people. Happy. In love. Not the balding loser who sat here now or the fat cow the woman had turned into.

The woman who I had promised to love forever so long ago.

"I'd die without you," I mumbled around the barrel.

Then I pulled the trigger.

The initial force jerked me backward. The gun barrel impaled the roof of my mouth. I felt blast open my head and heard the wet slap of my brains hitting the wall, turning the ivory flowered wallpaper crimson. Grey chunks of brain matter and eggshell splinters of my fragmented skull embedded themselves in the drywall. My right eye dribbled down my face as my bladder and sphincter let loose, staining the bed sheets.

The pain stopped abruptly, as if someone had flicked a light switch. One moment I was writhing in agony and trying to scream around the gun. Then there was nothing.

But I was conscious.

I wasn't dead. I'd fucked this up, too.

I pulled the trigger again. The second shot erased what was left of the top and back of my head. My face sagged down a few inches, making it hard to see clearly. Bits of skin and gristle dangled down my neck. The room stank of blood and shit and cordite.

The gunshots echoed throughout the house, drowning out my heavy breathing.

Letting the rifle slip from my numb fingers, I shuffled to the mirror and looked at the damage I'd inflicted. I had to shrug my shoulders a few times in order to get my face back up to eye level.

It wasn't pretty.

I should have been dead, yet there I stood. I reached behind me, letting my fingers play across the gaping hole where my brain had been. There was nothing. No bald spot, no scalp, no skull. Nothing.

The phone rang again. It sounded muffled, thanks to my one remaining ear. After four rings, the answering machine clicked on.

"Hi, honey." Carolyn. "I just wanted to see how you were feeling."

"My headache is gone." Laughing, I spat out a piece of myself. "I've cured the common headache."

"Anyway," she continued, "I've got to get back to work. See you when I get home. I love you."

"I'd die without you." My voice dripped with sarcasm.

Then it hit me—the reason that I was still alive.

So now I'm sitting here at the kitchen table, writing this while my insides dry on the bedroom wall. I'm almost free of this hell that is my life. Carolyn will be home soon, and I will fulfill the promise that I made to her so long ago.

———

STORY NOTE: This is another early tale. It suffers from that, at least by my reading, but I've always liked the opening sentence. Not much else to say about it, other than it was inspired by a late-night conversation with an old friend. I think of him whenever I re-read this.

Couch Potato

Adele didn't know much about zombies until they interrupted the Jerry Springer show. It happened during an episode about—well, Adele wasn't sure what it was about. She never paid that much attention to Jerry Springer. Her momma sure did, though. That was how Adele knew something was wrong. She'd been sitting on the floor, playing her four Disney princess dolls—Belle, Cinderella, Ariel, and Sleeping Beauty, all purchased for her by their neighbor, Mrs. Withers, at the Goodwill store ("and ain't a one of them black", the older woman had complained)—when the audience chants of "Jerry! Jerry! Jerry!" were suddenly interrupted by a monotonous, urgent tone. Her mother groaned, muttered a curse, and reached for the remote control. Adele was quietly hopeful. Momma got upset when her TV viewing was inconvenienced, but it was also the only time she tended to pay any attention to Adele.

The droning alarm continued, and letters scrolled across the bottom of the screen. Adele read them as they flashed past. E-M-E-R-G-E-N-C-Y... B-R-O-A-D-C-A-S-T... S-Y-S-T-E-M. She didn't know quite what that meant, but it sounded scary, whatever it was. Still muttering, Momma pointed the remote at the television.

"Wait, Momma. Maybe it's important."

Her mother turned toward her. The gesture was slow and exaggerated, as if she'd forgotten that Adele was in the room and was surprised to hear her voice. She didn't respond. Instead, she just stared at her daughter with a blank, indifferent expression, and then turned back to the screen.

Jerry Springer was gone now, replaced by the local news. The bar was still scrolling across the bottom of the screen, but the words were going by too fast for Adele to read them. Her mother began scrolling through the channels, but all of her favorite programs were gone, replaced instead by newscasters. Momma cursed. Adele listened. And that was how she learned about zombies.

The people on television said it was a disease. Adele knew about diseases. Cancer, the thing that had taken her Grandma away last year, was a disease. So was Momma's addiction to heroin, or at least, that's what some people said. But she'd never heard of the disease that was turning people into zombies. It was called Hamelin's Revenge. Adele hadn't understood what the name meant. She heard a pretty newscaster say it had something to do with the story of the Pied Piper, but the only version of that story Adele was familiar with was from an old Looney Tunes cartoon that she'd seen on one of the rare occasions when her mother wasn't watching television.

Apparently, the disease came from rats—dead rats, crawling out of the sewers and subways in New York City and attacking people. The people who were bitten got sick and died, and then they came back as zombies. And it wasn't just people and rats, either. Dogs and cats could catch it, too. So could cows, bears, coyotes, goats, sheep, monkeys and other animals. A few animals, like pigs and birds, were immune, and for that, Adele was glad. There weren't any pigs in Baltimore that she knew of, but she saw birds every time she went outside. She hated to think what would happen if they all turned into zombies.

All the shows that Momma liked—the court programs and soap operas and talk shows—were pre-empted by twenty-four hour news footage. She'd had no choice but to watch them, and as a result, Adele had watched them, too. Much of what she saw was confusing or scary, and in those first three days, it became a hodge-podge of horrific imagery. New York City was quarantined. National Guardsmen blockaded the bridges and tunnels and rail tracks, and fired on people trying to escape. Then the troops began fighting each other. The disease spread to other cities, and then to other countries. More and more people became zombies. The news said that all it took was one bite, one drop of blood, pus from an open sore or cut—any exposure to infected bodily fluid. People that died normal deaths stayed dead, but those who came into direct contact with the disease became zombies. A law was passed requiring the dead to be burned, and the television showed pictures of bulldozers pushing bodies into big, smoking pits. Chicago and Phoenix burned to the ground. Zombies overran an airport in Miami. A nuclear reactor melted down in China.

More and more people died every day, and then came back as zombies. There were also regular people—still living people—who were just as bad, if not worse, than the zombies. Adele knew all about bad people, of course. Her neighborhood was full of bad people (although there were some good ones, like Mrs. Withers next door, and her son Michael). But there were more bad people than good, and more zombies than either. The only thing that hadn't changed was that the police still didn't show up when people called for help. Now, the bad people finally had the opportunity to do everything they'd ever dreamed of.

Not so, Adele. Her dreams didn't involve rape or murder or robbery. All she'd ever wanted was for her momma to pay attention to her. But that didn't happen either. Not even when the power went on the third night. It was off for an hour before it came back on. Adele lay there in bed, hoping her mother would come in and check on her.

She didn't. Instead, Momma called the electric and cable companies to complain about the outage. Outside, the streets echoed with more gunshots and screams than usual. Adele fell asleep listening to Momma complain on the phone.

When she woke up the next morning, the power was back on again, but several stations had gone off the air.

Although Adele was only nine years old, she knew what a normal, loving family life was like. She'd seen plenty of examples on TV. She'd seen plenty of the other kind, as well. Often times, the people on the television used big words to refer to those bad relationships. One of the words was dysfunctional. Another was neglectful. In time, Adele came to understand that those words applied to her own home life, especially when compared against the lives of the kids on television. Those kids usually lived in nice houses, with one or two loving parents that took an interest in what they were doing, and talked to them, and played with them, and let them know that they were loved. Adele's mother didn't do those things. It wasn't that Momma was abusive. She was just neglectful.

Before the zombies had come, Momma's daily routine had been: wake up on the couch, fix, make coffee and light a cigarette, and then sit back down on the couch again. She'd sit there all day and watch television in between fixes. Occasionally, she'd make something to eat. Sometimes she'd even remember to make something for Adele to eat, as well, but Adele had become accustomed to making meals on her own. She liked school because she knew she'd get breakfast and lunch there. At home, she could never be sure. Adele put herself to bed most nights—bathed herself, put on her pajamas by herself, brushed her teeth, and read herself a bedtime story. She always told her momma good night. Occasionally, her mother would grunt in response. In rare moments, she might even spare a hug or a kiss on the cheek. But usually she just nodded, eyes glued to the television, cigarette smoldering between her fingers, discarded needle lying on the coffee table. Momma usually fell asleep on the couch at night. The television stayed on, even while they slept.

On the fourth day, Mrs. Withers sent Michael over to check on them. Momma didn't like the Withers family very much, on account the time Mrs. Withers had once threatened to call social services on her, but Adele liked the older woman and her son very much. They were always nice to her. Mrs. Withers always had a kind word and gave her hugs and smiles, and Michael could always make Adele laugh, and would talk to her about how school was going. Both took an interest in her, and for Adele, that meant everything.

When Michael knocked on the door, Momma's eyes barely flicked from the images on the television screen—footage of dead people and animals marauding through the streets of Camden. There was dried spit on Momma's cheek and she hadn't changed her clothes in days. Adele went to the door, peered through the peephole to verify that it wasn't a zombie, and smiled when she saw Michael.

So far, the worst part of the zombie apocalypse had been the loneliness and boredom. Staying cooped up inside the apartment, Adele missed her friends at school and the people she talked to on the block. She was no stranger to loneliness, of course. Living with Momma was a lot like living alone. But in the past, she'd been able to temper the loneliness with occasional interactions with others. Now, it was just her and Momma and the people on television, so seeing Michael made her happy.

He hurried inside and shut the door behind him, and advised them of the situation outside. Zombies were all over Baltimore, but it hadn't gotten as bad as some of the other cities yet. He'd heard that the National Guard and something called FEMA would have the situation under control soon. All they had to do was wait it out. Momma grunted in response to all this, and got mad and impatient when Michael reminded her to lock the door and barricade all the windows. Michael ended up doing it for them. Adele helped him as best she could, and when they were done, Michael slapped his forehead in mock surprise.

"I almost forgot!" He reached into his shirt pocket and pulled out a candy bar. Then he handed it to Adele. Smiling, she gave him a big hug.

"Thank you," she said.

"You're welcome." He hugged her back, and then sighed. "Adele, listen. Maybe you should come stay with me and my Mom. I could talk to your Momma about it. I don't think she'd mind."

Adele heard the tone in his voice, and her smile faltered. She knew what other people thought of Momma, and sometimes she felt that way, too, but still—it was her Momma, and she loved her.

"I can't," she said. "I'd like to, but I guess I better stay here with Momma."

"Maybe we can convince her to come over, too. There's safety in numbers."

Adele shook her head. "You know, Momma. She won't go."

"No, I don't guess she will."

"Then you should come."

"No," she repeated. "I need to stay here and take care of her."

Michael frowned. "Okay. But if you need anything, you come over. Check outside first. If you see anybody—zombie or otherwise—you stay inside. But if the coast is clear and you need us, you come hollering."

Adele nodded. "I will."

Michael gave Adele another hug and then left. Momma barely acknowledged the young man when he said goodbye. He made Adele promise to remain quiet and keep away from the windows, and told her to lock and barricade the door behind him, and she did.

Later that night, after she'd eaten her candy bar, Adele wondered what they'd do if they ran out of food. She never got the chance to find out, because they ran out of heroin and cigarettes first.

Adele woke to the sound of gunfire. That in itself wasn't unusual, even before the zombies. But the gunshots were right outside their apartment, and they went on for a very long time, punctuated with screams. Adele couldn't tell if the shrieks belonged to a man or a woman. When the sounds finally faded, she got out of bed and crept to the window. Michael had nailed it shut and put a blanket over it, preventing anyone from seeing inside. Adele lifted a corner of the blanket and cautiously peered outside. Several bodies lay in the street. She couldn't tell if they'd been living or the living dead. Now, they were just old school dead. Each one had been shot in the head.

Unable to sleep, Adele wandered into the living room. Even though Momma would most likely ignore her, she'd still get some comfort just from being in her mother's presence and not sitting there alone. The living room was lit only by the glow of the television. Momma had turned the sound low, so as to not attract attention from outside. Adele turned toward the couch and gasped. Her mother was gone. The blanket had been kicked to the floor and the pillow and couch cushions still held her impression. Adele glanced at the stained coffee table. It was littered with used needles, an overflowing ashtray, and empty, crumpled cigarette packs. Most telling was the television remote control sitting on the arm of the couch. Momma's lighter was gone, as were her shoes. Adele knelt down and reached under the couch, careful not to jab herself with any discarded needles that might be lurking in the darkness. She pulled out a slim cigar box that her mother used to hide her stash in. When she opened the box, there was a feint whiff of tobacco. The box was empty.

"Oh, Momma..."

She'd gone outside, in search of heroin or cigarettes, or more likely both.

Adele began to cry, not so much from sadness or fear. She felt those things, of course, but she felt another emotion, deep down beneath them, and it was that strange, unexpected emotion that caused the tears.

The emotion was relief.

Momma had left the door unlocked, so the first thing Adele did was lock it. She made herself a bowl of cereal. There was no milk in the fridge so she ate it dry. Then she did something she rarely had the opportunity to do—she picked up Momma's remote and changed the channel to something she wanted to watch. Two of the local Baltimore affiliates were off the air, and the third was showing news, but Cartoon Network was still on the air. She sat there, munching cereal and watching television, and was content.

She fell asleep in front of the television.

She woke to another noise outside. This time, it wasn't gunshots or screams. It was quieter—more discreet. At first, Adele thought she'd imagined it, but then the sound came again—a soft, subdued scratching at the door, followed by a thump. Wide-eyed, she pulled the blanket over her head. The fabric smelled like her mother. The noise came again, louder this time. Adele got up from the couch and padded across the room in her bare feet. Holding her breath, she glanced through the peephole.

It was Momma. She looked sick. Her eyes were glassy and drool leaked from the corner of her open mouth. As Adele watched, she raised one arm and scratched at the door again.

She must have found some, Adele thought. *She scored, and now she can't open the door. I'd better let her in and help her lay down.*

Adele's fingers fumbled with the lock. As it slid back, Momma pushed the door open so fast that Adele had to scurry backward to avoid being hit by it. Momma stumbled into the house, swaying unsteadily on her feet. Her lips were pale, and her eyes remained unfocused. She glanced at Adele, frowning in confusion, as if she wasn't sure who the girl was. That was when Adele noticed the bite on Momma's arm. There was an ugly, bloody, ragged hole where her bicep had been. The wound was white and red in the center, and bluish-purple strands of tissue dangled from it.

"Momma, you're hurt! Lay down."

Her mother's lips pulled back in a snarl. She reached for Adele and moaned. Drool splattered onto the floor. Adele had time to realize that Momma was neither high nor hurt. She was dead. And then Momma lunged for her, finally paying the attention that her daughter had craved for so long.

Screaming, Adele ducked her mother's outstretched arms and ran down he hall. She fled into her bedroom and slammed the door. Her mother's slow footsteps plodded toward her, but then stopped. Adele shoved her toy box against the door and stood there panting, waiting for the blows and scratches that would surely follow, but they didn't. If Momma was on the other side of the door, then she was quiet. Adele wondered if it could be a trick. Maybe Momma was lurking, waiting for her to come out. The zombies on television hadn't seemed very smart, but this wasn't TV. This was real life. This was her mother.

Adele tiptoed over to the far corner and slumped down to the floor. She kept her gaze focused on the door, waiting for it to burst open, but it didn't. She began to cry again—this time, because that feeling of relief was gone. She didn't know what to do. She couldn't escape through the window, because Michael had nailed them shut. But even if she could get the window open, there would be no escape outside. She was safer in here with one zombie than she was out on the streets with hundreds.

If she could make it over to Mrs. Withers' apartment next door, she'd be okay. She was sure of it. Michael and Mrs. Withers could help her. But the only way to get there was through the front door, which meant going past Momma. Taking a deep breath, Adele crept to the door again and listened. The only sound from the rest of the apartment was the television, which was still tuned to Cartoon Network.

"Momma?" Her voice, barely a whisper, was simultaneously hopeful and terrified.

Like she had when she was alive, Momma didn't answer.

Adele reached for the doorknob with one trembling hand and turned it. Then she slowly opened the door a crack, fully expecting her mother to barge into the room. When she didn't, Adele opened it wider and peeked out into the hall. It was empty. She shut the door again, and got dressed. She had a moment of panic when she realized that her shoes were in the living room, but then she found a pair of flip flops in her closet. When she was finished, Adele quietly rummaged through her toy box, and pulled out a small rubber ball. Then she opened the door again and rolled the ball down the hall. It bounced into the living room and vanished from sight. Still, there was no reaction.

Satisfied that her mother had left, Adele crept down the hall. The television grew louder as she neared the living room. When she rounded the corner, two things became immediately apparent. The front door was still hanging open...

...and Momma was sitting on the couch.

Adele stifled a shriek. Her mother sat slumped over on the sofa, her wound leaking onto the cushions. Flies flitted about the bite, landing on Momma's arm and then taking off again. Their droning buzz was noticeable beneath the noise from the television. If Momma noticed her, she gave no indication. The zombie's attention was focused instead on the remote control. Momma clutched it in one hand, and her thumb slid idly across the buttons, but she was holding it backwards and nothing happened. As Adele watched, the thing that had been her mother moaned.

Adele looked out into the street and saw that it was empty. She was sure it wouldn't be for long. If she was going to flee next door, she had to do it now. Taking a deep breath, she dashed into the living room and raced past her mother. She glanced back over her shoulder as she ran through the open door.

Momma hadn't even noticed.

––––––––

STORY NOTE: I've written a lot of zombie short stories over the years. *The Rising: Selected Scenes From the End of the World* collects a good chunk of them. This book (and the volumes to follow) collect the rest. This story was most likely the last one I'll ever write about zombies. Indeed, I'd thought I was already done with them before I wrote this one. Fact is, I'd run out of things to say with the undead. But then Christopher Golden asked me to write one more for an anthology he was editing. Chris is an old, dear friend, so I couldn't turn him down. And then I discovered that I had one more thing to say with zombies, after all.

Fade To Null

She woke to the sound of thunder, lying in a strange bed with no memory of who she was or where she was, and panic nearly overwhelmed her. Her stomach clenched. Her breaths came in short gasps. Frantic, she glanced around the room for clues, but familiarity eluded her. The room was small, equipped with a dresser, a writing desk, and a chair with one leg shorter than the others. Atop the dresser sat a slender blue-glass vase with some flowers in it.

The flowers soothed her, but she didn't know why.

She studied the rest of the room. Looming overhead were the cracked, yellowing panels of a drop ceiling. The carpet was light green, the wallpaper pastel. Framed prints hung on the wall—Monet, Kincaid, Rockwell. She wondered how it was possible that she knew their names but didn't know her own. The closet door was slightly open, revealing a stranger's clothes. There was only one window, and the blinds were closed tight. If the room had a door, other than the closet, she couldn't see it.

The sheets were thin and starchy, and rubbed against her skin like sandpaper. They felt damp from sweat. Clenching the sheets in both fists, she raised them slightly and peered beneath. She was dressed in a faded sleeping gown with a dried brown stain over one breast. What was it? Gravy? Mud? Blood? Except for her underwear, she was bare beneath the gown.

She considered calling for help, but decided against it. She was afraid—afraid of who, or what, might answer her summons. Despite the fact that the room seemed empty, she couldn't help but feel like there was someone else in here with her. Someone *unseen*.

The thunder boomed again. Blue-white light flashed from behind the closed blinds, and for a moment, she saw glimpses of other people in the room with her—a man, a woman, and a little girl. They were like the images on photo negatives, stark against the room's feeble light, but at the same time, flickering and ghostly—composed of television static. The man stood by her bedside, dressed in a white doctor's coat. A stethoscope dangled around his neck. He held a clipboard. The woman stood next to him, wearing a simple but pretty blouse. She seemed tired and sad. The little girl sat in the wobbly chair, rocking back and forth on the crooked legs.

"It's okay, Mika. Grandma is just having a bad dream."

The voice was distant. Muted. An echo. And female.

She tried to scream, but only managed a rasping, wheezy sigh.

The three figures vanished with the next blast of thunder, blinking out of existence as if they'd never been there at all.

Maybe they hadn't.

She was dimly aware that she had to pee.

When the drum roll of thunder sounded again, the drop-ceiling disappeared as quickly as the ghost-people had. Everything else in the room remained the same—the drab furnishings, the dim light—but in the ceiling's place was a purple, wounded sky. Boiling clouds raced across it, but she felt no wind. Although the temperature hadn't changed, she shivered. The pressure on her bladder increased. She relaxed, and felt a sudden rush of warmth. Then the violet sky split open, revealing a black hole, and it began to rain desiccated flowers.

'Flowers,' she thought. 'There are flowers on the dresser. Ellen brought them.'

Then she wondered who Ellen was.

Dried petals continued to shower the bed, tickling her nose and cheeks. She sighed. The feeling was not unpleasant. Then, as quickly as it had begun, the rain of flower petals stopped—replaced by something else. Her eyes widened in terror. A squadron of bulbous flies poured from the hole in the sky, buzzing in a multitude of languages. Their bodies were black, their heads green like emeralds. They circled the room in a swirling pattern. A flock of birds plunged out of the hole, giving chase. The thunder increased, inside the room with her now. The noise was deafening. The flies scattered and the birds squawked in fright. A black, oily feather floated gently towards her.

She tried to sit up, but her fatigue weighed her like a stone. All she could do was lie there and watch. Listen. Wonder.

Where was she? What was this? What was happening?

She thought again of the flowers. They'd been brought by... who, exactly? She couldn't remember. Someone. She thought it might be important.

The warmth dissipated. She was cold again. Her fear was replaced by a powerful sense of frustration in both her physical discomfort and her confusion. Why couldn't she remember anything?

Above her, the sky continued to weep. Now, strands of DNA fell in ribbons, forming puddles on the bed and floor. Life stirred within those puddles, writhing and squirming. The thunder changed into a voice—a deity, perhaps, screaming. It was a terrible sound. She clasped her hands over her ears and tried to block it out. She'd heard screams like this before. Perhaps she'd even made them, at one time. They sounded like the symphony of birthing pains.

A large puddle of liquid tissue had formed on the sheet in front of her, right between her legs. As she watched, something wriggled from the puddle—a one-inch tentacle, about the thickness of a pencil. There was an eyeball attached to one end of the tendril. It stared at her, and as she watched, the pupil dilated.

In the background, the deity was still screaming. She no longer cared. Her attention was focused on the tentacle-thing. The creature groped feebly at her gown, and then pulled itself forward. She slapped her hand down on it, pressing it into the mattress and grinding her palm back and forth. The tentacle squeaked—even though it lacked a mouth—and then lay still. She removed her hand. All that remained of the thing was a pinkish-white blob of mucus. Slime dripped from her hand.

Silence returned. The disembodied screaming stopped. So did the thunder. The flies and the birds turned to vapor. The hole in the sky closed up, and second later, the drop ceiling reappeared.

"Please," she whispered. "Please... please..."

Then, new voices spoke. A man and a woman.

"She used to love to paint. I thought bringing some of this might help, but she can't even hold the paintbrush."

"Yes. Her motor skills are decreasing rapidly."

"How long does she have?"

"In this stage of Alzheimer's, it is difficult to say. I've seen some hang on for years after the fourth stage has set in. Others go quickly. All we can do is keep her comfortable."

"I just hate bringing Mika to see her like this, you know? I'm worried about how it will effect her."

"That's understandable, Ellen. And while some studies suggest that it's beneficial for patients, we can't even really be sure that your mother is aware of the presence of those around her. I know it's not much comfort, but at least she's calm and peaceful, for the most part."

"Who are you?" she moaned. "Where are you?"

She closed her eyes and let her cheek loll against the pillow, wishing the sky would rain flowers again.

"Who am I?" she whispered. "Please..."

The voices disappeared.

At last, she slept.

When she awoke again, the room was dark and cold. She shivered. There were flowers on the dresser, but she no longer knew what they were.

————

STORY NOTE: This story started as just a fragment. That fragment was something I originally wrote for a multi-author collaboration projects—two dozen authors all contributing to a single short story. Unfortunately, the project never came to fruition. I no longer remember who was involved or what the premise was. All I know is that it was never published. Years later, after I bought a new computer and was in the process of transferring my files over to it, I ran across the fragment and re-worked it into this story. Alzheimer's has impacted my family in a very personal way several times. It's a truly terrifying disease. I find it especially scary because none of us really know what's going on inside the mind of the victim.

Babylon Falling

"We are so fucked!"

And they were.

Bloom coughed. Goggles protected his eyes, but they didn't prevent him from swallowing sand. Neither did his handkerchief, which was tied around his mouth and nose, and drenched with sweat.

He was perched atop an M-88 tank recovery unit, rumbling north toward Baghdad with an immense column of other vehicles from the 3rd Infantry. The convoy was nearly seven thousand strong. The M-88 held a two-man crew, and it was Bloom's turn topside. Myers stayed below, safe from the harsh desert conditions, bobbing his head to Led Zeppelin's "Kashmir." Myers played it over and over on a loop during the march.

"All I see turns to brownnnnnn," Myers sang, "as the sun burns the grounnnnnnnnnd, and my eyes fill with sannnnnd, as I scan this wasted lannnnddd..."

Bloom began to sing along, too. "Trying to find, trying to find where I've beeeee— ack!"

He choked as more grit blew into his mouth.

They'd left Kuwait City before dawn, driving past gorgeous luxury homes and seaside resorts unlike anything they'd ever seen back in the States. But soon, those faded from sight and the desert took over. The only thing for miles, other than camels and their nomadic herders, were massive power lines stretching across the horizon and oil pumps, thrusting into the earth. By midday, these disappeared too, leaving only the featureless brown desert. Even the lizards and birds inhabiting the wasteland vanished, hiding from the incoming storm. In Iraq's late spring, hot winds swept in from the north, raising clouds of sand and dust several thousand feet into the air. The locals called these storms shamals. A media embed in Kuwait City had told Bloom and Myers that this particular shamal was the worst in decades, with winds whipping across the desert at over fifty miles-per-hour, burying everything under a fine coat of yellow and brown. The storm had interrupted bombing missions and ground combat, but not their advance. They were given orders to roll, and roll they did.

Earlier that afternoon, their column had fallen under attack from an Iraqi artillery barrage, and one of the Paladin motorized howitzers caught fire and exploded. The crew escaped, but two of the soldiers were injured. One of them had suffered third-degree burns on his hands. Bloom cringed, remembering the smell, and the way the man's blistered fingers had resembled blackened breakfast sausages. Now, while shells were dropped on two Iraqi forward observation posts in retaliation for the attack, their section of the column had been ordered to wait.

Bloom took advantage of the delay. Myers replaced him at the gun, while he ducked inside. He wolfed down an MRE—Meal Ready to Eat (mixed with sand)—and then cleaned the grime from his face with a baby wipe, wincing as the alcohol came in contact with his red, wind-burned skin. Then he drank greedily from his canteen. Outside the M-88, Bloom heard artillery explosions rolling across the arid landscape. Soon, a report came over the radio that the opposition had been obliterated, and the lead forces were to hold their position to allow the rest of the division to catch up.

"We are so fucked," Bloom repeated, climbing topside to join Myers. "This goddamned sand is everywhere!"

"Could be worse." Myers's sounded tired. His laconic Texan drawl was even slower than usual. "Bad as these storms are, the temperature's only in the seventies. Imagine how this shit would be if it was mid-summer and a hundred and twenty!"

Bloom shrugged. "We'll be home by then. Won't have to worry about it."

Sharp and Rendell sauntered over; free for the moment while a mechanic unclogged the dust from their medical truck's engine. Sharp's pale skin and blonde hair were crusted with dirt, and when Rendell spat a wad of Copenhagen, Bloom noticed ugly blisters on chafed lips. A media embed trailed along behind the two soldiers, squinting against the blowing sand. His expensive sunglasses seemed to offer little protection.

"This sucks," Rendell moaned. "Why don't we just pave over this country and build some shopping malls?"

"That's how they'll know they're free," Myers said, nodding. "When they got a Starbucks and a Wal-Mart on every corner in Baghdad."

Sergeant O'Malley soon joined them, followed by Privates Williams, Sanchez, Riser, and Jefferson. O'Malley was older than the rest, and at thirty-two, a veteran of the first Gulf War. The younger men looked up to him. O'Malley was originally from Long Island. Like Myers, Sanchez hailed from Texas. Williams came from North Carolina, Jefferson from Mississippi, and Riser from Baltimore.

Shading his eyes with his hands, Jefferson surveyed their surroundings while another artillery explosion echoed across the plain.

"Look at it," he said. "This is Hell on earth, if you ask me."

"Can't be any worse than that garbage dump Bloom comes from," Myers said. "What's that city called? Trench-ton?"

Bloom punched him in the shoulder. "Trenton, asshole. And don't be talking shit about Jersey."

All the men laughed.

"What's going on back home?" O'Malley asked the reporter.

"Big protest in San Francisco," the media embed answered. "Martin Sheen and Sean Penn spoke at an anti-war rally."

Riser grimaced. "Does Martin Sheen think he really is the President? Somebody needs to remind him he just plays one on TV."

"What's Sean Penn famous for?" Williams asked.

"Fucking Madonna, apparently," Riser answered. "And that's all. He couldn't make a good movie to save his life."

"What about Fast Times?" Sanchez wiped his goggles on a clean rag. "He was pretty good in that."

"Oh, that took a lot of talent." Riser shook his head. "He played a stoned surfer. Not exactly academy award material, dude."

"My Daddy was protested against when he came back from Vietnam," O'Malley said quietly, his eyes focused on the sand dunes. "He served with the 82nd, saw a world of shit. Did his time, made it through, and came home. Got off the plane at the airport and they spit on him! He was so shocked that he just walked away. He walked. I think that fucked with him in ways the war never did, you know?" The others were silent, reflecting.

"I can't wait for one of these neo-hippie motherfuckers to spit on me," O'Malley continued. "Figure I owe them for him, and then some."

They waited for another hour, trying in vain to stay shielded from the shamal. With nothing to do, O'Malley gave them busy work. They checked and cleaned their gear—rifles, ammunition, body armor, helmets, Saratoga suits to protect against chemical agents, trenching shovels, sleeping bags, and gas masks. Their gas masks were to be within arm's reach at all times, and they'd been trained to don them instantly in case of attack; told there were nine seconds between life and death. So far, they hadn't needed to use them. They wrote letters home, tucked them away for safekeeping, and re-wrote their blood type on their helmets and sleeves.

The only thing they didn't do was sleep.

Eventually, the order came to move on. They proceeded on, into the shamal. The roads vanished amidst the storm, so they followed in the tracks of the vehicles ahead of them. The tanks and Bradley fighting vehicles could go faster, but the column moved at the speed of its slowest vehicle—a wagon train with everything from tanker trucks bearing fuel and water, to Humvees bearing young American soldiers. Radio chatter was kept to a minimum. Drivers focused on not driving off the roads.

The sandstorm's brutality increased. Topside again, Bloom wrapped his bandanna around his nose and mouth. He wished he had an asthma inhaler, some vapor rub, even an oxygen bottle—anything to make it easier for him to breathe.

They passed a hut, several unexploded cluster bombs from the previous Gulf War, and the wreckage of an Iraqi tank, before coming across a burned out observation post. Lying amidst the carnage were the charred remains of an enemy soldier. Bloom wondered if the blowing sand would cover up the corpse before the man's companions found him.

They encountered no further opposition. Occasionally, they came across Bedouin women and children, who waved as they rolled past. Bloom wondered what they were doing out in the storm, but decided that they were probably used to such weather. He debated throwing the kids some hard candy but decided against it—visions of the children being run down by the next vehicle in the convoy while they scampered for the treat ran though his head. Visibility was worsening, and it would be easy for a driver to miss the children bent over in the path of the column.

The storm stayed with them, a constant nuisance. Word came back that there were three Iraqi regular army divisions ahead, but that one of them had already surrendered. O'Malley told them that the commanders didn't anticipate any serious opposition in the south. The troops deployed there were mostly made up of unpaid, unfed conscripts— more than eager to toss their weapons aside and stand down in exchange for a hot meal. The wagon train was supposed to be a psychological offensive—an effort to convince the enemy that resistance was futile. Bloom had heard that the U.S. and British commanders even carried paperwork that allowed Iraqi commanders to sign and surrender their troops on the spot.

The winds reached seventy-five miles an hour. Riser cracked over the radio that they ought to rename the route the Hurricane Highway. This was greeted by laughter, and then a stern admonition to knock it off.

Bloom blinked the sand from his eyes, and tried to focus. "We are so fucked."

He was very tired.

It was almost nightfall when they came across the old man.

He stood along the roadside, propped up by a tall, gnarled wooden staff. Shrouded in colorful robes, only his leathery hands and face were visible. He watched them pass. His expression was impassive. Several of the soldiers waved at him, but he did not return the gesture. Rendell shot him the finger, but this, too, earned no reply.

When Myers pulled alongside him, Bloom stared into the old man's eyes. They were black, like two drops of India ink, and despite the blowing sand, the old man did not blink. Indeed, he seemed almost comfortable in the storm. As Bloom watched, the old man dropped his staff and gestured at the yellow sky.

"The fuck's he doing?" Myers called out.

"I don't know." Bloom was mesmerized by the actions. "Having a heart attack? Praying to Allah?"

The old man's stare never left his. Their eyes seemed locked together. As the M-88 rolled past, Bloom's head swiveled around, unable to break the connection. The old man said something, but the words were torn away by the howling wind. As Bloom watched, he knelt, and with one bony finger, drew a symbol in the sand. Then, another vehicle blocked Bloom's view, and the old man passed from sight.

"That was weird," Bloom muttered.

The M-88 swerved suddenly, and Bloom had to grab on tight to avoid falling off.

"Yo," he shouted. "What the fuck, Myers?"

"Sorry! Almost nodded off there for a moment. I'm fucking tired."

"Want to trade off?"

"We can't stop, man. You know that. Besides, you haven't had any more sleep than I have."

Bloom knew his friend was right. Exhausted and covered in dirt, they were both operating on pure adrenaline. So were the rest of the convoy. He also knew that they probably would not stop all night, and even if they did, there would be little time for sleep. Instead, the commanders would have them working all night repairing the vehicles that had fallen victim to the storm conditions. If they slept at all, it would be in short shifts.

Suddenly, without warning, the sandstorm increased with a shocking intensity. Furious winds rocked the lighter vehicles, buffeting them from side to side. Bloom's bandanna was ripped from his face, sailing away before he could grab it. Blowing sand gnawed at his nose and mouth.

"The hell is going on out there?" Myers asked.

Before Bloom could answer, the sun disappeared behind the dunes. The sky was bathed in a strange orange glow as the fading daylight filtered through the swirling dust. Bloom shivered, watching as the vehicles in front and back of them took on a spectral quality in the billowing sand. The ones further away faded completely from sight. Within minutes, the last of the light vanished, plunging them into darkness. The vehicles in the column turned on their headlights, but they did little against the storm.

Bloom gasped as the truck in front of them disappeared into the dense cloud. Then came the lightning. Thunder boomed across the sky. To Bloom, it sounded very much like artillery shells. He coughed, trying to breathe. The sand was in his eyes and nose and ears, and the more he coughed, the more sand he inhaled. He sneezed out dust. His eyes began to water, washing out clods of dirt and leaving balls of grit hanging from his eyelashes.

Something pelted him on the shoulder. Then another—hard.

Jesus, he thought, *did I just get shot?*

A moment later he realized that it was raining mud.

"Oh, fuck this! Myers, I'm coming down."

Abandoning the gun, he dropped down inside the vehicle, slamming the hatch shut behind him.

"Don't say anything," he warned. "It's only for a minute. Then I'll go back up."

"Couldn't say much if I wanted to." Bleary-eyed, Myers pointed to the radio. "Nothing but static the last ten minutes."

"You can't get a hold of anybody?"

"Nothing, man. Strangest fucking thing I've ever seen."

Myers tapped his fingers to the drums on the 'Kashmir' loop.

Bloom began to sing along again. "I am a traveler of both time and space—"

"Hey, who sings this?" Myers asked him.

"Led Zeppelin."

"Well, then shut up and let them."

Bloom punched him in the shoulder, grabbed a baby wipe, and cleaned more sand from his face.

Myers focused on the road. Bloom could tell that the combination of the sandstorm, fatigue, unfamiliar terrain, and now blackout conditions were working against him.

"You okay, Myers?"

"I can't keep my eyes open. I'm driving while standing up and I'm still falling asleep!"

"Let me take over."

"We can't stop, especially now. We'll get rear-ended."

As if to illustrate his point, the truck in front of them suddenly swerved back into view, veering off the path and vanishing again into the blackness.

Myers gasped. "Where the hell are they going?"

"They probably nodded off. Now let me drive!"

"I'm okay," Myers insisted. "Just chill, and help me watch ahead of us."

It was a long and dangerous night. The storm and fatigue drained the caravan in a way the Iraqi forces never could. Drivers fell asleep at the wheel and veered off their route. Soldiers behind them fought through on foot to wake the drivers and get them moving. Then another driver in the convoy would fall asleep, and the whole ordeal started over again. Traveling off-road, they'd lose sight of the vehicles in front of them and turn off in other directions.

The radios worked sporadically. There was mostly just the hiss of static, occasionally interrupted by a snatch of confused conversation or barked orders. The commander of an Abrams tank radioed that he was lost, couldn't see the rest of the convoy, and was almost out of fuel. Others were dispatched to find him, but nobody could locate him. Then the commander stopped responding.

Rendell wondered over the radio if their night vision goggles would help.

"NOD's can't see through sand—" O'Malley's curt reply was cut short by an explosive whine of feedback, and the radio went dead.

"The fuck is going on?" Bloom asked.

"Look at that!" Myers pointed out the window.

The tip of the radio antenna glowed with a ball of blue energy. Bloom grabbed the handset to ask if anyone else was experiencing the phenomena, and got shocked.

"Ouch!" He sucked at his tingling fingers. "What the hell is that?"

Myers shrugged, gaping at the phenomenon. "Static electricity? St. Elmo's Fire? Who knows?"

"How are we supposed to fight a war in this shit?"

"One thing's for sure. The Iraqi's ain't gonna be putting up a fight tonight."

Bloom fumbled in his pocket and produced a squashed pack of gum. "Want some?"

"No thanks. What I want is a smoke."

"Can't help you there." He unwrapped the stick of gum and chewed it happily, his parched mouth relishing the burst of flavor. He turned his attention back to the desert. He couldn't see anything. Blackness had swallowed up the entire column. He shivered. "It's cold in here."

"You shouldn't be cold. You've got five layers of dirt on you to keep you warm."

Bloom didn't reply. He wrapped his arms around his shoulders as another chill passed through him.

"Bloom?"

"Yeah?"

"It'll be okay. You'll be back in Trench-ton before you know it."

That was when the desert disappeared from beneath their wheels.

Bloom couldn't see anything other than darkness. It wasn't just black—it was the absolute absence of light. His face felt sticky. Wetness ran into his eyes. He placed a hand to his forehead and gingerly felt the edges of the wound. Myers moaned from somewhere to his left. Outside, the wind howled, rocking the M-88 back and forth.

"Myers? You okay?"

"Can't see..."

Bloom sighed in relief. At least he wasn't blind.

"I can't either," he whispered. "Must be the storm. Where are you?

"Over here."

Carefully feeling his way, Bloom crawled towards the voice. His palm flattened down on what felt like glass—the window.

"We're on our side. What the hell happened?"

"Don't know," Myers coughed. "The ground just disappeared. Maybe the storm blew us over."

"Somebody must have seen us wreck. Help's probably on the way."

His hand closed around Myers's leg.

"Quit feeling me up, or I'll make you my bitch."

"Fuck you, Myers. You okay?"

"Yeah, nothing's broken at least. Must've banged my head when we rolled. Got one hell of a headache."

"Me, too. My forehead's bleeding." Bloom wiped more blood from his eyes.

"How bad?"

"I can't tell. Not too bad, I don't think. I'm still conscious."

They sat quietly for a moment, letting their eyes adjust to the darkness. After a few minutes, they still saw nothing. Bloom had the uncomfortable impression that the blackness was pressing in on them, wrapping them in an embrace.

"This is no good," Myers said, finally. "Where's the night vision goggles?"

"I don't know. Everything got tossed around when we crashed. I told you we should have stowed everything like O'Malley said."

"Hang on."

There was a rustling sound. Then, Myers's lighter flared to life, illuminating them in its tiny circle of light. Bloom gasped. The darkness seemed to surround the flame, as if it wanted to extinguish it.

"Let me see." Myers's fingers probed his head, appraising the damage. "You're okay. It's not deep. Scalp wounds bleed like crazy though."

"Think we should put that out?" Bloom nodded at the lighter. "What if there are hostiles in the perimeter?"

"Fuck 'em. I need a smoke." He shook a cigarette out of the crumpled pack. "Besides, something just doesn't feel right..."

"The darkness?"

"Yeah. You feel it, too?"

Bloom nodded.

Outside, the wind shrieked in response, pounding the vehicle.

"I don't think help's coming," Myers said. "Not tonight, at least."

"Try the radio."

"Already did. It's dead."

"We are so fucked."

"Would you please quit saying that?"

"I can't help it!"

They crawled through the wreckage, salvaging what they could. When they were outfitted, Myers extinguished the lighter.

"You ready?" he asked.

"Let's do it."

They crawled outside into Hell. As they plunged again into the darkness, stinging sand lashed at their exposed skin, chipping the lenses of their goggles. The wind roared in their ears, and it was impossible to breathe, let alone speak. They communicated in sign language.

In the distance, they saw Sanchez and Riser struggling against the storm. Bloom and Myers found it hard to identify the two men at first, and had to watch carefully before they were sure. Bloom tried shouting, but the gale tore his voice away. He raised his arms over his head and waved. Barely visible, even from only a few yards away, the two soldiers made their way toward them. Wading through the sand, the four reached each other.

"What happened?" Myers shouted above the winds.

"We wrecked," Riser yelled. "One minute the road was there, and the next—fucking gone!"

Myers nodded. "Does anybody else know where we are?"

"Our radio's busted," Sanchez hollered. "How about yours?"

Myers slid his finger across his throat in a slashing motion.

Sanchez frowned. "Shit!"

"Well, what the hell do we do now?" Bloom coughed. "I don't see the rest of the convoy!"

"You can't see anything out here," Riser answered. "Our truck is toast! Let's head back to yours, and take cover till this blows over!"

They waded back to the M-88 and slipped inside. Myers pulled the door shut behind him, partially muting the wind. They sat clustered together in the feeble glow of a chem light, shaking the dirt out of their ears, nostrils, helmets, and boots. Riser removed his Kevlar vest, and sand poured from it.

"Shit," Sanchez muttered, banging his handheld GPS against his leg. "This thing's on the fritz too. Can't get any readings that make sense."

"It's this storm," Bloom said. "I've never seen anything like it."

Riser dumped the dust from his boots. "I don't think anybody has. This shit is Biblical, man."

They all stared at him.

"Think about it," he said. "We're in the cradle of civilization! It may be Iraq now, but this was Sumeria, wasn't it? This was fucking Babylon! This is where it all started."

"If that's the case," Myers said, "then I sure do wish God would send us a burning bush right about now."

"Fuck that," Sanchez replied. "I want him to send a couple Chinooks to fly our asses out of here."

"I just want to go home," Bloom said quietly. "I miss Jill."

"She your girlfriend?" Sanchez asked.

He nodded.

Riser yawned. "Me, too. All I want to do is go to Camden Yards, catch the O's, and drink a few cold ones. God damn, a cold beer would taste good right about now!"

Sanchez fumbled with his wedding band. "I miss my wife."

"I need a smoke." Myers searched his empty pockets again.

They sat in the darkness. All four men were disoriented, dirty, and exhausted. Outside, the storm continued, showing no signs of abating.

It was a long time before any of them slept.

When Bloom awoke, his tongue felt like beef jerky. His lips were cracked and raw. His puffy eyes itched, and he dug at them with balled fists. Then, he slowly opened them and looked around.

"Jesus!"

His shout woke the others. The entire bottom of the M-88 was covered in a layer of sand. They had fallen asleep sitting up, and while they slept, it had had piled up to their waists, obscuring everything. It was like sitting in cement, and they struggled to get free.

"Hey!" Sanchez glanced around. "Where's Riser?"

Frantically, they began digging with their hands, calling his name. Riser didn't answer. They found him seven inches down. His mouth, nose, eyes, and ears were filled with sand.

"Oh shit..." Sanchez ran his hand over his crew cut. "Riser."

Myers knelt, checking his pulse. "He's dead."

"You think so?" Bloom choked. "Sorry. This just sucks. Fucking Riser."

"He was short," Sanchez said. "Thirty-nine days and a wake up and he would have been out of here. He said when I got out, I could come to Baltimore and he'd show me around. They've got crabs there, supposed to be good—"

His sobs cut off the rest.

Bloom turned away, tears streaking through the dust on his face, as well.

Solemnly, Myers closed the dead soldier's eyes. "Rest easy, brother."

Later, Bloom and Myers ventured outside, while Sanchez stayed behind to guard the vehicle—and their fallen comrade.

The sky was clear. The piercing blue was broken only by a few wispy clouds. The wind had vanished, and the temperature was beginning to soar. No trace of the storm remained, except for the sand. Large dunes covered everything, obscuring their surroundings. The M-88 lay half buried on its side.

"No way we're getting that thing out of there." Bloom kicked at the desert in frustration.

"At least we got out. If that storm had kept up a few hours longer, we'd have been shit out of luck."

"Myers," Bloom began, hesitant. "Did you notice something last night?"

"You mean other than the weather?"

"Remember that old man, the one along the roadside? The storm didn't get really bad until after we passed him."

"What do you mean?"

"He said something—something in their language, and then he drew some funny symbols in the sand. Like he was doing magic or something."

Myers snorted, and spat a wad of mucous and dirt.

"Bloom, what the hell have you been smoking? Man, if your number comes up for a random piss test, you're looking at a dishonorable on your DD-214."

"I'm serious. That storm wasn't natural. And what about all that shit with the radios? That blue light? The darkness?"

"It was nighttime. Of course it was fucking dark. That don't make it magic. We've got enough trouble without inventing more."

"Forget it."

They explored the terrain in a steadily broadening circle, looking for anything that seemed familiar.

"Where the fuck is the road?" Bloom sat down on a dune. "Shouldn't there at least be tracks from the rest of the convoy?"

Myers shrugged. "Got covered up, I imagine. I don't see nothing that looks familiar. No buildings. Not even a tree."

"What's that over there?"

The sun glinted off a flat piece of metal. They approached it curiously.

"That's the roof of a truck," Myers said. "How the—"

"Shhh," Bloom silenced him. "Listen!"

Dim, muffled pounding came from somewhere beneath their feet. A voice called out from beneath the desert.

"Somebody's alive in there!" Myers began digging at the sand with his hands. "Go back to the truck! See if you can find the shovels, and bring Sanchez!"

"On it," Bloom said, dashing away.

"Hang on," Myers shouted at the ground. "We'll get you out!"

Bloom and Sanchez returned with a compact shovel and an empty coffee can. The three men dug in frantic silence, their bodies drenched with sweat.

Bloom knocked on the roof of the vehicle. "Hey down there! If you can hear me, we're digging you out!"

They kept at it, but their determined efforts quickly turned to frustration. For each scoop of sand they hauled away, more poured into its place.

"This ain't working," Myers moaned.

Sanchez stood up. "Hang on."

He ran back to the M-88 and disappeared inside.

"What's he doing?" Bloom asked.

"I don't know. Maybe he got heat stroke."

The burly Texan reappeared a second later, holding a fire axe over his head.

"Stand back," Sanchez warned, then swung the axe downward. There was a shriek of metal, and sparks danced over the sand. The trapped voice grew silent. He brought the axe down again, ripping a hole in the roof. He swung a third time. A fourth.

Five minutes later, Sharp stared up at them through the hole. His expression was a mixture of relief and sadness. Relief that he was saved. Sadness that Rendell, lying next to him, had met a fate similar to Riser's. During the night, when the air inside the buried truck grew thin, Rendell had fallen asleep and never woke up.

Having rescued Sharp, they grieved for their fellow soldiers. Exhausted and hot, each gulped greedily from their canteens, until Myers advised them to conserve their water. Since the others were

Privates, and he was a Specialist, and there were no Sergeants or Corporals to be found, command of the rag-tag squad fell to him.

"I think we need to face facts," he said as they huddled around him. "Either they don't know we're lost, or there's nobody left to find us. Either way, I don't reckon we'll get rescued anytime soon. We've got to make our own way out."

"Shouldn't we just wait here?" Bloom asked. "Dig some trenches and defend our position?"

"We could," Myers said. "But the way I see it, we're better off trying to find civilization—or at least a road. Even if they are looking for us, that storm messed everything up. They don't know our location, and neither do we. The radios are busted, so we can't call anybody, and we've only got enough rations for a day or two. I say we hoof it. Head due east and eventually we've got to come across a road or a village. Maybe even another convoy or platoon."

"What about Riser and Rendell?" Sanchez asked. "We just gonna leave them out here?"

"Yeah, unless you feel like carrying them over those dunes. Look, I know it sucks. They were my friends, too. Hell, Rendell and I went through basic together. But be realistic. We can't carry them. And we ain't doing them no good if we die out here, too."

They moved Riser's body to the medical truck, and then kicked sand over the roof to camouflage it better.

"We'll be back," Sanchez said to the ground.

"Count on it," Sharp added, quietly.

As they crossed the first dune, and stared out across the vast desert plateau, the opening chords of "Kashmir" ran through Bloom's head. He hummed along, until he found that it was smarter to save his breath.

They began to walk.

By midday, the desert gave way to palm trees and mud.

Bloom cheered, celebrating the change in landscape. "This is more like it!"

"What—this?" Sanchez scowled. "It's a fucking swamp, Bloom."

"Yeah, but at least there's no sand. The mud's hard packed.

Sharp paused, wiping the sweat from his brow. "This looks like Nassiriyah."

"Can't be," Myers replied. "I thought so too, at first, but we're too far west."

Trudging onward, they came across a rugged, narrow path winding through the mud.

"Anybody recognize this?" Myers asked.

Sharp and Sanchez shook their heads.

"Yeah." Bloom rubbed his calves. "It's a goat track."

"That's very helpful," Myers said. "Wherever we are, this path has been used recently. Look at the tracks."

He pointed at a pair of tire treads, baked into the ground.

"Not one of ours," Sharp said. "Too small."

There was a scuffling sound behind them. They whirled, raising their weapons in unison. A lone Iraqi man, barefoot and dressed in tatters, faced them. Two women in black robes, carrying bundles on their heads, and a boy and a girl in brightly colored rags, rounded the hilltop behind him. They all gasped in surprise.

"Are they civilians or militia?" Sharp asked.

Myers grunted. "Hard to say. The women and kids are civilians, but the guy could be wearing civvies to throw us off."

The man smiled a toothless grin, and mimed drinking from a bottle. Slowly, Bloom shook his canteen to show that it was empty.

"Speak English?" Myers asked.

The man stared blankly, still smiling. Then he held out his hands, and gave them the thumbs-up sign. The women and children joined him.

The man spoke. "Good... America."

Myers laughed, and after a moment, the others joined him, lowering their weapons. The young boy looked at the soldiers and said something barely understandable— "chocolate." It broke Bloom's heart not to have any to give him.

Myers walked forward and shook hands with the man.

"Thank for liberate us," the man said in halting English. "You great army."

"You're welcome." Myers paused, then rummaged in his pack and brought out two packs of MRE's. He handed them to the man, who looked at the gifts with puzzlement.

"Food," Sharp said, and then mimed eating. "Meal Ready to Eat."

"I thought we were here to make friends," Sanchez said. "Ain't gonna do it giving them those things."

The man turned and said something to the others. Then they all bowed in gratitude. The little girl ran up and hugged Myers around the legs. He shooed her away in gentle embarrassment, then spoke again.

"Can you tell us where we are? Is there a town nearby? Town?" The man thought for a moment, then nodded.

"Al-Qurna," he said, pointing down the road. "Eden."

"How far?" Myers asked.

"Eden," the man repeated, "Al-Qurna."

"Al-Qurna," Sharp mused. "I remember seeing that on the map."

One of the women whispered something in the man's ear. He seemed to consider her request for a moment, and then nodded. She stepped forward to Myers.

"We thank you for your help," she said in English. "My husband, his American is not so good. Mine is better."

"We're glad we could help," Myers said, smiling. "But why didn't you just tell us you spoke English to begin with?"

"Is not my place. That is my husband's choice."

Myers laughed. "If I tried that on my wife back in Nacogdoches, she'd likely whip me."

The woman smiled.

"Three miles that way," she pointed down the road, "is Al-Qurna. Is believed to be Garden of Eden, where Adam came to pray to God. Today it is, how you say— destroyed? Paving stones are broken, the walls full of bullet holes. The eucalyptus we call Adam's tree is dead. Every generation is taught that this was true Garden of Eden and this was Adam's tree, where he first spoke to God. Now is ruined."

"What happened to it?" Bloom asked.

"Saddam," she answered.

At the name, the man spat on the ground.

"The Baath party built shrine," the woman said, "for pilgrimage of tourists. After last time Americans come here, Saddam punished Al-Qurna for supporting you. They drained the water. Now the walls and floor of the shrine are cracked. The Garden is mud. Children fight with dogs there. But village elders will help you. Seek for them. Just do not go in the shrine. It is no place for uniforms and weapons."

"I understand," Myers assured her. "We'll be respectful."

Bloom gently asked, "Do you believe it's really the Garden of Eden?"

She was quiet, and Bloom worried that he had offended her. Then she nodded.

"I am Muslim, and I believe. No harm shall come to you there, from any Muslim. The Koran say 'if the Muslims capture them and take them to a place that has been prepared for them, they should not harm them or torture them with beatings, depriving them of food and water, leaving them out in the sun or the cold, burning them with fire, or putting covers over their mouths, ears and eyes and putting them in cages like animals. Rather they should treat them with kindness and mercy, feed them well and encourage them to enter Islam.' The village elders are Muslim, so this they believe, too."

"I hope you're right," Myers said.

She smiled. "In Al-Qurna, you shall find rest."

"I liked her quote from the Koran," Bloom said as they approached the village. "Reminded me of the way my Grandma used to quote the Bible."

Before the others could reply, gunshots rang out, followed by a woman screaming. Four more gunshots echoed in rapid succession, and then silence.

"What the—"

Four white SUV's roared over the hill and slid to a stop behind them. The tires gouged trenches in the mud. As the Americans pulled their weapons, nine figures dressed in black uniforms, their faces covered with black scarves, leapt from the vehicles, brandishing rifles of their own.

"Fuck," Myers screamed. "It's the Fedayeen!"

"Hold your fire," a voice called.

The old man who they'd passed on the road before the storm, stepped out from behind one of the vehicles.

"Hold your fire," he said again. His English was clear, and though he spoke softly, they could hear every word. "If you shoot, your friends die."

There was a commotion behind him, and several of the Fedayeen pushed forward, shoving O'Malley, Jefferson, and Williams ahead of them. The three were bound, and had been beaten badly.

"Drop your weapons," the old man said calmly, "or they die, and then you join them."

Cursing, Bloom considered their options. They were easily outnumbered. Myers must have realized the same thing, because he reluctantly ordered the others to lower their rifles.

Bloom put his hands up and turned to Myers. "Just remember the part of the Koran that the woman quoted to us."

As their hands were bound behind them and their rifles were collected, the old man smiled at him.

"Here, we do not read the Koran. Our book is much older. Come, we will show you."

Bound, gagged, and beaten, the Americans were brought to a building in Al-Qurna, and then herded through an underground passage in the basement beneath it. The complex beneath the village was staggering in its size. The prisoners soon lost all sense of direction as they were shoved down a maze of winding passageways and tunnels.

Finally, they came to a bunker built out of white sandstone. They were crammed together into a tiny jail cell with a red door and a rusted grate window that looked out on what could only be an interrogation chamber. Aside from the bloodstains on the floor, and a pile of dried feces in the corner, the only other thing in the cell was a coffee can for a toilet.

The men stood together in a tight knot as the door slammed behind them. When the bolt clicked into place, they realized that Jefferson was still outside

"What are you going to do with us?" O'Malley demanded through split lips. "I'm in command of this squad and I demand to know!"

The old man peered through the bars in the window.

"What we are doing? Electric shocks. Cigarette burns. Pulling out of fingernails, castration, rape, cut off your eyelids, your lips, hang you by your limbs from the fan in ceiling. Beating you with cables and hosepipe. Or maybe Falaqa, yes?"

"What's Falaqa?" O'Malley asked.

"We beat the soles of your feet with metal rod."

"That doesn't sound too bad," Sanchez muttered. "I got calluses."

"We will cut them off first," the old man said.

Williams stepped forward. "Hey, douche-bag. Ever hear of the Geneva Convention? You can't treat prisoners of war this way. They'll try you for war crimes!"

"But you are not prisoners of war," the old man answered. "You are sacrifices."

He nodded at the guards, and they immediately shot Jefferson in the back of each kneecap. As he collapsed to the ground, shrieking in pain, they pumped more bullets into his elbows, his hands, his legs, and finally his face. Gore sprayed across the alabaster sandstone.

O'Malley gripped the bars, unable to look away, while the others cursed and screamed. Bloom closed his eyes, turning away.

"That is one sacrifice," the old man told Williams. "Now, let us see about your mouth."

Before deploying to Iraq, the men had learned all about the Fedayeen. The name meant 'those ready to sacrifice themselves'. They were Saddam Hussein's most trusted paramilitary unit. Their duties included assassinating his enemies, and the capture, imprisonment, and torture of anyone deemed a dissident. The majority of their recruits were composed of criminals, pardoned in exchange for their service. One of their endurance drills was to survive on snake and dog meat. Their training included urban warfare and suicide missions. They reported directly to Saddam's eldest son, Odai.

"I want to speak with Odai," O'Malley shouted. He was strapped to a chair next to Williams, who had been tied to a gurney. Both men had been injected with a pharmaceutical grade of speed, so that they wouldn't pass out from the pain.

Ignoring him, the old man wiped blood from Williams's chin.

"This doesn't have to happen," O'Malley continued. "I demand that you let me talk to Odai. He's in charge!"

"No," the old man said. "Odai has been in hiding since the start of the war. The Fedayeen report to me, now."

"Okay..." O'Malley paused. "Then talk to me. Tell us what you want."

"I want you to be still," the old man said. "It is not your time to scream yet."

He nodded at two of the guards, one of whom was smoking a

foul-smelling cigarette. The two stalked toward O'Malley, and forced his mouth open. As he struggled, the smoking guard snuffed his cigarette out on O'Malley's tongue. O'Malley shrieked. Calmly, the guard lit another cigarette and then repeated the process. O'Malley's tortured cries turned to moans.

"Much better," the old man said, and with a yank of the rusty pliers, pulled another tooth from Williams's ruined mouth.

His gurgling scream echoed throughout the cells.

Bloom closed his eyes again and tried to think of home. Summertime on South Clinton Avenue. His father's extermination company. He was going to work for him when he got out. Jill, with her long, blonde hair. The week before he'd shipped out, they'd gone to see Linkin Park in concert. Afterward, they'd done it in the back of his parent's car...

Williams's shrieks, O'Malley's moans, and the old man's laughter shattered the visions.

"Leave them alone," Sanchez pleaded. "Stop it! O'Malley, hang in there, man."

O'Malley tried to answer, but the cigarette burns on his tongue made him hard to understand. He bunched his muscles, pushing against the restraints binding him to the chair, but the leather straps were stronger.

"Hey!" Myers rattled the bars of the cell.

The old man paused, dropping one of Williams's molars to the floor.

"You can't do this," Myers said. "It's not human."

The old man nodded. "Correct. Is not human."

He turned back to the quivering soldier and wrenched out the last tooth. Williams convulsed on the gurney, blood running from his mouth, but this time he made no sound. He was beyond sound. The old man appraised his handy-work. Satisfied, he selected an ice pick from the tools laid out on the table next to him.

"Now, we take your eyes, yes?"

Williams did not scream, so the others screamed for him.

The old man turned to the guards, and cocked his head toward O'Malley. Then he turned back to the prisoners.

"His eyes, too," he said.

His gnarled fingers reached out and held Williams's eyelid open.

Slowly, hypnotically, he waved the ice pick back and forth in front of the soldier's contracting pupil. Then, he jabbed it forward. At the same time, the two guards extinguished their smoldering cigarettes in O'Malley's eyes. Both men shrieked.

Myers turned away and vomited.

"You motherfuckers," Bloom shouted. "Oh you motherfuckers are so fucking dead when I get out of here! You are so fucking dead you sons of bitches—"

He stopped in mid-ramble, spying something hovering in the air, directly above the old man. Something formless and dark. It looked like a cloud, the size of a baseball. Colors for which there were no name swirled in the blackness.

The old man looked up, smiled, and then glanced back to the men in the cell.

"You see? It begins. He is coming."

Calmly, he plunged the tool into Williams's other eye. Williams's back arched up off the gurney, and this time he screamed so loudly that something tore in his throat. Blood poured from his mouth and eyes, pooling onto the floor. His mouth gaped like a fish as he continued to scream, but all that was generated was a tiny mewling whimper.

Then he was still.

"Why?" Bloom sobbed.

"We summon Kandara," the old man explained. "You are in Iraq. This was once Babylon. All of the great gods came from here. Dagon and Baal and Purturabo— all these belonged to us first. And there were others—Ob and Apu, Meeble and Kat—who came from else-where but resided here for a time. This is where magic was born. There are many books, much knowledge. You have bookstores in America where you can buy them in paperback. All this came from our lands."

"Magic..." Bloom's voice trailed off.

"Yes," the old man said. "Kandara is demon—what we call Djinn. There are

many Djinn. Some control animals or humans. Some grant wish-es and others destroy dreams. Kandara is great among the Djinn, and powerful. He commands the desert winds. You think the storm last night was bad, yes? Kandara will show your friends what bad storm really is! Even now, the rest of your army drives north. Kandara will go to meet them, and there he will destroy them. The desert will swallow even their bones."

"This motherfucker is crazy," Myers whispered.

"And you are the next one, I think," the old man answered. "Kandara must be summoned with pain, fed with suffering and anguish. Each of you feeds him until he is whole. When the last one is sacrificed, then may he be controlled, to obey the torturer's commands. The rules of summoning tells us this. The one who causes the most pain, the most suffering—this is the one that will bind Kandara to him, and Kandara will grant his wishes. And I wish for you to be gone from our lands. I will command him to destroy your 3rd Infantry. They will not reach Baghdad."

He wiped his bloody instruments on Williams's gore-stained uniform, and then gave orders to the guards. Williams and O'Malley's bodies were dragged away, and two Iraqi's approached the cell, their weapons drawn.

"Now you," the old man said to Myers, "and if the rest of you resist, we shoot."

"You're going to kill us anyway," Sharp said. "What does it matter?"

"Maybe yes, maybe no. We see how many more Kandara need. Maybe I not need to kill you all. He is getting big already, yes?"

Still floating in the air, the black cloud had tripled in size.

Bloom stepped forward. "Take me instead. Not him."

"Bullshit," Myers said calmly, and grasped his friend's shoulder. "You've got to get back home to that girl of yours. What's her name?"

"Jill," Bloom sobbed.

"Right. Jill. You get out of this and when you two have some rugrats, you name one after me, okay?"

He smiled, but Bloom said nothing.

"I need you to be strong for me, Bloom," Myers whispered. "Please."

Then they took him out of the cell.

The thing in the air swelled again. When Bloom glanced at it, he could see two small red dots in its center.

They blinked at him.

*   *   *

Myers was strapped naked to the gurney, and then a thin glass rod was shoved into his flaccid penis, via his urethra. After the tube had disappeared inside, the old man grabbed the organ with both hands and began to wring it like a dishrag, shattering the glass. Myers bucked against the restraints, grunting and hollering in the same breath.

The old man snarled, and one of the soldiers began to pummel the prisoner in the kidneys. Again and again the savage blows landed, until Myers's bladder let go. He howled in agony as the bits of glass were ejected with his urine.

"Listen," Sanchez whispered in Bloom's ear, "we've got to make a break for it! I've got my hands loose."

"How? Myers—they...Myers..."

"Get it together, man! Ain't nothing we can do for Myers or any of the others, except make these bastards pay."

"They'll shoot us if we try it," Sharp whispered.

"And they'll torture us if we don't," Sanchez said. His words were masked by Myers's screams.

In the torture chamber, three guards struggled with a hand-truck, on which sat a massive, industrial-sized battery charger. When they reached the gurney, the charger was plugged into an outlet. The room's single light bulb dimmed as they applied the first shock to Myers's nipples.

"I ain't going out like that," Sanchez continued. "When they open that door again, I'm rushing them. If you guys are with me, cool. If not, I'll try to do what I can for you."

"Fuck it," said Sharp. "I'm with you."

Sanchez began to undo the ropes around Sharp wrists. "Bloom? You in?"

Bloom stared in horror as Myers began to smoke and char. A long, keening wail came from his throat as his teeth shattered from the electricity jolting through him. After a horrifying second, Bloom recognized what Myers was saying.

"Trying to find, trying to find where I've beeeeeeeeee—"

Myers was singing "Kashmir", just like aboard the M-88.

"eeeeeeeeeeeeeeeeeeeeee—"

Simultaneously, they applied the jumper cables to his testicles and slashed his bulging throat with a box cutter.

"eeeeeeeeeeeeeeeeeeeeeeeeeeeeeeeeeeeeeennnnnnnnnnnnnn."

With his final breath, Myers hit that perfect Robert Plant wail that he'd always sought.

"Bloom?"

"I'm in," he snapped, so fiercely that both Sanchez and Sharp took a step back. "Goddamn it, I am so in!"

"Quick, let me see your wrists. Don't let them see us, though."

Above the gurney, Kandara took shape. Much bigger than a baseball now, its arms and legs were clearly visible, as were the malevolent red eyes, glowing like cinders in an otherwise featureless, obsidian face.

"You hear that, you fuck?" Bloom screamed at the creature. "I'm in!"

"Okay," the old man answered, as Myers's body was disposed of. "You can be in next."

Everything happened very quickly. Despite his time in country, Bloom had yet to experience real up close and personal combat. The only fighting he'd seen had been done from far away—bombing runs and artillery strikes. He wasn't sure what to expect. He thought that perhaps time would slow, like in a movie, and that everything would transpire in slow motion.

There was the click of the bolt on the door being thrown, and two guards entered, reaching for him. Then—chaos. Sanchez and Sharp were shouting, and Bloom was surprised to find himself shouting as well.

"Jersey in the house, you motherfuckers!"

They rushed forward, desperately grappling with the armed men. Even as Sanchez wrestled the rifle away from one of them, there was a loud explosion, and Sharp's stomach disappeared. He gasped, choking on his own blood, and then toppled onto his enemy, crushing him to the floor. The Iraqi struggled beneath him. Sharp clawed at the man's throat.

Bloom snatched a fallen rifle from the floor and glanced around. The other two guards scrambled, and Sanchez opened fire, mowing them down.

Bloom charged into the torture chamber. The old man backed toward the exit, hands raised in fear.

Kandara swelled, unmoving.

The door opened and two more guards ran in, spraying bullets indiscriminately. Sanchez lurched as rounds slammed into him, destroying flesh and bone. He slumped against the wall.

Crouching, Bloom fired back, the rifle jerking in his hands. The heavy staccato of automatic gunfire and the stench of cordite filled the room. The two guards fell beneath the barrage.

"Don't you fucking move," Bloom hollered at the old man. "Get away from that door!"

Cringing, the old man glanced up at the Djinn and began chanting. Bloom squeezed off one controlled shot at his feet, and the old man stopped.

"Lay down."

Bloom motioned toward the gurney with the barrel of his rifle. The old man complied, his bones and joints creaking audibly as he clambered atop it. Bloom lashed him down tight, smiling when the old man winced in pain.

He crept toward the door and listened. Silence. He opened it and peeked outside into the underground tunnel. More silence. They were alone, for now. He shut the door again and bolted it.

"I'm guessing that thing, that genie or whatever the fuck you called it, isn't full grown yet, since it didn't try to stop us."

"It is not bound to me yet," the old man babbled. "Only by causing the most pain can it be bound. Let me go, and I will see that it does not harm you."

Bloom's laughter sounded like the bark of a dog.

"I bet I can cause a lot of pain," he said. "Let's see just how much."

He tapped the old man's arm, searching for a vein. Then he emptied one of the speed-filled hypodermic needles into it.

"Don't want you passing out on me. We're gonna be here a while."

He picked up the box knife and got started.

Above him, Kandara trembled in ecstasy.

It took Bloom a long time to find a radio that worked, and even longer to contact the coalition forces. By then, he was hopelessly lost in the underground maze. While he'd been locked in the room with the old man, chaos had descended on Al-Qurna. He was stunned at the aftermath. Everywhere lay signs of the Hussein regime's fall—abandoned posts and equipment, shredded files, even the bodies of dead officers, gunned down by their own deserting troops. One room, behind a locked door that Bloom had to kick in, held row upon row of wooden shelves, lined with metal boxes. In each box was a plastic bag, containing the remains of previous Fedayeen victims. Some of the bags had identification cards stapled to them. Others did not. One held only a smashed skull. Another a severed hand. A third contained the desiccated remains of a newborn infant whose limbs. After that, Bloom stopped searching, afraid he'd come across what was left of his friends.

Deeper in the tunnels, he found two recently dug pits. Dozens of bodies had been thrown into the mass graves, in such haste that their killers hadn't even taken the time to cover them up. Most of the dead were women and children. Among them, Bloom recognized the woman who had helped them along the road. Tears rolled down his cheeks.

"Eden," he whispered.

He wept for her and he wept for his friends. He wept for Riser and Rendell, buried in the sand while they slept. He wept for O'Malley and Jefferson and Williams and Sanchez and Sharp. He wept for Myers.

He wept for himself.

Finally, he found an exit. Sunlight greeted him, shining down upon his face. He went outside to meet it, his tears drying in the heat.

"Oh, let the sun beat down upon my face..."

Humming a snatch of Led Zeppelin, he waited.

Eventually, he heard the hum of the rotors, and rose to his feet. Two Chinook helicopters buzzed toward him. He waved them down. Several soldiers disembarked, barking orders and securing the area while a medic checked on him.

"You're gonna be okay," the medic assured him. "What's your name?"

"Bloom. PFC Don Bloom, 3rd Infantry."

"The 3rd? Man, you're a long way from the rest of your company, friend. Lucky, too!"

"Why's that, sir?"

"Way I hear it, they're heading into some shit. Look's like you won't be with them when it hits. I'm talking major shit, right outside of Baghdad. Saddam's got the Revolutionary Guard heavily entrenched around the city. Look's like it's gonna be a big battle."

"They'll be okay." Bloom grinned. "I sent reinforcements to help them."

He passed out before the medic could ask him what he meant.

Beneath their feet, in a white sandstone dungeon hidden under the desert, the remains of something that had once been human lay scattered across the room. It was no longer recognizable as the old man. Bloom had taken his time and as he'd promised, he'd been very thorough.

The desert winds howled as Kandara raced north toward Baghdad.

STORY NOTE: I'm a veteran from a family of veterans. My great-grandfather fought in World War One. My grandfather and great uncle served in World War II. My father served in Vietnam. I served during the Cold War—which wasn't a war as much as it was a state of mind. Every male in my family has served. Hell, if you go back the family tree, distant relative Daniel Boone served (and we all know what happened to him).

I was lucky enough to see most of the Middle East during my stint with the navy, and it remains one of the most beautiful places I've ever visited, especially Israel and Egypt. It's a shame what Saddam's forces did to the Iraqi people and countryside (and what Bush and Cheney and Haliburton did to it later)—especially when you reflect that Iraq is pretty much the cradle of civilization. That's where it all started folks. That was the breeding ground for original evil. It's no surprise that Saddam came from that soil, and it's no surprise that greed and corruption rule that soil in the aftermath.

Anyway, this story came about as a result of those two experiences. It was hard to write—especially the torture scenes. I don't mean it was hard to type the words—I mean it was an emotionally difficult story to tell. It may well be one of the most brutal things I've ever written (excluding *Castaways* or *Urban Gothic*, perhaps), but I don't think it could have been told any other way. This was a story that couldn't be told in quiet, supernatural undertones. While writing the last half, it was common for me to do a few sentences, and then get up and wander away from the computer, reluctant to write the next. I absolutely *hated* what was happening to the P.O.W.'s, especially because I was the one doing it. But I'm happy with the way the story came out, and I hope that you are, too.

A Revolution Of One

I protected our country while you were sleeping.

You voted every week on who should win *American Idol*, frantically trying to insure that your favorite candidate would go on to the next round—yet you couldn't be bothered to go to the polling booth every few years to cast a similar vote for who should represent you in the House and the Senate. You knew the name of your favorite reality show contestant. You knew how old they were and where they'd gone to school and what things they liked—and more importantly, disliked. You followed them on Twitter and liked them on Facebook and were friends with them on every other social networking website, but you didn't know your current Congressman's first name, and the only reason you knew his last name is because you saw it on a sign in someone's yard a week before the election. On Election Day, you didn't have time to vote in the morning because you were late for work, and you didn't have time in the evening because you had to get home in time to see the *Biggest Loser* results. You got mad when the local news channel ran a scroll bar at the bottom of the screen with the election results for your district, because, as you said, nobody cares about that.

While you weren't voting, I voted for change, after a fashion.

Your indifference and stupidity stems from your ignorance—and ignorance is bliss. You stay silent because they want you to be silent. They feed your contentment and keep you pacified with a steady diet of movies, television, pop music, and video games. In social gatherings, you like to think of yourself as well-informed and politically-

145

aware, but you are not. You seem to think that if you watch the news or join in the latest cause-of-the week online, that you are making a difference, but again, you are not. Sure, you watch the news, but what is it that you see? Instead of showing you footage from the wars in Iraq or Afghanistan, or the deplorable state of our inner city neighborhoods or the rural areas of Appalachia, the media shows you pop starlets, sex scandals and celebrity marriages. You've never read the Constitution online, but your toolbar is full of links to funny animal videos on You Tube. When asked, you can't name the Bill of Rights but you can name all of the members of the latest boy band. You allow your children to idolize rappers who glamorize drug-dealing and murder and sexual promiscuity, and then act surprised when little Johnny gets busted for meth or little Janey ends up starring in a high school gymnasium gangbang, the grainy footage of which appears on all of her fellow students' cell phones. You watch the Grammy Awards, the Oscars and the Golden Globes. You watch police procedural dramas, hospital dramas and courtroom dramas. You watch sitcoms, documentaries and infomercials. You watch all these things, but you skip past C-SPAN.

While you were channel-surfing, I was paying attention.

You say that you are taking an active role. You say that you want your voice to be heard. You attend a Tea Party protest or an Occupy Wall Street rally, and while you are there, you buy a t-shirt and bottled water, both of which have a slogan on them, and then you take a picture of yourself at the event and post it online so that others can see how involved you are. You root for your political party like you root for your favorite football team, but while the NFL has thirty-two teams to choose from, the American political process only has one. You cheer for the Republicans or the Democrats without understanding that they are the same thing. You side with Fox News or with CNN and MSNBC, without ever understanding that all three are equally biased. The media doesn't report the news because there's no money in it. Instead, on the rare occasions when they interrupt coverage of that week's celebrity funeral, they simply parrot whatever their CEOs, shareholders, and friends in the government tells them to report on. Our wars, our economy, our crime rate, our social mores—all of these are reported on as a series of press releases, read to us by empty-headed, good-looking news readers. You loyally listen to Rush Limbaugh and Sean Hannity or Rachel Maddow and Keith Olbermann as if they were Jesus, Mohammed, Buddha and John Lennon, all come down from the mountaintop to impart some special wisdom on you, when all they are is empty, blathering, opinionated puppets. You identify as a liberal or conservative. You debate on message boards and at cocktail parties, regurgitating what you've read and heard. You blindly echo their talking points without daring to think for yourself, swallowing whatever propaganda they are required to feed you this week. And when you do it, you smile and pat yourself on the back, secure in your cleverness and intelligence and participation in something you think matters.

While you were feeling good about yourself, I got involved.

You worry about getting cancer. You worry about terrorism. You worry about Islamic radicals and Christian cults and other religious fanatics out there on the fringe. You worry about pedophiles and serial killers and crazed gunmen and online stalkers. You worry about your job and your house and what your co-workers think of you. You worry about whether your wife knows about your affair with that old flame, and whether your husband knows about what you did with that guy you met when you and your girlfriends went to Vegas for a weekend. You are afraid of black people. You are afraid of white people. You are afraid of brown and yellow and red people. You are afraid of the gays and the trans-gendered. Of atheists and agnostics. Of Communists and Socialists and Fascists. You are afraid of growing old. You are afraid that your children don't love you anymore. You are afraid that none of it mattered. You are afraid.

While you were being fearful, I was being brave.

You sat back and watched, doing nothing while our country was taken over by corporations and special interest groups, and our young men and women died in far-off lands for bullshit causes, and our jobs went overseas, and our courts became slow and ineffectual, and our children became illiterate, and our economy tanked, and our civil and human rights were trampled on and eradicated a little more each and every day. You couldn't be bothered to get out of your chair and run out into the street and protest. You lost that radical spirit, the revolutionary idealism that this country was founded on, a birthright that was reborn and renewed with every generation, until after the Sixties, when instead of asking what they could do for their country, people began asking what they could do for themselves. You swallow your antidepressants and turn the television up louder and go back to sleep, because you believe that you can't make a difference by yourself.

While you were sitting there, I got out of my chair and went to work at the lab. My employee badge has a red stripe, indicating the highest clearance and full access.

While you were doing nothing, I walked into the cryogenic lab, took two vials of a deadly, highly-communicable experimental virus that is projected to kill ninety-percent of the population, and released it into the world.

While you are part of the problem, I am the solution.

I am a revolution of one.

When this is over, perhaps there will be enough of us left to try again. Maybe the American Dream will live once more.

While you were sleeping, I saved our country from the likes of you.

———

STORY NOTE: Cemetery Dance asked me to write a story for an anthology of politically-themed horror stories that they were publishing. I agreed, but had no idea what to write. I sat down at the laptop a few days before the deadline, and this story came pouring out. It does a pretty good job at crystallizing my thoughts and feelings on the state of our country and our political process (except that I would never unleash a deadly virus and destroy the world). If you've ever wondered where I stand, politically—it's right here. I identify as a Libertarian, but I'm not even really that. I'm about as moderate and middle of the road as they come, and I hate what's become of political discourse and journalism in this country.

Full Of It

STORY NOTE: This is another very early tale, from the mid-Nineties. It was written for an annual event called The Gross-Out Contest. This was something that took place for years at the World Horror Convention. Authors would compete on stage to see who could tell the grossest tale. Contestants included authors such as Edward Lee, Michael Slade, Robert Devereaux, Cullen Bunn, Wrath James White, Rain Graves, Carlton Mellick III, Ryan Harding, and many others. Me, too. I was a three-time winner, and the first author to introduce "props" (such as the year I ate a dozen live night-crawlers on stage while reading an excerpt from this story). I apologize in advance...

The mountains stretched to each horizon. The forest's serenity was a welcome contrast from the bustle of the nation's capitol. Kaine took a deep breath of the crisp morning air. His body ached. He'd been crouched at the base of the pine tree all night, keeping a careful watch on the area.

The camp was silent this morning. The group of degenerates that collectively called themselves The Sons of the Constitution were asleep, dreaming of anarchy and New World Orders. Kaine kept a meticulous log of their movements, but did not act. That was against protocol. Lessons had been learned from Waco and Ruby Ridge. Those were mistakes that haunted.

This time, there could be no fuck-ups.

He was tired. His arms and legs felt like lead. Standing up, he shook himself and stomped the soft carpet of pine needles, fighting

149

off drowsiness. Through a break in the foliage, he spotted a hawk soaring overhead. The first rays of dawn shone down on his surveillance point. He thought of Melissa and the twins, and wished they were here to enjoy this peaceful moment. He missed them. She'd been upset when he couldn't tell her where he was going.

Kaine closed his eyes and listened to birdsongs.

Then, the tranquility was shattered by the staccato report of an assault rifle.

Clenching his binoculars, Kaine peered through the branches, staring down at the camp. Two men, dressed in camouflage, stood outside the cabin. One laughed as his companion took aim at the fleeing hawk, and squeezed off another burst. Kaine identified the first as Henry Berger—former marine in Vietnam, now an unemployed steelworker who blamed the government for his personal failings. The skinny runt shooting at the hawk was Owen West, a local West Virginian whose only contribution to the world was his talent for blowing things up. It had been West's handiwork behind the bombings in Norfolk and San Diego.

Engrossed in their actions, Kaine didn't hear the twig snap behind him. He didn't know he was no longer alone until the cold barrel of a gun was pressed firmly into the back of his head.

"Well, look at we got here, boys."

Then...*darkness.*

"You're full of shit," Barnes said. "Tell the truth, now. How many more agents do you have out there?"

Kaine lay crumpled on the hard-packed dirt floor of a utility shed. Jonathan Barnes, the notorious leader of the militia, and currently the most wanted man in America, strutted in a circle around Kaine. Six other men were in the shed with them, including Henry and Owen. All but Barnes had their weapons pointed at Kaine.

Kaine chided himself for being so careless. His actions were those of a rookie fresh out of Quantico. Now what? He wasn't due to make a report for another twelve hours. He was completely on his own out here. Escape was an impossibility. They'd trussed him up like a turkey. His hands and feet were handcuffed. The steel chafed his skin. Pain stabbed through his stiff arm and leg muscles.

"Look," he answered, affecting a southern accent, "I told you. I don't know nothing about no agents. I was hunting up here with my friends and I got lost. I was just going to ask you boys for help."

Barnes snorted. "What exactly were you hunting with a government issue handgun? How come you're not wearing an orange hunting vest? Let me guess. You left it in the truck?"

Kaine nodded.

"Don't you know that it's against the law to not wear your vest?"

The men laughed. Barnes continued.

"So what are you, cowboy? Seriously. United Nations? ATF? Eff Bee Eye? Black Lodge?"

"I don't know what you're talking about," Kaine said. "I was just—"

The rest of his denial was cut off as Henry's steel-toed boot smashed into his mouth. Kaine's lips were pulped. His vision blurred. Blood and drool dribbled down his chin. When his vision cleared, he glanced up at his captors' faces. They watched with gleeful interest, as if it were a movie or a football game.

Henry grabbed Kaine by the hair and jerked his head up. Blood spattered to the floor.

"You think we didn't see that black helicopter flying around up there? Country don't mean dumb, you son of a bitch!"

"Henry," Barnes interrupted, his tone calm, almost soothing. "It will be hard for him to answer our questions with a busted mouth."

"Sorry, sir."

Henry released him. Kaine sagged to the floor again. Barnes knelt beside him, smiling.

"You're just a soldier," he said. "Some of us used to be soldiers, too. They've brainwashed you the same way they do everyone else in this country. Why protect them? We've hurt no one. No one innocent. We just want to live our lives as free men, out here surrounded by God's glory."

He placed a finger under Kaine's chin and lifted his face toward him. Kaine winced in pain.

"So," Barnes continued, "why don't you tell us why you're really here?"

Kaine spat blood and teeth from the gaping ruin that had been his mouth, and then grinned at his tormentor. Ropes of crimson saliva dripped from his chin.

"Fuck you, scumbag." Each syllable was excruciating.

Barnes flinched. His cool demeanor vanished. Kaine tried unsuccessfully to roll aside as the burly leader aimed kick after vicious kick to his kidneys, ribs, hips, and back. Kaine howled.

"You're—full—of—*SHIT*," Barnes shouted, each word punctuated with another kick. "Full of it! I'll show you what we think of the people you work for."

He delivered one more kick. Kaine shrieked, feeling something tear at the back of his throat.

"Owen," Barnes said, "go and fetch me some rope. Y'all drag his sorry ass to the outhouse."

Barely conscious, Kaine struggled weakly as they hauled him across the rough ground towards a small, rectangular shanty at the edge of the clearing.

Giggling through Skoal-stained teeth, Owen handed the rope to Henry, who tied a loop around Kaine's feet, ignoring the agent's frantic kicks. Another militia member opened the outhouse door. A noxious stench wafted out to them. The group of men winced.

"Boy, don't that stink?" Owen laughed, holding his nose.

Barnes slapped a mosquito. "That's nothing compared to what this Fed is about to smell. I figure a piece of shit like this belongs with his own kind."

They shoved Kaine forward into the small outhouse. Even with his feet and hands shackled, he fought wildly. A stack of mildewed porno and survivalist magazines fell to the floor. His wrists, chafed raw by the handcuffs, grew slick with blood. He managed to dodge a wild kick from Henry, and sent a roll of toilet paper flying into the air. It left an unraveling trailer in its wake.

Despite his struggles, they managed to position him directly over the hole in the wooden bench. His head easily fit through the opening. Then they started shoving.

Kaine screamed.

He was a muscular man, and his shoulders became stuck. Henry pushed down on them with all of his strength. Kaine's skin ripped and tore. His blood provided lubrication, and inch-by-excruciating-inch, Kaine slid through the hole. His ribs snapped. Then his pelvis. Then he was through the hole, suspended only by the rope. His muffled screams echoed from below. The group laughed, and slowly let the rope slip through their hands.

Beneath the outhouse, Kaine whipped his head back and forth, coughing as the stench hit him. Each cough brought a fresh burst of pain in his chest. Reluctantly, he opened his eyes. He dangled head first, ten feet above the bottom of the pit. Below him lay a vast pool of feces and urine that had congealed into a partially solidified mass; toxic soup stewing amidst heaps of excrement and yellow pools. Clumps of toilet paper dotted the fetid landscape, as well as old leaves, flies, and mosquito larvae. The stink was overpowering. He gagged. Bile and blood splattered amidst the slime below.

Laughter drifted down to him as they lowered him closer. Kaine vomited again, trembling with nausea and terror. The putrid atmosphere solidified around him, pummeling his senses.

Above, Barnes pulled out a bayonet, displayed it proudly to the men, and then cut the rope.

Kaine plunged headlong into the sludge. Vileness coated him. It was in his hair and in his eyes. He opened his mouth to scream, and then it was inside him, filling his throat and lungs. He bobbed for a moment, and then sank below the surface.

His thoughts turned to Melissa and the twins. Then Barnes.

Then he thought no more.

The page crinkled as Owen turned it, drooling over Miss September's breasts. He grunted, straining. Despite his tremendous effort, he produced only a small fart.

Owen was anxious to finish his business. It had been a week since the government man had been dropped below, but he still didn't like taking a shit in the outhouse. Despite the numerous murders on his conscious, it still disturbed him to be taking a dump while a corpse rotted below. This confused Owen when he tried to figure out why it should bother him, and he didn't like being confused.

There had been no further sign of government surveillance, but they hadn't relaxed their guard. There was not one man in the camp who doubted that armed troops from the ATF or FBI could show up any day, clearing the way for the United Nations occupancy. All you had to do was watch the news to see what was going on.

Barnes was planning another bombing raid, this time at the FBI crime lab in Quantico. He'd been in touch with the other cells for the last week, meticulously going over the final details. Owen always grew apprehensive when a target date loomed.

He started to piss again, listening to his urine splashing into the pool far below. The sound struck him as funny, and he chuckled.

"Plop plop, fizz fizz, oh what a relief it is."

The trickle slowed, then stopped, and Owen decided that he was done. The hell with being constipated. He wanted to get back inside and finish his card game.

The swishing continued from below, even after he'd stopped.

Owen tilted his head and listened. His eyes grew wide. There it was again—a slithering noise in the darkness below. Rank air drifted up from the hole, followed by a bubbling sound. The foul stench grew stronger, and then there was a loud splash.

"Fuck this!" Grabbing his pants, he started to rise.

A brown tentacle exploded up from the hole, rushing between his legs and coiling itself around his waist. A putrid stink rolled off the thing, making him dizzy. Owen tried to scream, but the oozing tendril gripped him tightly. Only a terrified wheeze escaped his lungs as the air was pushed from them. Another, slimmer tentacle emerged, and wrapped itself around his head. Owen gagged, tasting shit in his mouth, and something else. Blood.

A third arm coiled around his flailing legs and pulled. Owen bent in half at the waist. The thing yanked again, the tentacles rippling with exertion. Strips of skin and hair were flayed from his body as it tugged him into the hole. Although he could not feel it, Owen heard his bones snapping. He screamed as the jagged edges poked through his skin.

Why can't I feel it?

He screamed again, and then he was gone. His scrawny frame merged with the nauseating mass as it absorbed him.

Henry and another man were on watch when the shrieks rang out. They drew their weapons and turned toward the outhouse. The ramshackle building shook violently. A thunderous rumble resonated below the ground.

"Go get Barnes," Henry shouted.

Then the four walls of the building exploded outward.

The thing that that stood illuminated in the moonlight defied description. Its shape changed constantly, shifting and running together to form new and more hideous designs. It towered above them, a malleable mountain of shit and piss and blood. Bits of solid matter floated within the heap like obscene driftwood—toilet paper, magazine pages, jewelry. Bones.

The creature's stench was overpowering. Both men coughed. Their eyes and noses burned from the gas.

"Go get Barnes," Henry repeated. "Damn it, Neil, I gave you an order!"

The other man, Neil, simply stood there gaping in fear.

Exasperated, Henry shoved him with his rifle stock. Neil barely glanced at him. He fumble with his rifle, aiming from the hip. Henry took aim, as well. The two opened fire, the white flashes from their muzzles lighting up the night. The rounds hit the creature and disappeared. As they watched, russet slime flowed into the bullet holes, sealing them within seconds.

The lights in the compound snapped on, flooding the clearing with a sickly yellow glow.

The wind shifted.

Henry's stomach revolted. He collapsed to his knees in the wet grass, vomiting.

Neil ran for the cabin, screaming for Barnes. Thick, ropy tentacles erupted from the middle of the thing and snaked across the yard after him. He shrieked as they twisted around his ankles and pulled him back toward the outhouse.

Barnes and the rest of the Sons of the Constitution rushed out of the cabin door. As one, they skidded to a halt, staring in disbelief as the thing *sucked* Henry into itself. Immediately, it swelled in size.

The assembled ranks dissolved in panic. Men dashed for the dubious safety of the trees while others blazed away with their rifles. The smell of cordite was quickly overpowered by the noxious fumes from the creature. One militia member was lifted off his feet as a foot thick tentacle wrapped around him and squeezed. He turned red, then purple. Blood burst from the pores of his skin. His screams turned into hoarse laughter as his eyeballs exploded from their sockets. Another man fired blindly, not spying the tendril snaking toward him until it was too late. He was whipped into the air, and smashed repeatedly into the hard earth. A third man was flung headfirst into an oak tree. His head burst like a melon.

Barnes shouted commands over the gunfire and screams. The rest of the men ran, leaving him alone. The thing shambled toward him on stumpy legs. Trembling, Barnes reloaded. He squeezed the trigger again, emptying the weapon. The bullets had no impact on the monster.

As he turned to flee, the creature fell upon him in one fluid motion, crashing overtop him like a wave, and crushing his body with its weight. Only his head remained free. He gasped, struggling in the quivering, putrid mass. His arms moved sluggishly, as if he were swimming in cement. Slowly, two tiny claw-like appendages formed. They wriggled towards his face, clamping each jaw and forcing his mouth open. His screams became gurgles.

The thing spoke. There was nothing human about the words it formed. The wet noises were created from flatulence. Each syllable had the gaseous resonance of a belch.

"NOW... YOU... ARE... THE...ONE... WHO... IS... FULL... OF... IT... BARNES."

It slithered into his gaping mouth, and then, Barnes was full of it indeed.

Two-Headed Alien Love Child

Kaine worked for the government. This was not something he revealed when meeting women or starting conversations. These days, with all of the paranoia and conspiracy theories, it was best to keep silent. When meeting women and starting conversations, Kaine introduced himself as an appliance salesman from New Jersey.

He'd served the department for thirty years, watching it grow from a tiny office into a sprawling bureaucratic monstrosity with buildings in every city of every state. He'd watched administrations rise and fall, witnessed cover-ups and exposes. He'd seen other divisions like the CIA and NSA hide their tracks repeatedly, but his division had *never* been covert. It worked with and among the civilians it was designed to help. True, in recent decades it had become slower and less efficient, but it still never failed to get the job done.

Getting the job done was something Kaine took very seriously. That was why he sat here tonight, listening to Neil Diamond while the rain beat upon the roof of his non-descript sedan. Sitting on a quiet suburban street in Idaho. Sitting outside the home of Sylvia Burns, a woman who, like thousands of young, unwed, or divorced mothers before her, was burdened by evil.

A blinding flash burst silently above the house like a miniature sunrise. Kaine glanced at the dashboard clock. *12:47 a.m.* Right on schedule. Then the clock flashed zeros as 'Sweet Caroline' dissolved into static. Outside, the streetlights dimmed, plunging the housing development into darkness. Kaine knew from experience that the neighbors would sleep undisturbed throughout the occurrence.

A ball of light appeared, soaring down from the sky and hovering just off the ground. A ramp descended and six diminutive figures walked out of the sphere. They approached Sylvia's bedroom window, and vanished into the house. After a few minutes, they reappeared, carrying a comatose Sylvia between them. The gray-skinned beings disappeared into the craft. The ramp began to recede.

Pausing only to smooth his tie, Kaine crept through the darkness, clutching an unregistered semiautomatic pistol in one hand, and a black briefcase in the other. Swiftly, he leapt onto the platform. The figures had retreated into the depths of the vessel. Kaine shuddered as he recalled Sylvia's description of the craft's interior.

The hatch closed behind him. Kaine examined the dimly lit corridor. A distant humming reverberated off the walls and floor. A bluish-green glow emanated from a doorway at the end of the hall. He examined the strange symbols scrawled across the door. Kaine placed the briefcase at his feet and touched the cold metal. It throbbed from deep inside, as if it were a living thing. Seconds later, the door slid open, revealing a nightmarish scene.

His client lay naked on a table, surrounded by dozens of the alien beings. They were vaguely humanoid, with two arms and two legs, but their heads were much larger than the rest of their bodies and their eyes were huge, dwarfing their almost nonexistent noses and mouths.

Kaine had seen them before. His mind flashed back to a supermarket tabloid from ten months ago: *WOMAN IMPREGNATED BY ALIEN ABDUCTORS.* Beneath the garish headline had been a photograph of Sylvia. Two weeks later, Kaine became her caseworker.

"Nobody move." He raised the pistol with one hand and unlatched the briefcase with his other. Kaine pulled a stack of papers out of the briefcase. The aliens cringed, fear flashing in their black eyes. Kaine held a document before him like a shield. "My name is Kaine. I am a Domestic Relations Officer, as well as the caseworker for the young woman you have strapped to that table."

He flung the paperwork toward the tightly clustered aliens, and undid Sylvia's straps. She clung to him weakly, as if waking from a dream.

"This, gentlemen, is a court order for child support. You are hereby ordered to appear in domestic court one month from today for a child support hearing. My client claims that you impregnated her; therefore, you are financially responsible for part of the child's welfare. Bring whatever pay stubs and supporting documents you may have with you. Also bring a copy of your most recent tax return. If you can not afford an attorney, one will be appointed to you by the state."

Still brandishing the gun, Kaine backed Sylvia towards the exit.

"The next time you decide to abduct and impregnate someone in my state, gentlemen, I suggest you remember that we do not go lightly on deadbeat dads. Good evening to you."

The door hissed shut behind them, leaving the aliens to stare at one another in bewilderment.

"Shit," said one. "We haven't fucked up this bad since Roswell."

———

STORY NOTE: Another very early story. I'm not sure where I got the idea. I think it stemmed from drinking a six-pack of beer while watching *The X-Files*.

Bunnies In August

One year later...

He shouldn't have come here. Not today. Especially not today.

This is where it happened, he thought. *This is where Jack died.*

Gary stood beneath the water tower. It perched atop the tallest hill in town, right between the Methodist church cemetery, and the rear of the tiny, decrepit strip mall (abandoned when Wal-Mart moved in two miles away), and a corn field. The tower was a massive, looming, blue thing, providing water to the populace below. Every time he saw it, (which was all the time, because it was visible from everywhere in town) Gary was reminded of the Martian tripods from *War of the Worlds.* When Jack was old enough to read the graphic novel adaptation, it had reminded him of the same thing.

"It looks like one of the robots, doesn't it Daddy? Doesn't it? Let's pretend the Martians are invading!"

The first tear welled up. Then another. They built to a crescendo. Surrendering, Gary closed his eyes and wept. A warm summer breeze rustled the treetops above him. His breath caught in his throat. He tried to swallow the lump, and found he couldn't. Sweat beaded his forehead. The heat was stifling. His skin prickled, as if on fire. As if he was burning. The wind brushed against him like caressing flames.

Blinking the tears away, he glanced back up at the water tower and wondered how he could bring it down. He saw it every day—on the drive home, from the grocery store parking lot, the backyard, even his bedroom window—and each time he was reminded of his son.

The tower's presence was inescapable. How to erase its existence—and thus, the memories? A chainsaw was out of the question. The supports were made of steel. Explosives maybe? Yeah. Sure. He was a fucking insurance salesman. Where was he going to find explosives?

He hated the water tower. It stood here as an unwanted reminder, a dark monument to Jack.

This was where it happened.

This used to be their playground.

Weekends had always been their time together. During the week, Gary and Susan both worked, he at the insurance office and she from home, typing up tape-recorded court transcripts. Jack had school, fourth grade, where he excelled in English and Social Studies, but struggled with Math and Science. Gary didn't see them much on weeknights, either. He'd had other... obligations.

Leila's face popped into his mind, unbidden. He pushed her away. *Get thee behind me, Satan.*

The weekends were magic. Once he'd waded through the mind-numbing tedium of domestic chores; grocery shopping, mowing the lawn, cleaning the gutters, and anything else Susan thought up for him to do while she sat at home all day long; after all that, there was Daddy and Jack time. Father and son time. Quality time.

Jack's first word had been 'Da-da'.

Gary had loved his son. Loved him so much that it hurt, sometimes. Despite how clichéd it may have sounded to some people, the pain was real. And good. When Jack was little, Gary used to stand over his crib and watch him sleeping. In those moments, Gary's breath hitched up in his chest—a powerful, overwhelming emotional wave. He'd loved Susan like that too, once upon a time, when they'd first been married. Before job-related stress and mortgage payments and their mutual weight gain—and before Susan's little personality quirks, things he'd thought were cute and endearing when he'd first met her, the very things he'd fallen in love with after the initial physical attraction, became annoying rather than charming. They knew everything there was to know about each other, and thus, they knew too much. Boredom set in, and worse, a simmering complacency that hollowed him out inside and left him empty. When Jack came along in their fifth year of marriage, Gary fell in love all over again, and his son had filled that hole.

At least temporarily...

Parental love was one thing. That completed a part of him. But Gary still had unfulfilled needs. Needs that Susan didn't seem inclined to acknowledge, and in truth, needs he wasn't sure she could have satisfied any longer even if she'd shown interest. Not with the distance between them, a gulf that had grown wider after Jack's birth. There were too many sleepless nights and grumpy mornings, too many laconic, grunted conversations in front of the television and not enough talking.

So Gary had gone elsewhere.

To Leila.

A crow called out above him, perched on a tree limb. The sound startled him, bringing Gary back to the present. The bird spread its wings and the branch bent under its wings. The leaves rustled as it took flight. Gary watched it go. His spirits plummeted even farther as the bird soared higher.

He stepped out from underneath the water tower's shadow, back into the sunlight, and shivered.

We beat the Martians, Daddy! Me and you, together...

"Oh Jack," he whispered, "I'm so sorry."

Gary felt eyes upon him, a tickling sensation between his shoulder blades. He glanced around. Through his tears, he noticed a rabbit at the edge of the field, watching him intently.

He sniffed, wiping his nose with the back of his hand.

The rabbit twitched its whiskers and kept staring. Gary felt its black eyes bore into him. He wondered if animals blinked.

The rabbit didn't.

"Scat." Gary stamped his foot. "Go on! Get out of here."

The rabbit scurried into the corn, vanishing as quickly as it had appeared. Gary studied the patch of grass where it had been sitting. The spot was empty, except for a large rock. Was it his imagination, or was the stone's surface red?

Maybe the animal was injured. Or dying.

His mind threatened to dredge up more of the past, and he bit his lip, drawing blood.

Gary checked the time on his cell phone. He'd been gone a long while. Susan would be worried. He shouldn't have left her alone, especially on today, of all days. But she'd insisted that at least one of them should visit Jack's grave. That was what had brought him here in the first place. He'd been drawn to the water tower without even thinking about it. Susan hadn't come with him to the cemetery. Said she couldn't bear it. She'd visited the grave many times over the past year, but not today. It had been left for Gary to do, and so he had.

He pressed a button, unlocking the keypad, and the phone's display lit up. It was just after twelve noon, on August fifteenth. But he'd already known the date.

How could he forget?

He trudged back the way he'd come, wading through the sweltering afternoon haze. Heat waves shimmered in the corners of his vision.

He shouldn't have come here. Not today, on the one year anniversary of his son's death. This was a bad idea. It was bad enough that he could see this stupid water tower everywhere he went. Why come this close to it? What was he hoping to find? To prove?

The wind whispered, *Daddy.*

Gary turned around, and gasped.

Jack stood beneath the water tower, watching him go. The boy was dressed in the same clothes the police had found him in.

Daddy...

His son reached out. Jack was transparent. Gary could see corn stalks on the other side of him.

"No. Not real. You're not real."

La la la la, lemon. La la la la, lullaby...

Gary shivered. Jack's favorite song from *Sesame Street*. He'd sung it all the time. All about the letter 'L' and words that began with it; a Bert and Ernie classic from Gary's own childhood.

"You're not there," he told his son.

Gary stuck his pinky fingers in his ears and closed his eyes. When he opened them again, Jack was gone. He'd never been there. It was just the heat, playing tricks on him. He lowered his hands.

Something rustled between the rows of swaying corn.

Gary didn't believe in ghosts. He didn't need to. Memories could haunt a man much more than spirits ever could.

He walked home, passing through the cemetery on the way, and his son's grave.

He stopped at Jack's headstone, knelt in the grass, and wept. He did not see Jack again. He did spot several more rabbits, darting between tombstones, running through the grass. Playing amongst the dead.

He tried to ignore the fact that they all stopped to watch him pass.

By the time he got home, Gary's melancholy mood had turned into full-fledged depression. He'd been off the medication for months now, ever since he'd stopped seeing the counselor. If he went inside the house, he'd feel even worse. Susan had been crying all morning, looking at pictures of Jack. He couldn't deal with that right now. Couldn't handle her pain. He was supposed to fix things for them, and this couldn't be fixed. Gary couldn't stand to see her hurting. Had never been able to.

He decided to mow the lawn instead. Even though he dreaded mowing, sometimes it made him feel better—the aroma of fresh cut grass and the neat, symmetrical rows. He went into the garage; made sure the lawnmower had enough oil and gas, and then rolled it out into the yard. It started on the third tug.

Gary pushed the lawnmower up and down the yard and tried not to think. Grasshoppers and crickets jumped out of his way, and yellow dandelions disappeared beneath the blades. He'd completed five rows and was beginning his sixth when he noticed the baby bunny.

Or what was left of it.

The rabbit's upper half crawled through the yard, trailing viscera and blood, grass clippings sticking to its guts. Its lower body was missing, presumably pulped by the lawnmower. Gary's hands slipped off the safety bar, and the lawnmower dutifully turned itself off.

Silence descended, for a brief moment, and then he heard something else.

The baby rabbit made a noise, almost like a scream.

Daddy?

He glanced around, frantic. A few feet away, the grass moved. Something was underneath it, hiding beneath the surface. Gary walked over and bent down, parting the grass. His fingers came away sticky and red. Secreted inside the remains of their warren were four more baby bunnies. The lawnmower had mangled them, and they were dying as he watched. Their black eyes stared at him incriminatingly. The burrow was slick with gore and fur.

Gary turned away. His breakfast sprayed across the lawn.

Despite their injuries, despite missing limbs and dangling intestines, the bunnies continued to thrash, their movements weak and jerky.

"Oh God," he moaned. "Why don't they die? Why don't—"

The half-rabbit dragging itself across the yard squealed again.

"Please," Gary whimpered. "Just die. Don't do this. Not today. It's too much."

Daddy? Daddyyyy? La la la la, lemon. La la la la lullaby...

Gary stumbled to his feet and ran to the driveway. Without thinking, he seized the biggest rock he could find, dashed back to the rabbit hole, and raised the rock over his head.

"I'm sorry."

He flung it down as hard as he could, squashing them. Their tiny bones snapped like twigs underfoot. Swallowing hard, Gary picked the rock back up again, ignoring the sticky, matted blood and fur that now clung to its bottom and sides. He stalked across the yard, tracked down the half-bunny and put it out of its misery, too.

Gasping for breath, he left the rock lay in the grass, concealing the carcass. His bowels clenched; then loosened. Kneeling, he threw up again. When it was over, he washed his hands and face off beneath the outside spigot.

This time, the tears didn't stop.

Gary wailed. One of his neighbors poked their head outside, attracted by the ruckus. When they saw his face, saw the raw emotions etched onto it, they ducked back inside.

Eventually, when he'd gotten himself under control, Gary went inside. He poured a double scotch, and gulped it down. The liquor burned his raw throat. He called out for Susan, but there was no answer. He found her in Jack's bedroom, sitting on their son's bed and holding one of his action figures. Her face was wet and pale. He sat down next to her, put his arm around her, and they cried together for a long time.

* * *

That night, Susan said she'd like to try again; she'd like to have another child. She murmured in his ear that it had been a long time since they'd made love, and apologized for it. Said it was her fault, and she'd like to try and fix things. Make them like they used to be, long ago, when they'd first been married. Every party of Gary stiffened, except for the part of him that could have helped insure that. When she noticed, and asked what was wrong, he told her that he didn't feel good. Too depressed. Susan pulled away. She asked Gary if he still loved her and he lied and said yes. She snuggled closer again, and put her head on his chest.

Gary thought of Leila and tried very hard not to scream. The guilt was a solid thing, and it weighed on him heavier than the thick blankets pulled over his body. He held Susan until she fell asleep and then he slipped out from underneath her. She moaned in her sleep, a sad sound. He went downstairs, turned on the television, and curled into the fetal position on the couch.

He'd never told her about Leila. As far as he knew, Susan had never expected. At one point, he'd thought the secret might come out. Leila had made threats. She was unhappy. Wanted Gary to leave Susan and be with her. He'd been worried, frantic—unsure of what to do. But then Jack had died and the whole affair had become moot. For the past year, he and Susan had both been overwhelmed with grief. And though Leila was no longer in the picture, and though Gary had tried very hard to be there for his wife and make the marriage work, he couldn't tell Susan now. She was a mother who'd lost her child.

He couldn't hurt her all over again.

Restless, Gary tossed and turned. The couch springs squeaked. Eventually, he needed to pee. Rather than using the upstairs bathroom and risk waking Susan, he went outside, into the backyard. He pushed his robe aside, fumbled with the fly on his pajamas, and unleashed a stream.

And then he froze.

In the darkness, a pair of shiny little eyes stared back at him. Although he couldn't see the animal itself, Gary knew what it was—the mother rabbit, looking for her dead children.

"I'm sorry," he whispered.

The eyes vanished in the darkness.

He went back inside and lay down on the couch again. Sleep would not come, nor would relief from the pain. It hadn't been this bad in a while, not since the month's immediately following Jack's death.

Gary stared at the television without seeing.

It was a long time before he slept.

That December, when Gary got home from a particularly harrowing day at the office, Susan was in the bedroom, holding the stick from a home pregnancy test. It was the second of the day. She'd taken the first that morning, after he left for work. Both showed positive; a little blue plus sign, simple in its symbolism, yet powerful as well. That tiny plus sign led to joy and happiness—or sometimes—fear and heartbreak.

Susan was ecstatic, and that night, after they'd eaten a romantic, candlelight dinner, and curled up together to watch a movie, and made love, Gary decided that he'd never tell her about Leila. Not now. He couldn't.

After all, he'd lived with the guilt this long.

He could do it for the rest of his life.

According to the obstetrician, (an asthmatic, paunchy man named Doctor Brice) Susan was due in August, within ten days of the anniversary of Jack's death.

On the way home from Doctor Brice's office, Susan turned to Gary.

"It's a sign."

"What is?"

"My due date. It's like a sign from God."

Gary kept silent. He thought it might be the exact opposite.

Two years later.

On the second anniversary of their son's death, with Susan's due date a little more than a week away, they woke up, dressed solemnly, and prepared to visit Jack's grave. Susan had picked a floral arrangement the night before, and both of them had taken the day off work.

Once again, the August heat and humidity were insufferable. Gary waded through the thick miasma on his way to start the car (so that the air conditioner would have time to cool the interior before Susan came out). He slipped behind the wheel, put the key in the ignition, and turned it. The car sputtered and then something exploded. There was a horrible screech, followed by a wet thump. The engine hissed, and a brief gust of steam or smoke billowed from beneath the hood.

Cursing, Gary yanked on the hood release and jumped out of the car. He ran around to the front, popped the hood, and raised it. The stench was awful. He stumbled backward. Something wet and red had splattered all over the engine. Tufts of brown and white fur stuck to the metal. A disembodied foot lay on top of the battery.

A rabbit's foot.

Guess he wasn't so lucky, Gary thought, biting back a giggle. He was horrified, but at the same time, overwhelmed with the bizarre desire to laugh.

The rabbit must have crawled up into the engine block overnight, perhaps seeking warmth or just looking for a place to nest. When Gary had started the car, the animal most likely panicked and scurried for cover, taking a fatal misstep into the whirring fan blades.

He glanced back down at the severed rabbit's foot again.

A bunny. Same day. Just like last year. With the lawnmower. He'd run over the nest, and then he'd... with the rock...

Susan tapped him on the shoulder and he nearly screamed. When she saw the mess beneath the hood, she almost did the same.

"What happened?"

"A rabbit. It must have crawled inside last night."

She recoiled, one hand covering her mouth. "Oh, that's terrible. The poor thing."

"Yeah. Let me get this cleaned up and then we'll go."

Susan began to sob. Gary went to her, and she sagged against him.

"I'm sorry. It's just..."

"I know," Gary consoled her. "I know."

She pushed away. "I think I'm going to be sick."

"Susan—"

Turning, she waddled as quickly as she could back to the house. Gary followed her, heard her retching in the bathroom, and after a moment's hesitation, knocked gently on the door.

"You okay?"

"No," she choked. "I don't think I can go. You'll go without me?"

"But Susan, I..."

She retched again. Gary closed his eyes.

"Please, Gary? I can't go. Not like this. One of us has to."

"You're right, of course."

Susan heard the reluctance in his voice.

"Please?"

Gary sighed. "Will you be okay?"

The toilet flushed. "Yes. I just need to rest. Remember to take the flowers."

"I will. Susan?"

"What?"

"I'm sorry."

He heard her running water in the sink.

"Don't be sorry," she said. "It's not your fault."

The graveyard was an empty, except for an elderly couple on their way out as Gary arrived. Despite the heat, he'd decided to walk to the cemetery rather than dealing with the mess beneath the hood of his car. By the time he reached Jack's grave he was drenched in sweat, his clothing soaked.

Panting, he knelt in front of the grave. Droplets of perspiration ran into his eyes, stinging them. His vision blurred, and then the tears began. They were false tears, crocodile tears, tears of sweat and exertion, rather than grief. Oh, the grief was there. Gary was overwhelmed with grief. Grief was a big lump that sat in his throat. But still, the real tears would not come.

But the memories did.

When he glanced up at the water tower, the memories came full force.

Grief turned to guilt.

*   *   *

"I mean it, Gary. I'm telling Susan."

"You'll do no such thing."

Leila's smile was tight-lipped, almost a grimace. "I've got her email address."

Gary paused. Felt fear. "You're lying."

"Try me." Now her smile was genuine again, if cruel. "I looked it up on the internet. From her company's website."

Gary sighed. "Why? Why do this to me?"

"Because I'm sick of your bullshit. You said you loved me. You said you'd leave her—"

"I've told you, it's not that simple. I've got to think about Jack."

"She can't take Jack from you. You're his father. You've got rights."

"I can't take that chance. Damn it, Leila, we've been through this a million times. I love you, but I—"

"You're a fucking liar, Gary! Just stop it. If you loved me, you'd tell her."

"I do love you."

"Then do it. Tell her. If you don't have the balls to, I will."

"Are you threatening me? You gonna blackmail me into continuing this? Is that it?"

"If I have to."

Gary wasn't sure what happened next. They'd been naked, sitting side by side on the blanket, their fluids drying on each other's body, the water tower's shadow protecting them from the warm afternoon sun, hiding their illicit tryst. He wasn't aware that he was straddling Leila until his hands curled around her throat.

Choking, she lashed out at him. Her long, red fingernails raked across his naked chest. Flailing blindly, his hand closed around the rock. He raised it over his head and Leila's eyes grew large.

"Gary..."

The rock smashed into her mouth, cutting off the rest.

He lost all control then, hammering her face and head repeatedly. He blocked out everything; her screams, the frightened birds taking flight, his own nonsensical curses. Everything—until he heard the singing.

"La la la la, lemon. La la la la lullaby..."

Jack. Singing his favorite song.

The boy stepped into the clearing. Believing his father was working that Saturday (because that was the lie Gary had told Susan and Jack so that he could meet up with Leila for an afternoon quickie in the first place—he'd even stayed logged into his computer at work so that if anybody checked, it would look like he was there working), Jack froze in mid-melody, a mixture of puzzlement and terror on his face.

"Daddy?"

"Jack!"

His son turned and ran. Jack sprang to his feet, naked and bloody, and chased after him.

"Jack, stop! Daddy can explain."

"Mommy..."

Unaware that he was still holding the rock, until he struck his son in the back of the head.

"I said stop!"

Jack toppled face first into the grass. He did not move. Did not breathe.

When Gary checked his pulse, he had none.

Something inside Gary shut itself off at that moment.

The rest of the memories became a blur. He dressed. Wrapped the blanket around Leila and loaded her into the trunk of the car, which he'd parked behind the abandoned strip mall, just beyond the cemetery and the water tower. Her blood hadn't yet seeped out onto the grass, and he made sure none of her teeth or any shreds of tissue were in sight. He'd thrown her clothes and purse inside the car as well.

Then he picked up the bloody rock, the rock that he'd just bludgeoned his son to death with, and threw it down a nearby rabbit hole.

He drove to the edge of LeHorn's Hollow, where a sinkhole had opened up the summer before, and dumped Leila's body. Gary knew that the local farmers sometimes dumped their dead livestock in the same hole, as did hunters after field dressing wild game. The chances were good that she'd never be found.

He cleaned his hands off in a nearby stream, then got back in the car and drove to the closest convenience store. He bought some cleaning supplies, paid cash, and then found a secluded spot where he could clean out the trunk. Then he returned to the office, unlocked the door, logged himself off the computer, and went home.

Then he went home.

The police knocked on the door a few hours later. Three teen-aged boys found Jack's body. One of them, Seth Ferguson (who was no stranger to juvenile detention) immediately fell under suspicion. When the police cleared him later that day, they questioned the local registered sex offenders, even though Jack's body had shown no signs of sexual abuse. In the weeks and months that followed, there were no new leads. The case was never solved.

The murder weapon was never found.

Daddy...

Gary sat up and wiped his eyes. Steadying himself on his son's tombstone, he clambered to his feet. His joints popped. He hadn't aged well in the last two years, and his body was developing the ailments of a man twice his age, arthritis being one of them.

Daddy?

"Oh Jack," Gary whispered. "Why couldn't you have stayed home that day?"

Daddy...

His son's voice grew louder, calling to him, pleading. Sad. Lonely.

Slowly, like a marionette on strings, Gary shuffled towards the water tower.

"Where are you, Jack? Show me. Tell me what I have to do to make it up to you."

Daddy... Daddy... Daddy...

The voice was right next to him. Gary looked around, fully expecting to see his son's ghost, but instead, he spied the rabbits. A dozen or so bunnies formed a loose circle around the water tower. They'd been silent, and had appeared as if from nowhere.

Penning him in.

Daddy. Down here.

Gary looked down at the ground.

Jack's voice echoed from inside a rabbit hole.

The same hole he'd thrown the rock into.

Gary's skin prickled. Despite his fear, he leaned over and stared into the hole. There was a flurry of movement inside, and then a rabbit darted out and joined the others. Then another. Whimpering,

Gary stepped backward. More bunnies poured themselves from the earth, and he felt their eyes on him—accusing.

Condemning.

"What do you want?"

Daddy.

Gary screamed.

They found him when the sun went down. He'd screamed himself hoarse while pawing at the ground around his son's grave. His fingers were dirty, and several of his fingernails were bloody and ragged, hanging by thin strands of tissue. He babbled about bunnies, but no one could understand him. The police arrived, as did an ambulance.

From the undergrowth, a brown bunny rabbit watched them load Gary into the ambulance.

When he was gone, it hopped away.

————

STORY NOTE: This story takes place in the same town as my novels *Dark Hollow*, *Ghost Walk*, *Take The Long Way Home*, and several short stories, and alert readers might recognize a few familiar places and people. The water tower exists much as I described it here, but it is far less sinister in real life. My oldest son and I used to play there when he was little. The mishap with the rabbits and the lawnmower is also based on something that happened in real life. I was mowing my lawn and accidentally hit a hidden nest of baby rabbits. It was horrifying and terrible and I felt guilty about it for months afterward. I channeled some of that into the story.

The Wind Cries Mary

Even in death, she returns to visit me every night.

If time mattered anymore, you'd be able to set your watch by her arrival. Mary shows up shortly after the sun goes down. She lumbers up our long, winding driveway, dragging her shattered right leg behind her like it's a dog. I often wonder how she can still walk.

Of course, all the dead walk these days, but in Mary's case, a shard of bone protrudes from her leg, just below the knee. The flesh around it is shiny and swollen—the color of lunchmeat. The wound doesn't even leak anymore. I keep expecting her to fall over, for the bone to burst through the rest of the way, for her leg to come completely off. But it never happens.

Her abdomen has swollen, too. We were never able to have children, but death has provided her with a cruel pantomime of what pregnancy must be like. I dread what will happen when those gases trapped inside of her finally reach the breaking point. Her breasts have sunken, as have her cheekbones and eyes. Her summer dress hangs off her frame in tatters. It was one of my favorites—white cotton with a blue floral print. Simple, yet elegant, just like Mary. Now it is anything but. Her long hair is no longer clean or brushed, and instead of smelling like honeysuckle shampoo, it now smells of leaves and dirt, and is rife with insects. Her fingernails are filthy and cracked. She used to take so much pride in them. Her hands and face are caked with a dried brown substance. I tell myself that it is mud, but I know in my heart that it's blood.

None of this matters to me. Her body may be changing, but Mary is still the woman I fell in love with. She is still the most beautiful woman I have ever known. She is still my wife, and I still love her. Death hasn't taken that away. It has only made it stronger.

We had fifteen good years together. Death does not overcome those times. Her body may be rotting, but those memories do not decay. I am sure of this. Why else would she return here, night after night, and stare at the house, fumbling at the door and searching for a way in? It can't be to feed. If it were, she would have given up by now—moved on to the new housing development a few miles up the road, where I am sure there are still plenty of families barricaded inside their homes, too scared or stupid to stay quiet for long. Easy pickings. I don't know what she does during the day. Certainly it isn't sleep. The dead never sleep. I assume she eats. Wanders, perhaps. But the question re-mains, why does she return here night after night? Mary doesn't know I'm in here. Of this, I am certain. Although she paws at the door and the boarded up windows, she can't see inside of our house. She can't see me or hear me. So why does she return?

The answer is simple. She remembers. Maybe not in the way the living remember things, but somewhere, rooted deeply in whatever is left of her brain, there is some rudimentary attachment to this place. Perhaps she recognizes it as home. Maybe she just knows that this was a place where she was happy. A place where she once lived.

Mary hated me the first time we met. It was at a college party. She was an art major. I was studying business. I was a drunken frat boy— a young Republican in training, the next-generation spawn of the Reagan revolution. Mary was a liberal Democrat, involved in a number of volunteer social programs. When she walked into the party, a blonde and a brunette were feeding me a forty-ounce of Mickey's through a makeshift beer bong. She glanced in our direction, then turned away. I was instantly infatuated. Not love at first sight, but certainly lust. Love came later.

I got her number from a mutual acquaintance. It took me two months to get a date with her. I was on my best behavior. The date lasted all night. We saw *Pulp Fiction* (I loved it, she hated it). We went to Denny's (I had steak and eggs, she had a salad). We went back to her place. We talked all night. Kissed a little, but mostly, we just talked. And it was wonderful. When the sun came up, I asked for a second date and got it.

We dated for years, and broke up a half-dozen times before we finally got engaged. It wasn't that we fought. We were just very different people. Sure, we shared some similar interests. We both liked to read. We both enjoyed playing *Scrabble*. We both liked Springsteen. But these were small, superficial similarities. At our core, we were different from one another. There are two kinds of people in this world—my kind, and Mary's kind. But we made it work. We had love. And we were happy.

Until Hamelin's Revenge. That's the name the media gave it, because the disease started with the rats. Hamelin, the village where the Pied Piper cured the rat problem once and for all. Except that in real life, the rats came back—infected with a disease that turned the dead into rotting, shambling eating machines. Some television pundit called them 'land sharks'. I thought that was funny at the time. I don't any longer. The disease jumped from the rats to other species, including humans. It jumped oceans, too. It showed up first in New York, but by the end of the week, it spread to London, Mumbai, Paris, Tel Aviv, Moscow, Hafr Al-Batin, and elsewhere. Armies couldn't fight it. You could shoot the dead, but you couldn't shoot the disease. Global chaos ensued. Major metropolitan areas fell first. Then the smaller cities. Then the rural areas.

Mary and I stayed inside. We barricaded the house. We had enough food and water to last us a while. We had weapons to de-fend ourselves. We waited for the crisis to pass. Waited for someone—anyone—to sound the all clear and restore order. But that someone never came.

Mary died a week ago. She'd gone outside, just for a second, to dump the bucket we've been using as for a toilet. A dead crow pecked her neck. Panicked, Mary beat it aside and ran back into the house. The wound was just a scratch. It didn't even bleed.

But it was enough.

She died that night. I knew what had to be done. The only way to keep the dead from coming back is to destroy their brain. I put the gun to her head while she lay still, but didn't have the courage to pull the trigger. I couldn't do that to her, not to the woman I loved. Instead, I cracked the door open and placed her body outside.

The next morning, she was gone.

That was when I put the gun to my own head and did to myself what I could not do to my wife. That should have been it.

But I came back anyway—not as a shuffling corpse. No, I am a different kind of dead. My body is decomposing on the kitchen floor, but I am not in it. All I can do is watch as it slowly rots away. I can't leave this place. There is no light. No voices from beyond. No deceased loved ones to greet me from the other side.

There is only me...and Mary.

I cannot touch her. Cannot follow. I've tried to talk to her, tried to let her know that I am still here, but my voice is just the wind, and she does not notice. Each night, I cry for us both, but I have no tears, so my sobs are just the breeze.

There used to be two kinds of people in this world. Now, in the aftermath of Hamelin's Revenge, there are two kinds of dead—my kind, and Mary's kind.

We made it work once before.

I wonder if we can make it work once again?

———

STORY NOTE: Just like a few of the other zombie stories in this collection, this story takes place in the same "universe" as my novels *Dead Sea* and *Entombed*. The story itself is a love story. It occurs to me that a LOT of my short stories that deal with zombies are, in fact, love stories. Not sure why that is or what it means about me...

The Resurrection And the Life

STORY NOTE: The following story is a remake of chapter eleven of the Book of John, which tells the tale of how Jesus raised Lazarus from the dead. My story is a decidedly different version than the one you'll read in the Bible. The main difference is the addition of Ob.

I'm assuming that you're already familiar with my novels *The Rising* and *City of the Dead*, in which Ob appears. If not, then a brief history lesson is required. Ob is an inter-dimensional being. He commands a race of similar beings known as the Siqqusim. The Siqqusim possess the corpses of the dead, reanimating them, wearing them like you or I wear a suit of clothes. They are zombies, in effect. Since the Siqqusim reside in the corpse's brain, the only way to defeat them is to destroy their dead host's brain, thus dispatching the Siqqusim back to the ether.

I got the idea for the story after being forced to go to church one Sunday morning. I was listening to a preacher talk about Lazarus' resurrection, and I thought, "So Lazarus was the first zombie..."

———

And so the Jewish priests accused the Rabbi, who was called Jesus, of blasphemy and tried to stone him. Jesus and his disciples fled Jerusalem for their very lives.

Escaping to the borders of Judea, they crossed over the Jordan River to the place where John had been baptized in the early days. There they set up camp, safe from the law, and Jesus began to teach again.

Many curious people came to the site over the next four days. Some just wanted to listen to what Jesus had to say. Others had heard rumors of miracles—that he'd made a blind man see, touched a lame little girl and commanded her to throw away her crutches, cast out demons, and walked across water. They flocked to the riverbank hoping for a glimpse, hoping to see something miraculous so that they could tell their children and grandchildren about it in years to come. They longed to say, "I was there the day Jesus of Nazareth made the sky rain blood. He split a rock with his staff and brought forth water. He touched your father's stump and his arm sprang forth anew. Serpents fled as he trod."

At first, they were disappointed. That emotion soon waned. Jesus performed no miracles during those four days. He didn't have to. No matter what their reasons for attending, once the throng heard him speak, they believed. His voice was melodious and assured, and the strength of his convictions shone through in every word. Unlike the prophets who held court in the desert or in the bazaars and alleyways, Jesus appeared sane. Likeable. His charisma was infectious.

When John had taught on this same riverbank in earlier years, he'd prophesied about the Messiah. Many of the older members in the crowd had heard John's predictions regarding Jesus, and after listening to Jesus speak they said, "Though John never performed a miraculous sign, all that he said about this man, Jesus of Nazareth, was true. He really is the Son of God. The Messiah walks among us."

On the fifth day, a messenger from the Judean village of Bethany crossed the border and entered the camp. Word spread through the crowd that he was seeking Jesus. Worried that the messenger might actually be an assassin sent by the priests, Peter, one of Jesus' disciples, met with the man and demanded that the message be given to him instead.

But Jesus overheard this and granted the messenger an audience, telling Peter, "If any come seeking me, you must show them the way."

Jesus and the messenger drew away from the others, and Jesus offered the man water and bread, saying, "I can feed your hunger and thirst, if you will only partake."

When he was sated, the man delivered his message.

"Rabbi," he said, "I have tidings from Mary and her sister, Martha, who reside in the village of Bethany. It concerns their brother, Lazarus."

Jesus knew Mary, Martha, and Lazarus very well. All three were dear and faithful friends of his. Many months ago, as Jesus and his disciples were traveling through Judea, they'd come to a village where a woman named Martha opened her home to them. Jesus taught from Martha's home for many days. Her sister, Mary, had sat at his feet and listened to what he said. Martha had been unable to partake in the teachings because she was distracted by all the preparations that had to be made in order to feed all twelve of Jesus' entourage. She'd come to Jesus and asked, "Lord, don't you care that my sister has left me to do the work by myself? Tell her to help me!"

When he heard this, Jesus said, "Martha, you are worried and upset about many things, but only one thing is needed. Mary has chosen what is better, and it will not be
taken away from her."

At first, Martha had not understood his meaning, but when at last the knowledge dawned on her, she laughed.

The sound had filled the Son of God's heart with happiness.

He loved them both, and loved their brother Lazarus most of all, for he was a good man and had not been offended when Mary poured perfume on Jesus' feet and wiped them with her hair. Lazarus had understood the symbolism and blessed it with his acceptance rather than demanding blood.

Jesus smiled at the memory.

"Lord?" The messenger shuffled his feet in the sand, unsure if Jesus had heard him.

"What news from Mary and Martha?" Jesus asked. "What news of Lazarus?"

"The sisters have commanded me to say, 'Lord, the one you love is sick'."

When he heard this, Jesus patted the messenger's hand. "This sickness will not end in death. No, it is for God's glory so that God's Son may be glorified through it."

Jesus loved Martha, Mary and Lazarus. Yet when he heard that Lazarus was sick, he stayed where he was two more days, teaching upon the banks of the Jordan.

"Surely, he will go to aid his friends," whispered Judas. "He would not let death claim a man such as Lazarus."

"Our Lord cannot return," Peter said. "Have you forgotten, Judas? Bethany is in the heart of Judea. We have just fled that place for our very lives. To return now would mean certain death."

On the seventh day, just as the sun rose over the hills, Jesus called his disciples together. They sat around the fire and shared a wineskin and bread. The assembled crowd was still sleeping. Many of the people who had come to hear Jesus out of curiosity had ended up staying, forsaking their farms and families so that they could gain knowledge and understanding.

When they had broken their fast, Jesus said to his disciples, "Let us go back to Judea."

"But Rabbi," Paul exclaimed, "a short while ago the Jews tried to stone you, and yet you are going back there?"

Jesus nodded. "We must return. Our friend Lazarus is sick."

"Then we shall travel under the cover of darkness," Matthew suggested.

"No, Matthew," Jesus said. "That is not the way. Are there not twelve hours of daylight? A man who walks by day will not stumble, for he sees by this world's light. It is when he walks by night that he stumbles, for he has no light."

Paul stood up. "I still do not think it is a good idea, Lord."

Judas poured river water on the campfire and stirred the ashes. The rest of the disciples grumbled among themselves.

Jesus insisted. "Our friend Lazarus has fallen asleep; but I am going to Bethany to wake him up."

"Lord," Luke said, "if Lazarus sleeps, then he will get better. We should let him rest."

"That is not the sleep I speak of. By the time we arrive, Lazarus will be dead. And for your sake, Luke, I am glad that I was not there in time, so that you may believe."

Luke frowned. "I do not understand."

"I know." Jesus smiled. "But enough talk for now. Let us go to him, and all will be made clear."

Jesus stood up and prepared to leave. He moved amongst the crowd, wishing them well and imparting his blessing. Some of the people wept when they heard that he was leaving, for they knew what the Jewish priests would do if he were caught.

Jesus reached the bank of the river and turned around.

He called out, "I go to Judea."

"Then you go to your death, my Lord," Judas whispered.

Thomas, who was also called Didymus, said to the rest of the disciples, "Let us also go, that we may die with him."

When they arrived, Lazarus had already been dead and in his tomb for four days, just as Jesus had predicted.

Bethany was less than two miles from Jerusalem, and many Jews had come to Martha and Mary to comfort them in the loss of their brother. They brought whispers and gossip of Jesus' arrival—how he and his followers were approaching in broad daylight, marching down the main road in plain defiance of the priests. When Martha heard that Jesus was coming, she went out to meet him, but Mary stayed at home.

Jesus greeted Martha. "It is good to see you."

The distraught woman did not return his smile, nor would she meet his eyes.

"Martha, do not be troubled," Jesus said.

"Lord, if you had been here, my brother would not have died. But I know that even now God will give you whatever you ask."

"And what would you have me ask of my Father, dear Martha?"

Martha lowered her head again. Her voice was barely a whisper. "That He not have taken Lazarus from me."

"Your brother will rise again," Jesus told her.

Martha nodded. "I know he will rise again in the resurrection at the last day."

"But," Jesus said, "I am the resurrection and the life. He who believes in me will live, even though he dies; and whoever lives and believes in me will never die. Do you believe this, Martha?"

"Yes, Lord," she replied, "I believe that you are the Christ, the Son of God, who was to come into the world."

"Then let not your heart be troubled. You will see your brother again. Now where is Mary?"

"She is at our home, Lord. I should make haste there as well, to prepare for you and your disciples."

Sighing, Jesus eyed the crowd that had gathered to see him. "We shall follow along behind you as we are able."

Martha ran home ahead of them. Mary was still in mourning,

and had not moved from the straw mat in the corner. She was surrounded by many friends, all of them offering comfort, and yet no comfort did she find.

Martha went to her sister's side. "The Rabbi is here and he is asking for you."

When Mary heard this, she got up quickly and went out to meet him. The people who had been comforting Mary noticed how hastily she left. They followed her, assuming she was going to the tomb to mourn her brother there.

Jesus and his disciples had not yet entered the village, and were still at the place where Martha had met them. Jesus was giving an impromptu lesson to the assembled crowd. When Mary reached the place and saw Jesus, she fell at his feet and wept.

"Lord," she cried, "if you had been here, my brother would not have died."

Mary's friends grew sullen and whispered among themselves about the influence Jesus had on her. Several of them began to cry as well, overcome with sorrow for their friend, Lazarus. They felt bad for the two sisters. Both had believed until the very end that this son of a carpenter—this Nazarene—would somehow save Lazarus. But he had not.

And now Lazarus was dead.

Jesus was deeply moved by their tears, and his spirit was troubled.

"Where have you laid him?" Jesus asked.

"Come and see, Lord," Mary replied. Her face was wet, her eyes red.

They walked along the road and Jesus wept.

As they passed by the sisters' house, Martha joined the procession, assuming that Jesus wished to bid his respects to the deceased. More villagers followed along, and the disciples grew nervous, certain that word of their presence would each the priests in Jerusalem soon.

One of Mary's friends watched Jesus cry, and said, "See how he loved Lazarus! He did not mean for him to die."

But another of them said, "Could not he who opened the eyes of the blind man have kept this man from dying? That is what we were told would transpire. That is what the sisters believed."

Jesus did not respond. His tears fell like rain, spattering the dry, dusty ground.

Father, he prayed, *forgive me that I did not want to return to Judea. I knew what awaited me here—the beginning of the end. I was fearful of death. I am sorry. I now follow your will, though I am still afraid.*

They came to the tomb, a cave with a massive stone blocking the entrance. Even with the entrance sealed in this way, the smell of rot and decay hung thick in the air.

"Take away the stone," Jesus said.

"But, Lord," said Martha, "by this time there is a bad odor, for he has been in there four days."

"Did I not tell you that if you believed, you would see the glory of God?"

"Yes."

"Then take away the stone."

Several of the disciples did as he commanded, grunting with the effort. They rolled the boulder away, revealing a yawning, black crevice. The stench that wafted out was horrible and many in the crowd turned away. The foul miasma did not seem to bother Jesus. He stepped towards the opening and looked up into the sky.

"Father," he said, "I thank you that you have heard me. I know that you always hear me, but I say this for the benefit of the people standing here, so they may believe that you sent me."

He moved closer still. He trod on old bones and his sandals crushed them into powder. Jesus bowed his head in prayer. The crowd watched, fascinated.

Then Jesus shouted, "Lazarus, come out!"

No one moved. They stared in shocked silence as a sound came from inside the tomb—a soft whisper, cloth on rock. A bent form shuffled towards the entrance and many of the onlookers were afraid. Somewhere near the back of the crowd, a child began to cry.

A cloud slid over the sun, and when it had passed, the dead man staggered out of the tomb, his hands and feet wrapped with strips of soiled linen, and a bloody cloth around his face. His bodily fluids had oozed into the rags, crusting them with gore.

Gasping, the crowd shrank away. But Mary, Martha, and the disciples surged forward, shouting with joy.

Jesus said, "Take off the grave clothes and let him go."

They stripped the dirty linens from Lazarus's body and when his sisters saw his face, they wept with happiness.

"Oh, brother," Mary cried. "You are returned to us. We are blessed. Truly, the Lord is mighty."

Lazarus stared at them, blinking, as if trying to remember who they were. Then he smiled.

"Hello, my sisters. It is good to see you."

Jesus twitched, as if startled. His disciples noticed his reaction, but no one else among the crowd did. They were too busy celebrating Lazarus's resurrection. Mary and Martha knelt at their brother's feet and kissed his hands. Lazarus ignored them, his gaze settling on Jesus.

"Thank you," the dead man said, grinning. *"Thank you for this release."*

Jesus did not reply. He tried to appear happy but his smile faltered. His demeanor troubled the disciples, and they pulled him aside.

"What is it, Lord," asked Mark. "Are you not happy to see our friend?"

"He is not our friend," Jesus whispered.

"But Rabbi," Judas said, "this is Lazarus that stands before us, resurrected by your will and strength. This is a sign of your testimony."

Jesus shook his head. "This is not what I summoned. This is something else."

"What, Lord?" Matthew glanced back at the crowd, watching Lazarus move among them.

Jesus frowned. "Speak softly, so that none other shall hear. This is not our friend Lazarus. Something else inhabits the temple of his body. Something that it is not given to me to have power over."

Luke was incredulous. "Lord, even the demons submit to us in your name. You have power over everything."

"No," Jesus replied, "I have given you authority to trample on snakes and scorpions and to overcome all the power of the enemy; nothing will harm you. However, do not rejoice that the spirits submit to you, but rejoice that your names are written in heaven. I saw Satan fall like lightning from heaven. I saw his army fall with him. But there were Thirteen that did not fall, yet neither did they serve my Father. That is because my Father did not create them. These Thirteen came from... before. Great among the Thirteen is Ob, the Obot. He is Lord of the Siqqusim and it is given to him the power to reside in the dead."

"Then cast him out, Lord," Judas said. "Force him to flee our friend's body."

"I cannot," Jesus said, "for as I said, I have no power over him."

"But why is he here?"

"My Father is displeased, for I feared to enter Judea again."

Frowning in confusion, the disciples watched Lazarus and the Jews. The dead man moved spryly, his limbs showing none of the stiffness that came with death.

"I am hungry," Ob croaked with Lazarus' mouth. *"Who among you shall feed me?"*

"We shall prepare a great feast for you, brother," Martha cried, "to celebrate your return to us."

"Yes," Mary agreed. "We shall all feed you."

Ob smiled at this news, and stared at Jesus.

"Will you not come dine at my sister's table?" Ob asked, laughing.

"I will not."

"You will miss a rich meal." Lazarus put his arm around Mary's shoulder and leaned close to her. *"Delicious and succulent. Truly a tantalizing feast."*

Jesus stirred. "Come and walk with me, Lazarus. Let us give thanks together for your return."

Ob's smile faltered. Noticing that the crowd was watching him, he held his head high and walked over to where Jesus stood. The disciples drew away from them, leaving the two alone.

"You befoul this body," Jesus spat. "You defile my Father's glory."

Ob leaned close, his stinking breath hot on his adversary's face. *"Your Father is disappointed with you, Jesus. Since the day you turned fourteen, you have known this time would come. When the angel appeared to you and revealed your destiny, you were distraught. Since then, you have accepted God's will. You knew that in this, your thirty-second year, you would be asked to work this miracle. You would be asked to intercede on behalf of your friends. You would return to Judea, be betrayed by the one you call Judas, and die at the hands of the Jews. You knew your Father's will, and yet you balked. You delayed, because you did not wish to return. Did not wish to set these events into motion. And thus, He has sent me so that you will not forget—it is His will that you serve.*"

"You lie."

"*I am not the Master of Lies. That is your older brother, the Morningstar.*"

Jesus glanced over Ob's shoulder. Martha and Mary were waiting.

"If you harm them," he whispered, "then know this. I will—"

"*Do nothing,*" Ob interrupted. "*That is what you will do. Nothing. But never fear, Nazarene. I am forbidden to harm them. If I do, I shall be returned to the Void. Your Father may be powerless against me, but He has human agents who know the way.*"

They glared at each other, unblinking, and it was Jesus who looked away first.

"I understand now," Jesus told his disciples. "My Father's will has been made clear to me. I understand why He commanded us to return to this place. I understand all that will transpire. And know this, Judas. I forgive you."

Judas was taken aback. "Forgive me, Lord? For what? Do you not know that I love you? That I serve you faithfully?"

Jesus's smile was sad. His eyes grew wet again. Instead of responding to Judas, he bid farewell to the sisters and told his disciples to follow him.

"Where are we going, Lord?" Thomas asked.

"I must go into the desert and pray. We cannot be here after dark."

"Lord," Peter insisted, "we must stay and fight him."

"No," Jesus said. "My Father has forbidden it. What happens next is His will."

That night, there was a great celebration in the village, and all hailed Lazarus's return. After the celebrants had fallen asleep, satiated on lamb and duck and wine, Ob moved among them and began to feed. He plucked sleeping babes from their mother's breasts and drank their blood. He then turned to the mothers, nuzzling at their teats as they slept, before sinking his teeth into the soft flesh. Screams ripped through the night.

His only regret was that his army—his Siqqusim—could not join him.

Ob's feeding frenzy continued. He ripped the arms from men and wielded the severed limbs like clubs, striking at others. He chewed the face off a beggar, tore into stomachs, gouged eyeballs and ate them like grapes, bit into Adam's apples as if they were real apples, and left a trail of gore and offal behind him. Bethany became a place of slaughter. He licked the scabs of lepers, skewered children on spears, and even feasted on the livestock and pets.

When he was satisfied, Ob vanished into the night, intent on finding the necessary ingredients to open a portal and free his brethren from their imprisonment in the Void.

The cries of the dying and wounded drifted into the desert, and when Jesus heard them, he wept again.

Many of the Jews who had come to visit Mary, and had seen what Jesus did, put their faith in him after the resurrection. But when the first light of dawn lit upon the massacre, they went to the Pharisees and told them what had occurred. None of them thought to connect Lazarus to the crimes.

The chief priests and the Pharisees called a meeting of the Sanhedrin.

"What are we accomplishing?" they asked. "Here is this man, Jesus of Nazareth, performing many miraculous signs. If we let him go on like this, everyone will believe in him, and then the Romans will come and take away both our place and our nation. But now comes news of a massacre at Bethany. Surely, this Jesus has loosed a demon upon us, as punishment for speaking against him."

Caiaphas, the high priest, spoke up. "The Romans shall do nothing. I have a plan. It is better that one man should die for the people than that the whole nation perish. We shall slay this Rabbi, and we shall slay this demon he has summoned forth. We shall also slay this man, Lazarus, whom has returned from the dead. That way, there shall be no loose ends."

So, from that day on, they plotted to take the life of Jesus, and Lazarus's life as well, although they did not know he was possessed by a demon.

When word of this reached Jesus, he called his disciples together. "We can no longer move about publicly among the Jews. Instead, we will withdraw to a region near the desert, in a village called Ephraim."

And so they did. Mary and Martha wondered what had become of their brother. When Jesus and his disciples disappeared, they assumed Lazarus had gone with them.

Meanwhile, Ob roamed the sands and mountains of Judea, raiding and feasting in the night and hiding during the day, plotting to unleash the Siqqusim.

When it was almost time for Passover, many came to Jerusalem for their ceremonial cleansing. The crowds kept looking for Jesus, and as they stood in the temple, they asked one another, "What do you think? Isn't he coming to the Feast at all?"

The chief priests and Pharisees had given orders that if anyone found out where Jesus was, they should report it so that he could be arrested.

Eventually, Jesus returned to Bethany. His spirits seemed low, and he did not teach. The sisters gave a dinner in his honor. Much to Mary and Martha's delight, Lazarus arrived as well, and reclined at the table with Jesus. They could not understand why the disciples met his arrival with dread and shrank away from him. They assumed it was because of his cleanliness. Lazarus's flesh, while not marred, was sallow and ripe. Mary put a few drops of pure nard, an expensive perfume, on her brother's head. Then she poured some on Jesus' feet and wiped them with her hair. The house was filled with the fragrance.

Judas objected. "Why was this perfume not sold, and the money given to the poor? It was worth a year's wages."

"Leave her alone," Jesus said. "It was intended that she should save this perfume for the day of my burial. You will always have the poor, Judas, but you will not always have me."

Ob laughed, loud and boisterous. The dinner guests were shocked, but Jesus ignored him.

"The hour has come," Jesus continued, "for the Son of Man to be glorified. Unless a kernel of wheat falls to the ground and dies, it remains only a single seed. But if it dies, it produces many seeds."

"And one day," Ob interrupted, *"all will die, and the seeds of my kind's revenge shall be sown."*

Jesus's demeanor changed. He whirled on Lazarus.

"Silence your tongue!"

Ob leaned close and whispered, *"Caution, Nazarene. I am forbidden to harm the sisters, but your Father said nothing of your precious disciples. I can eat their bodies in remembrance of you."*

Ignoring him, Jesus turned back to his listeners. "The man who loves life will lose it, while the man who hates life in this world will keep it for eternal life. Whoever serves me must follow me; and where I am, my servant also will be. My Father will honor those who serve me."

There came a loud, insistent knock at the door. All of the assembled jumped, startled. The knock came again. Mary opened the door. A priest and four soldiers pushed into the home.

"Where is Jesus of Nazareth?"

"I am he."

"And where is Lazarus of Bethany?"

Ob rose. *"I am he."*

The priest appraised them both. "And you, Jesus, claim you brought this man, Lazarus, back from the dead."

"I did, by the Glory of God."

"Then you blaspheme."

"If you have eyes," Jesus said, "let them see. Follow me."

He strode past the armed men, and they did not molest him. The priest followed him outside, along with the disciples, the sisters, and the other guests. Ob remained inside.

Jesus turned back to the house. "Lazarus, come forth."

Ob's host body's legs moved without him willing them. He glanced down in panicked confusion.

"What is this?"

His arms and hands defied him and opened the door. Against his will, he strode out into the streets and cursed Jesus' name.

"What trickery is this?"

"No trickery," Jesus said. "I cannot command thee, but it suddenly occurs to me that I can command the flesh you inhabit."

Many among the crowd were confused by the exchange between the two men, but did not intercede.

Jesus turned to the priest. "I brought this man back from the dead. Is he not now marked for death because of it?"

The priest nodded.

"And if I did it again," Jesus asked, "would you not then believe?"

"What are you saying, Rabbi?"

"Carry out your sentence. Slay him. Then I shall bring him back and you shall see."

"Wait," Ob shouted. *"You cannot—"*

The priest nodded at the soldiers. "Make it so."

Mary and Martha averted their eyes, but were not afraid, because they had faith in the Lord.

A soldier stepped forward, armor clanking, and thrust a spear into Lazarus's chest. Ob grasped the shaft and grunted. The crowd gasped.

"He lives," they murmured. "He does not fall."

"His head," the priest commanded. "He cannot survive that."

Ob's eyes grew wide. *"No. Strike not my head. Do not—"*

A second soldier drew his short sword and ran it through the back of Lazarus' head. He pushed hard, pierced the skull, and slid it the rest of the way in. Lazarus dropped, and Ob was dispatched. He screamed with rage, but none save Jesus could hear him.

As he fled, Ob's spirit whispered in Jesus' ear. *"You know what fate your Father plans for thee. I shall be there, waiting. And after your spirit has fled, when your discarded flesh hangs from the cross, I will take it for my own. On the third day, when you rise from the dead, it shall be me inside your bag of skin and blood and bones. You may be the Life, but I am the Resurrection."*

The priest looked at the corpse lying in the street and said to Jesus, "Now, if you are who you say, bring him back."

Jesus folded his arms. "I will not. For you have eyes, but do not see. I am the resurrection and the life, but your lack of faith blinds you."

"This Rabbi is touched in the head," the priest said. "Nothing more. He is not the Messiah. He is a simple madman."

After the priest and soldiers had departed, and Mary and Martha wept for the second time over their brother's fallen form, Jesus turned to the disciples.

"Now my heart is troubled, and what shall I say? 'Father, save me from this hour?' No, it was for this very reason I came to this hour. Father, glorify your name!"

Then a voice came from heaven, "I HAVE GLORIFIED IT, AND WILL AGAIN."

Some in the crowd thought the voice was thunder. Others said it was an angel.

Jesus said, "This voice was for your benefit, not mine. Now is the time for judgment on this world; now the prince of this world will be driven out. But when I am lifted up from the earth, I will draw all men to myself. You are going to have the light just a little while longer. Walk while you have the light, before darkness overtakes you all. For one day, it will. Darkness will descend upon this entire world, and shall not be lifted. That shall be the time of the Rising, when the Siqqusim are unleashed upon the Earth. Put your trust in the light while you have it, so that you may become sons of light, and not be left behind as the dead."

When he had finished speaking, Jesus left Bethany and hid himself from them. In the desert, powerless to act against Ob, he turned to the ways of man. He performed a secret spell, passed down from Solomon, taken from one of the books from before man, and cast Ob's disembodied spirit into the Void with the rest of his kind.

Judas, who was hiding behind a stone, saw Jesus work the forbidden rites and was appalled. He had believed his Rabbi to be the Son of God, and had believed that Jesus's powers came from the Holy Spirit. But now, here he was working arcane magicks. At that moment, Judas' heart was filled with resentment, and he vowed to turn Jesus over to the priests.

And in the Void, Ob wailed and raged and waited for the death of light and the time of the Rising.

Stone Tears

Something splashed in the water hard enough to rock the small boat. Nelson LeHorn reached out and grabbed the sides of the craft. His knuckles turned white.

"Don't let it spook you," Hodgson said. "Probably just a channel cat."

"I ain't spooked. Just surprised me, is all."

"They get big in here. Heard tell of ones on the bottom that are longer than a man. I'd love to catch me one of them. Bet they put up one hell of a fight."

Nelson didn't respond. He stared out over the dark river, watching the moonlight reflect off the waves. Behind them, the launch near Wrightsville faded into the gloom. The lights of Columbia and Marietta twinkled on the far side of the shore. For the most part, the Susquehanna flowed quietly. The silence was broken only by the swells lapping gently against Hodgson's boat, and the droning hum of the small motor, as Hodgson guided them towards their destination.

A bat darted overhead, catching their attention. It was followed a moment later by the shadow of a hawk.

Nelson knew it was an omen.

He just didn't know what it meant.

Nelson LeHorn had never been much of a water person. He'd taken his family to Ocean City, Maryland once, when the kids were young. Matty, Claudia and Gina had loved it. They'd have stayed in the ocean for the entire weekend, if he and Patricia had let them. But

Nelson was wary of so much water. That wide, unbroken expanse made him uneasy for reasons he couldn't explain. He much preferred the small fishing pond on his farm, and the thin stream that ran through his property.

It occurred to him that his dislike of water was funny, in a way, since water had been involved in his introduction to Hodgson, who now ferried him across the river.

Ten years before, when Richard Nixon was still in office and American troops were still in Vietnam, Hodgson and some other employees of the Gladstone Pulpwood Company had been clearing trees on Nelson's property. Crops were bad that year, on account of too much rain. To make some extra money, Nelson sold off some timber. He had plenty. His farm was surrounded by acres of forest and deep, dark hollows.

Hodgson had been cutting through the trunk of an old, gnarled sycamore when the chainsaw hit the knot. Suddenly, it snapped back and caught him in the chest and shoulder, slicing through his shirt and deep into his flesh. Nelson, who had been working in the barn at the time, was alerted by the shouts of Hodgson's co-workers. When he arrived on the scene, the man was lying on the forest floor, unconscious and in shock. Hodgson bled profusely, but the ground around him was nearly dry, as if the forest's roots were sucking it up. Still, Nelson knew that if they didn't stop the bleeding, Hodgson would never live long enough to make it to the hospital. He'd told the co-workers to apply pressure to the wound as best they could, and then dashed back to the house.

The Gladstone employees must have figured he was going to call 911, which he did, but they were surprised when Nelson returned a few minutes later with a piece of paper, a pen, and an old, brown book called *The Long Lost Friend: A Collection of Mysterious and Invaluable Arts and Remedies For Man As Well As Animals* by John George Hohman. Hohman had written the book in 1856. It was a curious mix of German and Hebrew mysticism, Dutch herbal recipes, and Egyptian lore collectively known in the Central Pennsylvanian region as powwow. Hohman was considered a powwow magician.

So was Nelson LeHorn, as his father was before him, and his grandfather and great-grandfather, as well.

Nelson knelt beside the injured man and referred to the book. Then he wrote the name of the four principal waters of the whole world—Pison, Gihon, Hedekiel, and Pheat—on the sheet of paper. While the men watched in bewilderment, he placed the paper on the wound. He then whispered, "Blessed wound, blessed hour, blessed be the day on which Jesus Christ was born, in the name."

And just like that, the bleeding stopped.

Hodgson's co-workers were amazed. Many of them had, of course, heard of powwow magic, given its long-standing connection with the region's folklore. But this was the first time any of them had actually seen its methods in action. Nelson modestly brushed aside their questions and comments, and urged them to get Hodgson up to the house before the ambulance arrived.

That was how they'd met. Hodgson got worker's compensation and disability from the accident, and rather than going back to cutting trees, he bought a small place in Wrightsville along the river and spent his days fishing from his little bass boat.

And once a year, indebted to the man who had saved his life, he ferried Nelson out to the middle of the Susquehanna River, and landed on the shore of Walnut Island.

"Pretty out tonight," Nelson said.

"Yeah," Hodgson agreed. "It is. Wife's probably pissed as shit at me right about now. Nice night, like tonight, and I'm out here, instead of back home. Especially with them saying who shot J.R. on *Dallas* tonight. You ever watch that show?"

"Can't say that I have. I read, mostly. My family's been bugging me for that cable television. Imagine—paying for TV. Dumbest thing I've ever heard of. What's next?"

"I hear you. I wouldn't have fooled with it at all, but the wife made me get it. Twenty bucks a month! But we get fifteen channels. She loves her shows. Likes me to rub her feet while we watch them, which is why she'll be pissed that I'm out here."

"I'm sorry about that. Like I've told you before, you shouldn't feel obliged. What I done for you, I'd do for anybody. If these yearly trips make trouble for you at home, I won't ask no more. It's just that you're the only fella' I know with a boat—only one I trust, anyway."

"Oh, don't worry about it. To be honest, I like to get away once in a while. And she's used to it by now. Alls I got to do is show her my scar and remind her of what you did for me, and she gets over it quick. But she thinks it's pretty odd that you go night fishing every year on this day. I don't tell her what we really do out here, of course—I don't tell no one, just like you asked."

"I appreciate it. More than you know."

"Least I can do. I've got to wonder though, if you don't mind me asking—what's your wife think about it?"

Nelson frowned. "Patricia? She's fine with it. Why wouldn't she be?"

"Don't know. Figured maybe she wasn't privy to all the powwow stuff."

"She knows it well. Even helps me with it sometimes. Her Daddy practiced powwow, same as mine. And she knows what today's date is, too, and why it's so important to me."

"Why is it so important?" Hodgson asked. "I mean, I know you can't tell me what you get up to out there on Walnut Island, and I'm not sure that I even want to know. But I always wondered about the date? Is it one of them equinoxes or something?"

Nelson was quiet for a moment. He watched another bat dive down towards the water, snatch a lightning bug in mid-air, and then flit away towards shore. Another omen, and still, he couldn't divine any meaning from it. When he looked back at Hodgson, Nelson sighed.

"I don't reckon it will hurt to be straight with you. You've done right by me over the years. Not to mention you've brought me out here each year, and never asked why."

Hodgson nodded, encouraging his passenger to continue. His expression was eager.

Nelson pointed at Walnut Island, looming out of the darkness. "You ever hear of the petroglyphs out here?"

"No, can't say that I have. What's that—some kind of oil drilling place?"

Nelson laughed. "How in the world did you come up with that?"

"Petro. Ain't that what the Brits call gasoline?"

Nelson, who had never been out of the tri-State area in his life, and whose knowledge of the United Kingdom's modern culture was limited to Margaret Thatcher, the occasional British sitcom on PBS, and a band that his son, Matty, listened to (Deaf Leopards or something like that) had no idea, but he didn't admit it to Hodgson.

"Petroglyphs," he repeated. "They're pictures and symbols carved into the rocks out here. Some of them were made by the Indians."

"Which ones?"

"Take your pick. The Susquehannocks, of course. The Iroquois. The Algonkians. There's a bunch that were carved by white men, too—sort of like Civil War-era graffiti. Some were made by prehistoric man, long before the Indians came. And a few are even older than that."

"How can they be older than prehistoric man?"

Nelson ignored the question. "There used to be a lot more of them out here. But back in the Thirties, when they built the Holtwood and Safe Harbor dams, a lot of the petroglyphs ended up underwater. Some archeologist folks managed to save a few. Dug them out with a big pneumatic rock drill and put them on display at the Pennsylvania Historical Museum. But to see the rest, you've got to put on a diving suit and swim around down there with those big catfish you mentioned earlier."

Hodgson shuddered.

"The only ones left above water," Nelson continued, "are on Big Indian Rock, Little Indian Rock, and Walnut Island. And since the County Historical Society, the Museum Commission, and the State don't like folks traipsing around on the islands, I have you bring me out here at night."

"Could we get arrested for it?"

"I don't know. Reckon we'd get fined, at least."

Hodgson paused, seeming to consider this. "So, every year, you come out here to look at some rocks?"

"Sort of. There's one petroglyph in particular that I come to see."

Hodgson stroked his mustache. "Well, I don't guess it's any weirder than the Arabs making their pilgrimage to Mecca, or all that carrying on the Baptists do during those tent revivals."

Nelson smiled. "It's something I have to do. That's why Patricia don't get mad at me. Cause she understands."

"So her daddy practiced powwow just like yours did, huh?"

"Both her parents did. They were both great healers."

"Yours, too?"

Nelson shook his head. "No. Just my father. My mother went away when I was younger. Daddy caught her with another man, and there was hell to pay. My father had a wicked temper."

"That so?"

"Yep. He worked powerful powwow, though. Hexed the river witch over in Marietta once, after he found out she'd put a blight on our cattle. Hexed a man who he caught stealing from our root cellar one year, too. Fella' went blind and deaf."

Hodgson grinned, bemused. "Sounds like your Daddy wasn't one to piss off."

"No, he wasn't."

"And he really did all of that? Actually hexed people?"

"Sure. Loathe as I am to admit it. Like I said, he wasn't a nice man."

"And it really works?"

"It worked on you well enough, didn't it?"

Hodgson shrugged. "I reckon that's true. But that was healing. Hexing is something different, right?"

"It all comes from the same source. And it don't matter who you are and which kind of powwow you practice—sometimes, you're called upon to do the other. That's one of the prices."

His companion nodded, but Nelson could tell from Hodgson's expression that he didn't really understand, and was just humoring him.

They fell silent again as they approached Walnut Island. Lightning bugs twinkled on the shore. When they were close enough, Hodgson shut off the engine, and the silence deepened. Using an oar, he guided them in the rest of the way. The bottom of the boat scraped along the rocks. He hopped out and dragged it up onto the bank.

"I'll wait here for you, like always."

Nelson shook his hand. "Appreciate it. I'll be back soon as I can."

"Take your time. It's a nice night. I don't mind waiting."

Nelson took off his orange life vest, and pulled a small, plastic bag from the boat. It rustled, catching Hodgson's attention.

"What you got there?" he asked. "Magic stuff?"

Winking, Nelson wagged his finger at the man. "A magus don't ever reveal his secrets."

He removed his orange life vest, grabbed the flashlight from the boat and then headed off into the island's interior. An empty beer can, a torn pair of women's panties, and the burned-out remains of a campfire told him that someone else had been there recently. Frowning, Nelson continued onward. Birds rustled nearby, disturbed by his intrusion. The lightning bugs disappeared as he approached. Somewhere in the darkness, an owl hooted. Otherwise, the island was silent. Lifeless.

The gentle breeze cooled the sweat on his neck. The plastic bag slapped against his thigh with each step. The flashlight beam bobbed up and down.

Walnut Island was small, little more than a large outcropping of bedrock covered with sparse trees and vegetation, and he didn't have to go far before encountering the petroglyphs. Some were clearly recognizable—animal tracks, birds, deer, bear, foxes, snakes, trees, and human faces. Some depicted scenes of everyday life—a hunter with a bow, a mother with her baby, a group attending to a field of corn. There were abstract designs—spirals and geometric shapes. Others were of more mysterious figures—bird-men, goat-men, reptile-men, a massive serpent (that many, including Nelson, thought depicted Old Scratch—a legendary giant water snake rumored to haunt the Susquehanna River), and a snail-like creature with a headdress. There was a smattering of what looked like Chinese, Hittite, and Cypriot characters. He'd seen those before but hadn't mentioned them to Hodgson. No sense in confusing the man. Nelson knew better than to argue with the popular conception that Columbus had been the first non-Indian in America.

Amidst all of these petroglyphs was a smattering of modern graffiti. Its presence angered Nelson. There were declarations of love, crude little hearts, names, dates, and genitalia, not to mention the numerous pentagrams and swastikas, all carved by stoned teenagers who hadn't the slightest understanding of the latter two symbols' true meanings or power.

He passed by all of the petroglyphs with barely a cursory glance. He was seeking another.

In the center of the island was a huge slab of rock. The flashlight beam trailed over it as he neared the spot, illuminating a life-sized petroglyph of a woman. The figure was about five and a half feet tall, naked, and incredibly lifelike and detailed. Her hair, facial features, and even the blemishes on her skin had all been painstakingly recreated. Unlike the other carvings, erosion and vandalism had not faded or damaged the petroglyph.

Nelson cleared his throat.

"Hello, Mom. Happy birthday."

Nelson opened the plastic bag and took out a bouquet of fresh followers—tulips, roses, petunias, Queen Anne's Lace, and daisies. All of them had been grown on his farm, and all of them had been picked by his hand that morning. He talked to the carving for twenty minutes, telling her what her grandchildren had accomplished in the last year, and of how much he missed her. He repeated his annual promise that some day, he'd figure out a way to bring her back again. Then he leaned over, kissed the rock on the cheek, and said goodbye.

As he made his way back to Hodgson's boat, rainwater leaked from the corners of the petroglyph's stone eyes.

STORY NOTE: Regular readers will note that this is not the first appearance of Nelson LeHorn. He first appeared in my novel *Dark Hollow*. This story takes place years before the events that occur to him in that book. Hopefully, it gave you a little more insight into his character and his motivations.

The Susquehanna River petroglyphs are real, as are Walnut Island, Big Indian Rock and Little Indian Rock. I was unaware of them until several years ago, when a local reader mentioned them in a post on my message board. Since then, I've become fascinated with them. Some replicas of the carvings are on display at the Indian Steps Museum, located in Airville. If you're ever in the area, the museum is worth visiting. Much like the characters in this book, I have undertaken a midnight journey to see the real, remaining petroglyphs. They are, quite simply, awe-inspiring, even despite the ravages of time, nature and human vandalism. To the best of my knowledge, however, there is no life-sized carving of a human female.

If you're interested, there are also two very good books examining the petroglyphs. The first one is *Petroglyphs in the Susquehanna River near Safe Harbor, Pennsylvania* by Donald A. Cadzow. As the title suggests, it is dry, academic reading—especially for the novice. But that doesn't make the material it presents any less fascinating. The second book is *Indians in Pennsylvania* by Paul A. W. Wallace. Both books were published by the Pennsylvania Historical and Museum Commission, and are (as of this writing) still in print and available at various locations, including online.

Red Wood

"You ever fart while a chick was going down on you?"

Groans and laughter drowned out David Allen Coe's lament about the woman who had never called him by his name.

"Smitty," Frank Lehman said, "you are one sick son of a bitch!"

The big man grinned, his double chins wiggling. "No, I'm serious. Have you?"

"Not me." Luke shook his head.

Smitty leaned forward between the driver and passenger's seats. Frank, riding shotgun, shoved him back.

"How about you, Glen?" Smitty asked.

Concentrating on the dirt road in front of him, Glen chuckled. "No, Mr. Smith, I can't say that I have."

Smitty frowned. "Knock off that Mr. Smith shit. Christ, you boys have known me for thirty years!"

Luke took a swig of beer. "Even if Glen or Mark did fart while a chick was going down on them, they're not going to say it in front of their old man."

"That's right," Frank said. "I brought these boys up better than that."

Luke and Smitty looked at Mark, mashed into the rear passenger's side door.

"How about it, Mark?" Smitty nudged him in the ribs with his elbow. "You ever bust one while getting head?"

"He's never even got head," Glen teased, eyeing his younger brother in the mirror.

"Screw you." Mark took a sip of cold coffee from his travel mug. Despite the alleged roominess of the SUV, he was uncomfortable. He'd been stuck in the back with his father's fat co-worker and his older brother's friend for the past two hours, the last

twenty-five minutes of which had been spent on one narrow, winding back road after another. He wished that he'd brought along his laptop or something else to occupy him.

"Well," Smitty said, "I have. Did it while Linda was gobbling my knob. Spread my legs and just let it rip. Then I held her head down there and laughed my ass off!"

"It's no wonder she divorced you," Frank said.

"Fuck it." Smitty dismissed the comment with a shrug of his shoulders. "She never had a sense of humor anyway."

Luke twisted around behind him, fumbling with the cooler lid. "Does anybody want another beer? They're still—"

Glen slammed the brakes. The Explorer skidded to a stop, kicking up dust in its wake. Luke pitched forward, bouncing off Glen's seat. Smitty was thrown into Mark,

crushing him against the door, and popping the lid from his mug. Coffee soaked through Mark's jeans. In the front, Frank clutched the dashboard and cursed.

"What the hell are you trying to do, Glen?" Luke shouted. "Break our fucking necks?"

"What happened?" Smitty asked. "Deer run out in front of us? Don't tell me you got one before season even started!"

"See for yourselves." Glen opened the door. He glanced over at Frank. His father was breathing heavy, his face ashen. "You okay, Dad?"

"Yeah," Frank wheezed, "I'm fine. Just startled me a bit, is all."

The older man grasped his door handle and swung it open. The others followed, walking to the front of the vehicle.

A massive oak tree, its trunk rounder than even Smitty, had fallen across the road. Beneath its splintered branches lay the carcass of a deer. The animal's belly had ruptured and its hind legs were splayed. The rest of the deer was obscured by the gnarled tree-trunk.

"Shit," Smitty gasped. "You weren't kidding."

The other's stared. Glen straddled the tree, yelping in pain as he clambered over it.

"What's wrong?" his father asked.

"Splinter," Glen said, rubbing his thigh. "Damn tree bit me."

Glen knelt down, parting the branches to get a better look at the deer, and then whistled softly.

Mark frowned. "What?"

"It's a twelve point. What a waste." Glen let the branches fall back in place and stood up.

"Probably the only deer we'll see during this whole trip," Luke said. "We ought to take it with us. Have some venison in the morning before we go out hunting."

Frank shook his head. "It's no good. This happened early this morning, maybe even last night, judging by the condition of the corpse. Meat's spoiled by now, for sure."

"Grab that axe out of the trunk," Glen said. "Let's get to work on this tree before it gets dark. We've still got another two miles to the cabin."

He threw the keys to Mark, and his younger brother disappeared around the back.

"Why don't we just park off to the side, grab the stuff, and walk it?" Frank asked.

"No, Dad," Glen said. "I don't think that's a good idea."

"Oh, for God's sake. You're worse than your mother! It's only two miles."

"Forget it, Dad," Mark said, returning with the axe. "Besides, Smitty would never make it."

Smitty scowled at him, and then turned to Frank. "That's a real smart mouthed kid you got there. Like father, like son. Both assholes."

Frank, Glen, and Mark laughed.

The brothers and Luke took turns chopping at the tree, while Smitty supervised them from his seat on the bank. Each time Frank made an effort to help, he was gently rebuked by his sons. Finally, after they cut the fallen trunk down to size, he ignored their protests and helped drag the tree sections and the deer carcass out of the way. By the time they'd tossed the final branches into the ditch, he was panting and pale.

"Fucking Agent Orange," he wheezed, clutching his side.

The others said nothing. Glen's and Mark's eyes met.

They got back into the vehicle and drove on in silence.

*   *   *

A mile down the road, Luke asked, "What do you guys think did that?"

"I'd say lightning," Frank speculated. "Except that it didn't really look like it had been struck."

Glen and Mark sat quietly, lost in their own thoughts.

"It wasn't a deadfall either," Smitty said. "Leaves were still green. Ain't that weird? Two days after Thanksgiving and the leaves hadn't changed color yet."

"We're here," Glen said, pulling to a stop in front of the cabin.

Frank had built the deer camp in 1970, three years after returning from Vietnam. He'd been coming here with Smitty ever since. Glen started joining them when he'd turned fourteen, along with Luke, whose father never hunted.

Mark had never been a hunter either. He'd tried, just like any male who grew up in central Pennsylvania had tried. Hunting was a required rite of passage, from the orange vest and hat down to the mandatory hunter safety course in junior high school.

The year Mark turned fourteen, he'd gone along hunting with his father, brother, and their friends, and had been miserable. They'd gotten up at four in the morning and left the relative warmth and comfort of the cabin, so that they could find a spot. This involved trekking into the woods in the dark. The others had glared silently each time he'd stepped on a branch or rustled the leaves under his feet. It had been cold—the type of cold that soaked through your feet and fingers no matter how many pairs of socks you wore. He couldn't wear gloves, he was told, because they'd interfere with the trigger and safety on his rifle. The cold made his ears sting, and he'd longed for nothing more than to go back to the camp and crawl into his sleeping bag. They'd positioned him at a tree and left him there, each going off to find their own spot. And so he had waited. And waited.

And waited.

By the time the sun had dragged itself reluctantly above the horizon, Mark's extremities were throbbing and numb. Bored and miserable, he'd made his way back to the cabin, alone. They'd found him there that evening, reading a *Micronauts* comic book and happily munching potato chips. His father and Glen had both gotten deer— a spike and a four point, respectively. Smitty had missed one, and Luke, succumbing to buck fever, had killed an old toilet somebody had dumped in the woods.

That was the last time Mark Lehman ever went hunting.

Until now, he thought, grabbing his gear from the back.

He glanced at his father. Frank beamed with excitement as he surveyed the rolling woods and fields that he'd hunted for so long.

Mark tried to forget that his father was dying.

He rummaged around in the back of the Explorer, fishing out his camera case and untangling it from the other gear. Glen stepped up beside him and grabbed a sleeping bag.

"I'm glad you came along," Glen said.

"Yeah, well..." Mark didn't look up. "I promised you and Mom I would."

"It means a lot to him. You know how Dad is. He'd never say it out loud, but he's really happy you're, even if the only scope you're using is that camera lens."

He playfully punched Mark's shoulder, and then grabbed a rifle and slung a sleeping bag over his shoulder. Then he grew quiet.

Mark looked up. His brother was crying—his face twisted with silent grief.

"This'll be the last trip," Glen said, "and I—"

He broke off and turned away as Luke approached them.

"Your Dad really looks happy, guys," Luke whispered. "I think this trip will do him some good."

They nodded in agreement; both afraid to speak aloud lest their voices fail them.

"Hey, Mark," Smitty called. "Grab my stuff, will you?"

Frank shook his head. "Grab it yourself, you fat fuck."

They got the gear, and clomped up the stairs onto the porch. A vacant hornet's nest hung from the eaves. While Frank searched for the right key, they surveyed their surroundings.

The cabin sat along a seldom-used dirt road. After passing the cabin, the road led to the old LeHorn farm, but the farmhouse and buildings had long been empty. Nelson LeHorn had killed his wife in 1985, and then disappeared. His children were now scattered. His son, Matty, was doing time in the Cresson State Penitentiary. His daughter, Claudia, was married and living in Spring Grove. And his youngest daughter, Gina, taught school in Brackard's Point, New York. Because the old man was legally still alive, the children were unable to sell the property—so it sat abandoned, providing a haven for rats, groundhogs, and other animals.

Behind the cabin, and to its right, lay miles of vast woodlands, untouched by the explosive development that had marred other parts of the state. Across the road was more forest, this portion used by the Gladstone Pulpwood Company for its paper mill. As employees of the company, Frank, Smitty, Glen and Luke had permission to hunt the land. To the left of the cabin stretched a vast expanse of barren cornfields. The rolling hills had not been worked or plowed since LeHorn's disappearance.

Beyond the fields lay an area known as LeHorn's Hollow, and beyond that, more dense, expansive woodlands. That area was apparently off-limits. From the cabin's porch, bright yellow POSTED signs were visible, hanging from a few of the hollow's outer tree-trunks.

"Did somebody finally buy the LeHorn farm?" Mark pointed at the signs.

"No," Frank said, twisting the key in the lock. "Those were left over from when LeHorn was still here. We can ignore them."

"He was an odd one," Smitty said. "He didn't have a problem with us hunting on his land, but he always kept that hollow and the area around it posted. He'd get madder than shit if he even saw you walking along the edges between the trees and the corn. Really protective of it. Always wondered if he had a moonshine still or a plot of marijuana down there."

"I guess he was odd," Frank agreed, shoving the door open and stepping inside. "He'd have to be wouldn't he? After all, he killed his wife."

"Threw her out the attic window," Glen said.

"Shit," Smitty said. "That doesn't make him odd. I wanted to do that a time or two when I was married."

They shuffled inside the cabin and put their gear down. It was a rustic, simple building, with one large living area, complete with a wood burning stove, a couch that had never been new, a card table, several folding chairs, a portable radio, and a nineteen inch black and white TV with a coat-hanger antennae. A kitchenette stood off to the side, and two bedrooms were in the back, each with two bunk beds.

Glen glanced out the back window. "The outhouse is still standing."

"Good," Smitty said. "I've gotta take a dump. I'll go break it in for the year."

He left, farting as the screen door slammed shut behind him. The others chuckled amongst themselves, and then unpacked. Luke cleaned his Remington 30.06, ramming the rod repeatedly down the barrel, and Mark cleaned his camera, wiping the lens rhythmically with a cloth. They grinned at each other.

"Let's see if we can get the Penn State game," Frank said, and tried the TV. Static greeted him as he flipped the dial. Finally, he gave up in frustration. "We'll try it later."

Glen fished some batteries from his bag, and put them in the radio. Minutes later, Ozzy Osbourne filtered through the speakers.

"God damn devil music," Frank said. "Find a country station. Not this noise."

"You had your way on the drive here, Dad," Glen said. "And this isn't noise. You want noise, try listening to what Little Mikey likes. Limp Biscuits or something like that."

"Don't know why you let my grandson rot his brain with that stuff, either."

"If it was up to me," Glen said, "he wouldn't be listening to it at all. Cheryl lets him get away with it."

Mark chuckled. "You sound like Dad did when Mom let you listen to Judas Priest and Iron Maiden."

Glen grinned, shaking his head.

"Hey, Dad," Mark said, "remember when Reverend Smith told you that KISS stood for 'Kings In Satan's Service' and you threw away our albums?"

Frank shifted on the couch. "Don't start with that again. I've apologized over and over for that. Christ, that was years ago!"

"Good years, though." Glen said.

They fell silent, reflecting.

Luke cleared his throat. "I still say that's why Mark started listening to rap. You sent him from bad to worse, Frank!"

"Oh yeah," Glen groaned. "We'd be in my room cranking up Motley Crue, and Mark would be squirreled away with Ice T."

"My wife had on *Hollywood Squares* the other day," Luke said. "Ice-T was one of the guests. Had him on there with Elmo from Sesame Street."

"The guy used to sing about killing cops, and now he's hanging out with Elmo?"

"Yep." Luke nodded. "We're getting old."

The song ended and the announcer advised them they were listening to Central Pennsylvania's home for classic rock. Then Bon Jovi wailed about loving somebody always.

"When the hell did Bon fucking Jovi become classic rock?" Glen asked.

"When my generation started dying off," Frank said. "The World War Two crowd are almost gone. It's our turn now. Like it or not, you boys are in charge. I just hope you do a better job of it than we did."

A loud crack split the air, followed by Smitty's scream.

Glen jumped. "The fuck—"

"Maybe a snake bit him on his fat ass," Luke said.

They dashed outside and ran towards the outhouse. Mark, Glen, and Luke pulled ahead. Frank stopped, leaning against the side of the cabin and catching his breath. Then, when he saw what had happened, he began to laugh. The others soon joined him.

A muffled shout came from inside the outhouse.

"Quit laughing and get me the hell out of here," Smitty yelled.

A lofty elm towered over the outhouse, just on the edge of the forest. A broad, thick branch had broken off and landed at the door of the outhouse, effectively trapping Smitty inside. The walls trembled as he slammed against the door. For all of his considerable effort, the limb did not budge.

Chuckling, they cleared it out of the way. Red-faced, Smitty waddled out, holding up his pants with one hand.

Glen doubled over with laughter. "I bet that scared the shit out of you, didn't it Smitty?"

"I wish it had," Smitty said, buckling his belt. "But I can't go at all, now. My butthole is squeezed up tighter than a virgin."

"Some Jim Beam will fix that," Luke said.

"Lead on, young man. Lead on."

They walked back up to the cabin, while the limbs along the tree line stretched away from the evening sun, seeking darkness.

It was a good night.

They played poker and blackjack and war, and switched back and forth between the country station and the classic rock station. They cheered Penn State, cursed them when they lost to West Virginia, and swore at Luke in between when he snapped the antenna while trying to adjust the picture. They drank beer and ate potato chips and beef jerky and the leftover turkey their wives had packed. Frank fried potatoes with onions and sausage, and they devoured them eagerly, washing the meal down with more beer. Cholesterol did not exist during hunting season. They spoke of deer past, their antlers hanging on the walls around them, and recounted previous trips to the cabin. They talked cars and politics and football and how the union was screwing them worse than the company, and how Mark had it made, working as a magazine photographer in New York City. Glen brought out the tequila and the cards were forsaken for more talk—of glory days, of women other than their wives, and eventually—the war.

Frank and Smitty both grew maudlin after that, and when Luke commented that he figured watching *Platoon* was pretty close to being there, Frank and Smitty just stared at him quietly.

Soon, however, they were laughing again, as all of the tequila Luke had consumed came back up on the front porch. They rolled him into his bunk, where he promptly passed out, the first official casualty of the night.

They laughed long into the night, and Glen and Mark both thought that they hadn't seen their father look this alive or this happy in a long time.

They retired before midnight, knowing that four in the morning would come quickly. Smitty stayed awake long enough to drain the tequila, and then, only his great,

racking snores disturbed the stillness outside.

None of them heard the car drive past at a quarter to three, heading toward the LeHorn place.

*   *   *

"There's some," Jason said, scowling at the Explorer parked in front of the hunting cabin. "Bastards."

"Remind me again," Joe said, yawning in the back seat, "why we're up at three in the morning?"

Debbie frowned. "Remind me why you have to come along every time Jason and I go somewhere."

"Because you love me," Joe said.

Debbie took a sip of her mocha latte and glared at Jason. "We go to the P.E.T.A. rally, and Joe comes with us. We try a romantic evening at home, and Joe's downstairs playing Playstation. We went to Ocean City for the weekend, and Joe shared a hotel room with us!"

"Don't start," Jason said. "Joe was my friend long before I started dating you."

"Besides," Joe said. "I've got the weed."

Furious, Debbie stared out the window at the dark fields and trees. She wished they could just leave Joe along the side of the road. It was an ongoing battle between them. Her girlfriends asked why she put up with it, and there were times when she didn't know herself. But she loved Jason. It was hard to find a guy that would go along with her to spike trees at a logging project or help deface an animal-testing laboratory.

The Depeche Mode tape ended, and Debbie pressed the seek function on the radio. Snatches of disembodied voices cut through the backwoods-induced static. She heard an infomercial for hair replacement medicine, the twangy strains of a Jerry Reed song, and either a preacher or a conservative talk show host. It was hard to tell which.

"Solomon tells us in Ecclesiastes nine, verse three," the preacher or talk radio host said, "that there is an evil among all things that are done under the sun..."

Jason groaned.

"Chapter eleven says for thou knowest not what evil shall be upon the earth, and if the tree falls toward the south, there it shall be."

Debbie clicked the radio off.

"Reception is for shit back in these hills," Jason said. "We're just about there anyway."

In the back, Joe's face was lit with an orange glow as he fired up the bowl. He took a deep hit, coughed, and then offered it to Debbie. She ignored him pointedly.

"Come on, baby," Jason urged. "Smoke the peace pipe and make up."

"I don't want any pot. Christ, we just woke up an hour ago! I need more latté."

She stretched her feet out and kicked the bag between them. Cowbells jangled inside.

"I still don't see the sense in this," Joe said. "Traipsing around in the woods in the dark, ringing cowbells a few hours before dawn? What's that going to accomplish?"

"It will alert the deer, and scare them off," Debbie said. "Then, when the hunters get out to the woods, there won't be anything for them to shoot."

"Except for us," Joe said.

Jason laughed. "We'll be long gone by then, dude."

They rounded a turn and there was the LeHorn farmhouse, eerily silhouetted in their headlights.

Jason whistled. "Man, this place is really falling apart."

"Is it true that Nelson LeHorn used to sacrifice animals down in that hollow?" Joe asked.

"No," Jason said, "that's all bullshit. Local legend. I mean, the guy was your typical Pennsylvania Dutch farmer. Sure, he slaughtered pigs and cows, but what farmer doesn't? It's only because he killed his wife that people say shit like that."

"I don't know," Joe said. "Brad Speelman used to date Gina Le-Horn, and he said he saw a copy of *The Long Lost Friend* inside the house once. Some books in German and Latin too. You know—spell books. Something called *Daemonolatvian* or something like that."

"Brad Speelman is an idiot," Debbie said. "*The Long Lost Friend* is nothing more than a book of folklore and remedies. Like how to cure rheumatism and snake bites. Heather has one. She got it from her grandma before she died."

Joe grinned. "Isn't Heather that crazy goth chick that thinks she's a witch?"

"She's Wiccan," Debbie said. "And she thinks you're an asshole, too, Joe."

"Fuck you!"

"Knock it off, both of you!" Shutting off the headlights, Jason gripped the wheel. "Dude, do me a favor and stay in the car. We'll go do our thing, okay?"

He tossed Joe the car keys.

"It's cool with me bro." Joe smiled, reloading the bowl from his plastic bag. "You kids have fun."

Debbie grabbed the bag and they both got out, softly shutting the car doors behind them. Holding hands, the walked across the overgrown yard and into the barren cornfield.

"Watch out for old man LeHorn," Joe called after them.

Debbie responded with her middle finger, not looking back.

Joe watched the darkness swallow them up, then leaned back, kicked his feet up on the seat, and stretched out.

"Spooky place."

He looked around. The distance between the house and the barn was one long shadow. The fields reminded him of NASA's pictures of the Mars landscape. The buildings and the car sat under watchful stars, with nothing moving. Far away in the distance, a tree loomed, tall and menacing.

Menacing, Joe thought. *How the hell can a tree be menacing? Must be the weed.*

Joe closed his eyes and fell asleep.

"Why are we whispering?" Debbie clutched Jason's hand.

"I don't know," he admitted. "Everything just seems so small out here. Quiet."

"Only for a few more hours. Then it'll be nothing but gunshots and rednecks."

"Well, let's fix it so there's nothing for them to shoot at." He paused, gazing up at the night sky. "It's beautiful."

"Yeah, it is."

They trudged on in silence, drawing closer to the hollow.

Debbie shivered inside her fleece jacket. "It's so cold out here, though."

"Well, how about when we're done, I warm you up?"

"We can't." She let go of his hand and sped up, walking past him. "You had to bring Joe along."

"God dammit, Deb—"

Approaching the tree line, Debbie pulled a cowbell out of the bag. Parting the low branches, she stepped into the darkness. The branches rustled back into place.

Sighing in exasperation, Jason hurried to catch up with her. Inside the forest, he heard her cowbell. It sounded farther away than he would have guessed.

"Hey, Debbie, wait up! You've got my bell in that bag, too."

When she didn't respond, Jason swore, wondering again why he went along with Debbie's animal rights nonsense. Hell, his father hunted, and he wasn't a bad guy.

The things I do just to get laid on a regular basis...

He pushed through the branches and thorns, stepping into the forest. The ground sloped steadily downward. There was no sign of Debbie, and the cowbell was silent. The stillness was disturbing. To Jason, it felt like the hollow was holding its breath.

"Debbie?"

The tree limbs rustled softly above him, but no breeze disturbed them. Somewhere below him, farther down in the hollow, a twig snapped. It seemed as loud as a gunshot in the stillness. Jason jumped, backing up a few steps. Another twig snapped, followed by the rustle of leaves.

"Come on, Debbie, quit messing around! Where the hell are you?"

As if in answer, the cowbell rang sharply, but farther down the hill. He stomped off in that direction, and more twigs snapped directly behind him. He began to half jog, half slide down the slope. Ahead of him, the cowbell pealed continuously.

"Give it a rest!" Thorns tore at his jacket. "I think the deer got the message."

The clamor continued. Oddly, it now sounded as if it was coming from above him.

Jason barreled the rest of the way down the slope, splashing through a half-frozen stream. Icy water flooded his sneakers, chilling his toes. Gasping, he jumped to the other side.

The cowbell echoed off the trees surrounding him, but there was no sign of Debbie. He spun in a circle as the shrill ringing grew frantic.

Then he looked up.

And screamed.

Debbie dangled fifteen feet above him, her blue fleece now crimson and tattered. A gnarled tree limb jutted from between her breasts, and another had punched through her abdomen. The cowbell hung from a third branch. As Jason shrieked her name, the branch shook back and forth, ringing the bell again.

Something snapped behind him—something bigger than a twig.

The bell continued to ring long after his screams had ceased.

Mark awoke to his father shaking his shoulder. He blinked sleep dust from his eyes.

"What time is it?"

"Four o'clock," Frank told him. "Better get up before your brother and Luke drink all the coffee."

Yawning, Mark sat up, shivering as his bare feet hit the cold floor. The others were already dressed, decked out in flannel shirts, camouflage jackets, and bright orange hunting vests. Glen and Luke sipped coffee while Frank laced up his boots.

Bleary-eyed, Mark looked around the cabin. "Where's Smitty?"

"Outhouse." Luke cocked his thumb. "He's sick as a dog. Too much tequila."

"We weren't going to leave you any bacon or eggs," Glen said, "but Dad insisted."

"So what's the plan?" Mark pulled jeans on over his long johns.

"I figure I'll work the hollow," Luke said. "Smitty can walk the cornfields and between us, we ought to flush something."

"We'll head across the road," Frank said. "Over to that ridge that runs along the top. Hook up with that logging road the trucks use, and then work our way back down to the LeHorn place."

The door opened and Smitty walked in, followed by a frigid blast of air.

"Colder than a witch's titty out there," he huffed.

"You look like hell," Frank told him. "Feel any better?"

"I'll live," the big man replied, wincing as Glen shoved a plate of eggs and bacon floating in grease under his nose.

Impatiently, they allowed Mark ten minutes to get dressed and eat. He grabbed his camera and the rest of their rifles. Then they stood on the porch, basking in the cold, blue pre-dawn world.

"See you guys back here this evening." Frank nodded to Smitty and Luke.

"First one to get a buck cooks tonight, right?" Luke asked.

"Well, then we know it won't be you," Glen said, stepping off the porch.

Luke headed across the field toward the hollow. Smitty trailed behind him. Glen, Mark and Frank crossed the road and stepped into the woods. The last thing they heard was a flatulent blast from Smitty, followed by Luke telling him that he'd scare all the deer away if he kept it up.

Then the forest consumed them.

"BRRRRAAAAAPPP!"

"Oh for Christ's sake, Smitty." Luke winced. "What the hell did you eat yesterday?"

"It's that fucking tequila." The big man clenched his teeth. "Rot gut stuff has my stomach in an uproar."

"Keep it up, and you'll scare the deer away for real. They can smell that, you know."

"It'll clear up. Just got to get it out of my system."

They trudged through the field. Desiccated cornhusks crunched softly under their feet.

"It sucks about Frank," Luke said. "Glen told me the doctors can't do anything."

"Yeah." Smitty panted. "Frank doesn't talk about it much, but I'm guessing we won't be doing this again..."

Luke was silent for a moment. "If I was Frank, I sure as hell wouldn't still be working. I'd be out here enjoying myself every day."

"Me, too. That's Frank, though. He never did mind those seven-day shifts. The man likes to work."

"I'm glad Glen convinced Mark to come along."

"Yeah," Smitty said. "Still, I think it's funny that he brought that camera along, instead of a gun."

They both laughed.

"BRAAP—"

Somewhere in the blue glow that was not true darkness but not yet daylight, a bird chirped in alarm and took flight. The stars, though dimming, were still visible.

"I love this time of morning," Luke whispered.

Smitty didn't reply. Luke turned and found that the big man had stopped walking. Smitty crouched, grimacing in pain and clutching his prodigious stomach with one hand. His Marlin 30-30 dangled loosely by his side.

Then Luke smelled it. "Jesus, Smitty!"

"I think I shit myself, man. I'm gonna head back."

"Okay," Luke said through bursts of disgusted laughter. "I'll stay in the field, around the edges of the hollow, until you get back. Maybe a buck will come out, looking for some corn."

Smitty nodded weakly, sweat beading on his pale face. He shuddered.

Luke backed away in disgust, and his partner shambled back the way they'd come.

Luke watched him go, and then faced the hollow.

He walked toward it.

"I want you boys to promise me something."

"What's that, Dad?" Mark asked, sidestepping a knobby, moss-covered trunk.

"I want some of my ashes scattered up here at the cabin."

The woods were silent, save for their soft footsteps in the undergrowth and a few birdcalls.

"Um..." Glen stammered.

"Dad," Mark said, "don't talk like that. There's new advances being made all the time—"

"Oh, bullshit, Mark." Frank spat on the ground. "Sorry. That came out sterner than I meant to sound."

They halted. Mark kicked aimlessly at a root jutting from the ground. Glen crooked his rifle between his side and his arm and moved from foot to foot, trying to keep warm. Father and sons finally met each other's eyes, their breath fogging the air between them. Mark sniffed, from both the cold and his own emotions.

"Sorry," Frank apologized again. "I didn't mean to snap. But you sound like your mother, bless her heart. We've been over it with the doctors at the V.A. and at Johns Hopkins. I brought that shit back from the war, and it's been killing me ever since. I'm luckier than most. Some guys died right away. The cancer took them quick. At least I got to live a full life. I got to marry your Mom and see you two grow up. I wouldn't trade that for anything. The guys on that wall in D.C. and the ones that died of cancer after the war never got that chance."

"What about the chemo?" Glen asked.

"Didn't work," Frank replied. "And they can't cut it out either. Two months ago, it was the size of a raisin. Now, it's the size of a grape. Right smack dab in the middle of my brain. Two months from now, it'll be big as a golf ball."

"Shit," Glen said.

Frank placed an ungloved hand against the rough bark of a maple. "I feel like this tree—old. You could cut me open and count my rings. 'Here's where he was the high school quarterback, and here's where he got married, and these two are from when he became a Dad.' You know, I bet some of these trees saw this country settled. They were here with the Indians, and maybe even before that. But even trees die eventually. They rot out from the inside—just like I am."

The brothers said nothing.

"Now, promise me that you'll make sure it gets done."

"You and Mom bought those plots at Bethlehem Church," Mark reminded him. "What about those?"

"You can still put a little bit of me there." Frank smiled. "Your mother would have a fit otherwise. But just do me a favor and bring some of me along up here. Let Smitty come too. And Luke, if he wants."

Both sons nodded, wary of speech lest their voices crack.

They walked on in silence, so that the deer wouldn't know they were coming.

All of them were glad to use that excuse.

Dawn arrived.

Luke stuffed a pinch of Kodiak between his lip and gum, and snapped the lid back on the plastic can. Returning it to his jacket pocket, he rubbed his hands together briskly, then put his gloves back on and picked up the rifle.

The sun shone brightly now, a cold orb rising over the forest and fields. There were still shadows about him, especially at the tree line between the hollow and the cornfield, but even those would evaporate within the next half-hour.

In those shadows, something skittered.

Luke spotted it immediately and froze—patient and unmoving. His mouth filled with tobacco juice, and he swallowed, rather than spitting and announcing his presence. He held his breath.

Beneath the outstretched limbs, a shape emerged. He saw four legs, a mid-section, and then a head. And what a glorious head it was! Even enveloped in the murk as it was, Luke could spot the rough outline of a rack. His pulse sped up. It was a big rack— possibly a twelve-point or more.

Fuck me, he thought. His finger twitched on the trigger.

The deer bent its head, as if to sniff the ground, and Luke strained his eyes to see it better. It was useless, he realized in frustration. The shadows were too thick. He pondered a shot, but the buck stood close to the trees, almost entwined with the ones on the outer edges. Then, with a blur and a whip of branches, it vanished into the forest. Luke glimpsed a fragmentary telltale flash of white as it ran.

"White-tail, baby!"

Thumbing the safety off, he quick-stepped towards the hollow. Approaching the space where the deer had disappeared between the trees, he heard it, just beyond his line of sight. It snorted, and he caught a glimpse of it again. The sunlight had not yet penetrated the hollow, but he spied the deer's dim outline beneath the trees. Carefully, he raised the Remington to his shoulder and sighted. The deer snorted again and turned towards him. He still couldn't see its features, but he was sure the buck was staring directly at him.

He squeezed the trigger. The rifle bucked between his armpit and shoulder. It was a good pain. The deer dropped in the shadows beneath the trees. The shot echoed in his ears, rolling across the field. The others would hear it, and Luke grinned in anticipation. He'd gotten the first one. With a whoop, he crashed into the hollow, running to his unmoving kill.

The tree limbs swung shut behind him.

As he approached it, the deer stirred. Luke brought the rifle up to shoot it again, then paused, gaping. Something was wrong with the deer, because—

Because it wasn't a deer.

On the ground in front of him, the thing he'd mistaken for a twelve-point buck was unraveling itself. A coiled mass of roots and vines had twisted themselves together, mimicking a deer. Now the simulacra untied itself. The tendrils snaked back into the ground and foliage. Two roots rubbed against each other, reproducing the snorting sound he had heard. Vines whispered across the ground, rustling the dry leaves at his feet.

Something cracked behind him.

Head pounding, Luke whirled around, just as a misshapen tree limb swung toward him. It dealt a vicious blow to his mid-section. The surrounding branches splintered in tune with his ribs. He soared backward, crashing into another tree. His teeth clamped down on his tongue, and warm blood filled his mouth, mixing with the tobacco. He gagged, then screamed.

On all sides, the trees moved toward him, the dirt rippling at their advance. He ducked as a branch swiped at his head, and then spied the rifle. Even as he lurched toward it, more branches and vines swooped down, knocking both him and the Remington aside. Luke rolled through the leaves, loam filling his nostrils and mouth. He swallowed his plug of tobacco. His breath came in sharp, jagged spurts, and when he tried to scream again, all he managed was a harsh wheeze.

A mammoth, ancient oak towered over him, blocking out what little sunlight remained. A massive limb, sporting leafless branches at all angles, stabbed downward. He rolled aside just in time, but it grazed against his side where his shirttail had pulled out of his pants. The rough bark was like sandpaper, and blood welled around the bits of wood that ground into the wound.

More trees surrounded him. Luke spotted a dead girl impaled near the top of one.

How did she get up there, he wondered as shock set in. A cowbell dangled from another branch, jingling crazily. Then the trees were upon him, encircling him where he lay. Their blows fell like leaves, and Luke had one last, disjointed thought.

Timber...

Then he thought no more.

Whipping and coiling across the leaves, the roots swarmed toward him like worms, burrowing through cotton and flannel, and sinking into the soft, pliable flesh. Deeper they sank, struggling for the marrow. Then they began to drink.

Within minutes, Luke's body began to change shape. Folds of baggy skin drooped around newly-hollowed bones. His face collapsed in upon itself. Finally, all that remained of him was a loose bag of flesh, sucked dry of all fluids and marrow and tissues.

A satisfied sigh went through the forest.

Gagging from his own stench, Smitty heard the distant rifle shot as he reached the outhouse door.

"Fucker got one." He groaned, and then collapsed on the rough bench, shivering with a mixture of nausea and queasy pleasure as his bowels let loose.

He listened for more shots, but none followed.

Joe awoke in the backseat, gloom filtering through the car windows. Disoriented, he glanced at his watch. It was eight in the morning. There was no sign of Jason or Deb. He closed his eyes and lay back down. They were probably screwing in the woods and had fallen asleep. It would serve them right if a hunter stumbled across them now.

Still—something wasn't right.

He opened his eyes squinted at his watch again. Eight o'clock in the morning. So why was it so dark in the car?

Joe bolted upright.

Trees surrounded the car.

"The fuck?"

He patted his pocket, reassuring himself that both the keys and his weed were still there. He blinked, then looked again.

Jason had parked the car between the old farmhouse and the barn. That space had been vacant the night before, covered only by dead grass. Now, it had turned into a forest.

He stared uneasily at the trees. The panic didn't set in until they began to move closer.

"Holy fucking shit. Oh, fucking sweet mother of fuck!"

He sprang over the seat, frantically fishing the keys out of his pocket. A tree limb smashed down on the hood, denting it. A second tremendous blow caused the metal to crumple.

Hands trembling, Joe slid the key into the ignition and turned it. The engine turned over smoothly, despite the battering. More limbs hammered down upon the car now. The sound was terrifying. The roof buckled under the force, and the rear window imploded, spraying shards of safety glass all over the back seat where he'd been sleeping only minutes before.

He slammed the car into reverse and floored it. The rear bumper collided with a tree trunk, and Joe was thrown into the steering wheel. Whimpering, he put the car in drive and pressed the pedal again. A knotty elm and two slender birches pressed against the front fender. The tires spun uselessly.

Joe glanced to his right just as a tree limb drew back, unnaturally bending in the middle. He scrambled to the passenger side, flinging the door open just as the tree limb punched through the driver's side window. Wiry, wooden fingers grappled for him.

He tumbled out of the car and hit the ground running.

The trees swarmed the car. More rolled towards him.

The car lasted longer than Joe did.

Frank aimed, carefully lining the deer up in his scope. He squeezed the trigger and the deer jumped. It sprawled on the ground, then leapt to its feet and loped toward the cabin.

"Shit!"

"I think you hit it, Dad," Glen said. He stepped out from behind a tree several yards away.

Mark followed him. All three hovered over the spot where the deer had been. A slick of blood proved the shot had been true.

"Let's track him, boys," Frank said.

Eyes to the ground, they followed the wounded prey.

For the fifth time that morning, Smitty found himself wishing that Frank had thought to stock the outhouse with more magazines. The *Field & Stream* issue he was flipping through was two years old, and he'd read it before—and once more in the last half-hour. His buttocks were numb, but each time he stood, another cramp gripped him, forcing him to collapse back onto the seat. He longed for a copy of *Hustler*.

Something thudded against the door. Startled, his sphincter let loose again.

With one foot, he pressed against the door. It didn't budge.

"Not another fucking tree limb!"

Beneath him, in the foul pit, something moved.

Smitty glanced down between his legs just as the root rushed upward. He exhaled in pain as it slithered inside him, burrowing deep. Gasps turned to screams, then high shrieks as it wormed its way through his intestines. The skin on his extended belly began to swell around his navel. It darkened, purple, then red, as it split open. Smitty screamed one long, uninterrupted wail as the root sprouted from his stomach and began to coil around him.

Then more roots were upon him—clenching, tearing. Drinking.

Piece by piece, shred by shred, he was dragged down into the hole.

Mark was the first to notice the road.

Eyes to the ground, they'd followed the blood trail almost back to the cabin. Alert for the spatters of crimson, he saw something peculiar. The dirt road peeked up from the middle of the forest floor.

"I think we missed the cabin," he said. "Isn't this the road?"

Frank and Glen looked up in confusion.

"What the hell?" Glen gaped. "Dad, that's not part of our road is it?"

"It can't be. We're still in the—"

Smitty's distant scream cut short Frank's reply. They ran, glancing about them in bewilderment.

"That is the road," Mark shouted. "But we came out farther down."

"The road doesn't cut through the forest," Frank yelled.

"Look!" Glen pointed. "There's the cabin. What the fuck is going on, Dad?"

Smitty's screams had taken on an inhuman quality. Mark shuddered at the sound. Nothing human could make that sound. He thought of the sound the deer made when his father had shot it.

The cabin stood amid an instant forest. They watched in disbelief, then horror, as the outhouse was crushed beneath a savage onslaught of battering limbs and trunks. Smitty went silent.

Then the trees surrounding them erupted with life. Mark and Glen bounded onto the porch and turned. A limb clutched the back of their father's jacket, yanking him to a halt. A sea of brown and green flowed toward them. Mark leaped from the porch and sprinted toward his father. Grabbing the branch with both hands, he snapped it in half, freeing Frank. His father lurched forward, and the tree shuddered. Then it crawled toward them.

Regaining the porch, they piled through the door and slammed it shut. The rustling from outside was unlike anything they had ever heard. The thrashing branches raked against the walls and roof. The leaves hissed like rattlesnakes. The cabin shook under the attack. They huddled together in the center of the room as angry branches thrust themselves through the windows, grasping at items and withdrawing.

Finally, as quickly as it had begun, the assault stopped.

"I knew," Frank gasped, chest heaving. "I knew we built this thing solid."

They waited.

"Eventually," Glen said, "somebody will have to come. The game warden maybe? I mean, if we're not back by the end of the week, Mom will start to worry. She'll call somebody."

His words were slurred. Mark supposed his were, too.

The trees had tried two more assaults. The first had come an hour after their imprisonment, and the second that first night. Their father's craftsmanship had withstood both.

Their father, however, had not.

The air was different now. It felt electric and heavy, and had the sharp tang of ozone, like just before a thunderstorm.

The air had killed their father. Not the Agent Orange spiraling through his system. The air.

"Mom will come looking for us," Glen babbled. "Or Luke. Luke's probably bagged a big old buck by now, Mark. He'll drag it back soon, and then we'll be saved."

As the second day of the siege had worn on, the three of them had become nervous and irritable. Mark hadn't noticed at first. The current situation allowed for those feelings. But all three of them then suffered excruciating headaches and had trouble breathing. Frank struggled especially hard. Each labored breath became a struggle for him. And then Mark had noticed the ozone smell. He remembered a term from college—hyper-oxygenated.

The trees had surrounded the cabin in a tight ring. Then, they had begun to accelerate their photosynthetic processes, pumping out pure oxygen.

Mark remembered something else from college. Oxygen was flammable.

Frank had died an hour ago. His chest gave one final, heroic heave and then stopped. Mark was silently glad that his brother's sanity had gone before his father had.

"It's the second day of deer camp, and all the guys are here..." Glen sang happily, staring at nothing.

Mark closed his father's eyes and wept. All it would take was just one spark.

"We drink our beer and shoot the bull, but never shoot no deer."

Mark crawled towards the stove. Rising to his feet, he felt around, searching. Alerted by the sound of his movements, branches began to skitter outside. Beneath his feet, roots clawed under the hardwood floor, looking for an entrance into the cabin. They had shoved mattresses and dressers against the broken windows, and now they creaked and rattled as they were pressed against from outside.

"It's the second week of deer camp..."

Mark's fingers closed around a box of wooden matches. Hands shaking, he opened it, spilling them to the floor.

Outside the pounding began.

"Pure oxygen, Glen. That's what they're pumping in here. And all it takes is just one spark."

Glen stopped singing and looked up. "Daddy's sleeping."

"Why don't you go to sleep, too, big bro?"

"Okay, Mark. I'm very tired." He closed his eyes.

Mark lit the match.

———

STORY NOTE: Another early story, and the start of my LeHorn's Hollow mythos, which eventually led to the novels *Dark Hollow* and *Ghost Walk*. This story takes place between "Stone Tears" and *Dark Hollow*. The next story takes place after those two novels.

The cabin is based on my family cabin, built by my father on a plot of land in West Virginia that's been in our family for generations. And much like Mark in this story, I'm not a hunter. They took me deer hunting when I was fourteen, and I escaped back to my Dad's truck, where they found me later reading *Micronauts* and *Rom* comic books.

The Ghosts Of Monsters

The moon peeked down through the treetops.

"That's weird."

"What?"

"The moon is red."

Roy shrugged. "Yeah, I know."

"Wonder what made it do that?" Sally mused. "Pollution, maybe?"

"It's a hunter's moon," he explained. "That's what my daddy and my grandpa used to call it."

"Were they hunters?"

Smiling, Roy nodded. "Best damn hunters you've ever seen."

"How about you? Do you hunt?"

"Sure."

"Ever hunt *here?*"

"In LeHorn's Hollow? Nope, not yet. I usually hunt in Adams County, out by Gettysburg. I need to find a new place, though. There's too much posted property and the game are all skittish."

Roy ducked under a low-hanging branch and then pulled it out of the way until Sally had passed by. Then he performed a mock bow, making a sweeping gesture with his arm.

Sally giggled. "Thank you, sir."

"My pleasure."

They continued down the narrow, winding trail, heading deeper into the forest. The woods were dark and still. There were no birds or insects. Neither one of them minded. That just meant that their impromptu midnight stroll was mosquito-free.

Roy gripped the flashlight in one hand, moving the beam back and forth in front of them. An old blanket was tucked into the crook of his arm. His other hand held Sally's. Her long, pink nails grazed against his skin, making him shiver with excitement. The crotch of his jeans seemed to grow smaller—more confining. His erection strained against the zipper.

"This isn't really the hollow," Sally said. "That's miles from here, near that ghost walk where all those people died last year. The real hollow is all burned down now."

"Yeah, but this is still part of the same forest. People call it Le-Horn's Hollow, even if the actual hollow isn't there anymore."

"How come you never hunted here?"

Roy shrugged. "Never had the chance before. I live all the way out in Hanover. I don't get to this side of the county very often."

"So what brought you out this way tonight, then?"

He shrugged. "I don't know. Tired of drinking at the same old bar, I guess. Needed a change of scenery. Figured I'd see how things looked out this way."

Sally gave her hips a little shake. "And have you liked what you've seen?"

"So far."

"Me, too. I'm glad you decided to have a drink in my regular bar."

"You go there often?"

"Every Friday night. You come back next week, and I'll be waiting. Maybe we can do this again."

"Well, we didn't do anything yet."

"The night is young."

Roy smiled. His erection grew harder.

"So, are you married?" he asked.

"Nope."

"Boyfriend?"

She shook her head. "Nah. Only men in my life are my father and my two brothers. You'd like them. They're big hunters, too."

"Oh, yeah?"

"Yeah. Every year, they take a week off work for deer season and go up to Potter County."

Roy paused, let go of her hand, and lit a cigarette. He offered Sally one, but she declined.

"Don't worry," he said. "I've got some of those Listerine thingies in my pocket."

She took his hand again and squeezed. "I don't mind. And besides, those things burn if you—"

"What?"

She seemed flustered. "If you put one on your tongue, and then go down on somebody, it burns."

Roy's laughter echoed through the darkness. When he shined the flashlight on Sally, she was blushing.

"Don't laugh." She punched his arm playfully.

"Don't worry. I won't put one on my tongue if you don't want me to."

She arched an eyebrow. "Is that a promise of things to come?"

"We'll be doing more than that, soon as we find a good spot."

"I still don't understand why we had to come all the way out here."

"Well, not to be rude, but I don't want to get stuff on my upholstery."

"What kind of stuff?"

Now it was Roy's turn to seem flustered. "You know. Bodily fluids..."

Sally snickered. "You're really something, Roy. I'm glad I met you tonight."

"So am I."

"Still, I don't know why we couldn't have just spread that old blanket out in the cab of your truck."

He swept the flashlight beam in a wide arc, letting it glide across the dark tree trunks and boulders. "And miss all this ambience?"

"Aren't you afraid of the monsters?" Sally teased.

Roy snorted in derision. "What monsters?"

"Oh, come on. You've never heard all the legends about these woods? The Goat-Man who plays his pipes at night and seduces women? That writer guy from Shrewsbury supposedly went nuts while working on a book about him."

"Writer guy—the one who escaped from the nuthouse last year and killed those people on the ghost walk?"

"Yeah."

"Well, he was bat-shit crazy."

"But he wasn't the only one who was supposed to have seen the Goat-Man. And there's more. The black hound dog with red eyes. Balls of light that float around through the forest. Ghosts. Demons. And some people say that the trees move on their own."

"It's all bullshit," Roy said. "There's no such thing as monsters."

"You don't believe any of the stories about this place?"

"Well, I know that a lot of people have died here over the years. But that doesn't mean it was monsters. It was just people acting like people. Human beings are evil enough. We don't have to invent stories about monsters. Why? Don't tell me you believe in that stuff?"

Sally pouted. "I don't know...a little, maybe."

Roy stopped in the middle of the trail, and shined the beam across the ground. He released her hand, sat the flashlight down on a rock, and unfolded the blanket. "This looks like a good spot."

"You read my mind."

"Come here."

He pulled her close. They kissed, tongues entwining hungrily. Their hands explored each other's bodies. Sally shivered.

"You cold?"

She nodded, nuzzling his chest. "A little. And a little nervous. I mean, we just met."

"You sure that's all?"

"Well what else would it be?"

"I don't know. Maybe you're afraid of the Goat-Man."

She hugged him tighter. "You've got to admit, it is a little creepy out here at night."

"Don't worry," he said. "There are no monsters in LeHorn's Hollow."

Then he pulled out the knife and stabbed her in the neck. He let her body sag onto the blanket, and watched it jerking and twitching. Sally's eyes were wide. She clawed at the hilt jutting from her throat, and made faint gobbling noises. Her hands grew slick with her own blood. Roy could no longer contain his excitement. He pulled down his zipper and let his erection bob in the cool night air.

"No monsters," he repeated. "Just hunters, like me. The monsters are all ghosts now. I'm the real thing."

STORY NOTE: This was written for the special lettered edition of *Ghost Walk*. It takes place a year after the events of that book. I think it has a real Richard Laymon and Ed Gorman vibe to it, which pleases me to no end.

Slouching In Bethlehem

Joe woke up when Mary screamed.

For a moment, he couldn't remember why he was lying in an alley. It all came back to him with her second scream. Joe shut his eyes, stuffing his fingers in his ears to block the sound. He wished that he could fall back asleep.

Nearby, the cardboard walls of their makeshift home rustled. He considered rushing inside and stopping what was happening, but they needed the money. Instead of stopping it, he shuffled out to the sidewalk, draining the last of the cheap wine. He flung the bottle into the gutter, broken glass crunching inside the brown paper bag.

There was a dull ache in his head, where the stranger had touched him before he fell asleep. He leaned against a lamppost, trying to clear his mind. The street was deserted. Traffic in Bethlehem, Pennsylvania was never exactly abundant at this time of night, but he found himself wishing now that someone would drive by.

A yellowed scrap of last week's newspaper floated by. Joe spied the headline in the moonlight: HEROD SUSPECTED IN TWELFTH NEWBORN MURDER

Herod, the serial killer terrorizing the small city with a wave of infanticide, was one of the things they didn't have to worry about when living on the streets. Violence in the Middle East, the gutted economy, the new law calling for mandatory census participation, who the President was banging in the Oval Office—none of these things mattered out here. He'd assured Mary of this time and time again. All that mattered was the two of them—and scoring crack from Andre or one of the other hustlers.

Mary cried out again. Joe wasn't sure if it was from pleasure or pain, fear or ecstasy. He wasn't sure that he wanted to know. In contrast, the stranger inside the cardboard shelter with her was silent.

Life in the alley behind the adult video store had been good until this moment. They hadn't always been homeless, of course. Joe had once worked as a carpenter, and Mary had been a waitress. They'd been poor, but shared a love for one another.

And a love for crack.

It was that second love that had eventually brought them here. The descent led from their run-down apartment to a series of shelters—each one more heinous and decrepit than the last—before finally depositing them on the streets, in the shadow of Bethlehem's abandoned steel mills.

They tried to find refuge in one of the vacant factories or warehouses, but tribes of other homeless people had staked those out, and viciously defended them. Strangers were not welcome there, so Joe built a shelter out of cardboard boxes and scrap wood, using what little remained of his carpenter's skills.

When the gnawing pain in their stomachs became too much, they went to the soup kitchen, or the alley behind the Chinese restaurant. When hunger was replaced with the need for nicotine, they waited outside the courthouse; circling like scavenger birds as the yuppies exited their cars, lit up, took three quick puffs, and then deposited the remainder on the sidewalk before entering the building. On a good day, they could gather the half-smoked equivalent of a carton.

More important than hunger or nicotine, though, was the constant craving for more rock. That need had been especially bad when the stranger arrived.

From the moment his long shadow slid down the alley, Joe knew he wasn't from the hood. A silhouette in streetlights, the stranger stood tall and proud, seemingly unaware that he was in the worst section of the city.

Unaware or unable to care. Joe couldn't tell which, and didn't really give a fuck. The guy was probably an easy mark.

"Yo," Joe said, "you got some spare change?"

The figure stepped deeper into the alley. "Perhaps, I can offer you something better than spare change."

Joe caught a trace of an accent, but couldn't identify it.

Mary gripped Joe's forearm. "I don't like the looks of this guy. I bet he's a cop."

"How about that?" Joe asked. "You five-oh?"

"I am a soldier." The stranger spread his arms, palms turned upward, and smiled. "I have fought the Babylonians and the Sumerians, and bathed in Assyrian blood. I soared through the clouds while the first deluge covered the Earth, and while Sodom and Gomorrah burned—and again for Hiroshima and Nagasaki."

Joe had only a dim knowledge of anything past Fifth Street, but he nodded as if he understood.

"You a fighter pilot, then? Well, God bless you for that."

"God does indeed bless me, for I serve His will." The man moved closer, and his shadow covered them. "He is about to bless you, as well."

"How's that?"

"What is your name?"

"Joe."

"And this is your woman?"

"Yeah, Mary's with me."

"I would like five minutes alone with her."

Mary shrank back against the wall.

Joe jumped up, his fists clenched. "What kinda' shit you been smoking, talking to us like that?"

"I've no quarrel with you, friend. Indeed, I have traveled far to reach you. Farther than you might imagine. Do not misunderstand. My request is simple. Allow me five minutes with your woman, and you will both be richly rewarded."

Joe turned to Mary, and saw the fear and disbelief in her eyes. He crouched down beside her.

"We need the money, baby," he said. "Andre ain't gonna give us no freebies. We're both jonesing. Dude only wants five minutes. Says he'll pay."

Mary frowned. "So you're my pimp now? Fuck you!"

"It ain't like that, Mary. You know I love you. But we got no choice. We need to score and we need money to do it. It's just one time. Five minutes, baby! Five minutes and then we can find Andre and hook up."

Before she could answer, he turned back to the stranger.

"Five minutes, right?"

"Correct. I will not harm her."

"You got a deal."

"Excellent." The stranger stepped forward. His hand darted out, fingers pressing into Joe's forehead.

"Sleep."

Joe's last thought, before collapsing to the pavement, was that he hadn't asked the stranger how much he was paying.

Quivering in the darkness, Mary held the stranger tightly even after it was over.

"Damn," she whispered. "That wasn't what I expected. What's your name?"

The man smiled, slipping back into his business suit. "It is never wise to ask for someone's name. Names have power. That is one of the most important universal laws. It is better to ask what one prefers to be called."

She shook her head and stretched, relishing the feeling of satisfaction that washed over her. "So what are you called, then?"

"I am called many things. It depends on many factors. Some call me Djibril, of the El-Karrubiyan, those brought near to Allah. Others call me Gabriel, of the Cherubim."

"Cherubim," she repeated, pulling her soiled jeans over her scabbed, scrawny legs. "Never heard of it. You a stock broker or something?"

"Hardly." His laughter was melodious.

"Well, now that you told me your real name, doesn't that give me power, like you said?" Visions of blackmail swam in her head. Headlines trumpeting: WALL STREET TYCOON IN TRYST WITH HOMELESS WOMAN. She finished dressing.

"I have indeed given you power, Mary, but not as you suspect. You are highly favored by our Lord, and unto you has been given His highest blessing. Even now, you are with child—His child. You are to name him Prosper, for his birth will usher in a new age of prosperity for those favored by the Lord, even at the worst hour. His middle name is to be Christ, which means teacher, for that is what he will be. He is to educate the world, before the trials begin. Understand something. We are undoing a terrible mistake. The Trinity has been split asunder for too long now. We are rejoining it."

She stared at him in disbelief. Deep inside, she felt his seed. It wasn't cold and slimy and didn't drip down her thighs like Joe's did. It pulsed, throbbing as it burrowed inside her—and suddenly it burned. It felt like the john had ejaculated molten lava.

"You're crazy."

Gabriel turned to face her. "No, I am tired. Very tired. And yet, I am not anxious for it to end. I shall—miss...all of this." He waved his hand in the air. "The time draws near, and I've but one more role to play, now that we've finished. But that must wait until the trumpet sounds."

The burning in her loins subsided, and Mary wondered idly if he'd given her some disease. She finished fastening her bra, and then looked up to ask him.

The stranger was gone.

Sighing, she reached beneath her jeans and panties to scratch. Her fingers brushed against her still swollen sex, and she shivered with an aftershock of pleasure. Her finger slid deeper, and then she gasped, withdrawing it in disbelief.

Her hymen had grown back.

Had it not been for the swelling of her abdomen, and the fact that her periods stopped, Mary wouldn't have believed she was pregnant. There was no morning sickness, and no cravings—neither pickles and ice cream, or crack and cigarettes.

They'd scored from Andre immediately after the transaction with the stranger. When Joe had passed the makeshift soda can crack pipe to her, Mary became violently ill. Cigarettes and liquor had the same effect. She quit all three.

Spring turned into sweltering summer, and the headlines reflected the change in the weather. Two terrorist cells had been discovered in Los Angeles and Miami, both within days of acting on their plots. The construction of a new Globe Corporation skyscraper had stalled, delayed by union battles. In Brackard's Point, New York, a rapist was on the loose, wearing a Casper the Ghost mask and a smile. A bus driver in Philadelphia fell asleep at the wheel, plowing into a crowd of people waiting for him. In San Francisco, medical workers reported that the number of young, gay males actively seeking HIV-positive partners to infect them was at crisis level proportions. In Chinatown, a back-alley abortionist had been charged with selling discarded fetuses to medicine men. Overseas, the news was even worse. The President of New Palestine and the Prime Minister of Israel swore they were committed to peace, even as their armies slaughtered innocents on both sides, and now it appeared as if Saudi Arabia, Egypt, Syria, Iran, and the rest of the Middle East would be joining the fray, backed by weapons from the re-communized Soviet states. Four million people were dead of AIDS and Ebola on the African continent, and SARS had claimed half that number in Asia.

But in Bethlehem and surrounding towns, Herod overshadowed all of this.

Twenty-seven newborn male infants were dead, butchered like livestock. Police were no closer to catching the killer, or if they were, they weren't telling the press. Armed guards had been posted at maternity wards across the United States, despite the fact that all of the slayings had taken place in or near Bethlehem. On the cable news networks, the politicians and media talking heads argued over who was responsible and what could be done. Some called it terrorism. Others cried serial killer, or even a team of predators. The country was paralyzed, terrified. The Herod slayings were worse than a suburban sniper, worse than a schoolyard shoot-out, even worse than a hijacked airplane flying into a building. The psychological and emotional scars ran deep, and people wondered if this truly was the beginning of the End Times.

Nine months later, in a cardboard shelter in the alley behind the adult video store, Mary's water broke. Joe made preparations to take her to the clinic.

At the entrance to the alley, another shadow fell across them.

STORY NOTE: Another early tale. Prosper Johnson (the baby Mary is carrying) is important to my overall Labyrinth mythos, although readers haven't seen much of him yet. As of this writing, he only appears in one other short story, and is mentioned a few brief times in other novels. Suffice to say, you'll be seeing more of him, and of the serial killer known as

Herod. In fact, look for Herod's path to cross that of The Exit (the serial killer featured earlier in this collection). Gabriel has since popped up in *Take The Long Way Home*, where he indeed had something to do after the trumpet had sounded.

Marriage Causes Cancer In Rats

"It's terminal, Mr. Newton."

Harold stared across the desk. "I'm sorry?"

"Your cancer. Chemotherapy and surgery would be ineffective at this point. Had we caught it earlier, perhaps... I don't understand, Mr. Newton. You had substantial health insurance. Why didn't you come in earlier, at the first sign?"

"I thought they were cysts," Harold told him. "I used to get them all the time when I was a kid. But they were always benign. Just calcium and fatty tissues, they said. It wasn't until the one showed up on my—well, my penis, that I got scared. Can't you cut them out?"

"Not at this point. The cancer has metastasized."

"I think God is trying to kill me," Harold said.

The doctor gave him a puzzled half-smile.

On his way to the car, Harold's vision blurred. He stopped, took several deep breaths, and closed his eyes, waiting for it to pass. Then he opened his eyes again, slid behind the wheel and put the key in the ignition. His hands were trembling.

For the first time in a week, he thought of Marcy, and of Harry Jr. and little Danielle.

And Cecelia.

He began to sob.

*   *   *

On the way home, he called headquarters in Dayton, and told his Regional Manager that he needed a few weeks off, and that somebody else would need to fill in as Store Manager for him. He confided about the cancer, but not the prognosis. The RM agreed that Will, Harold's Assistant Manager, was the obvious choice.

Then Harold stopped into the store and advised Will that he would be running the show. He explained to his sales staff that they'd have to sell big screen TV's and DVD players by themselves for the next few weeks, and that Will was in charge while he was gone.

He didn't tell them about the cancer, but he could see the pity reflected in their eyes just the same. Harold knew what they were thinking: *Poor guy. He's still taking their deaths pretty hard.*

Harold felt the scream welling up from deep inside, and he left the store before it could escape. In the parking lot, the shakes returned and he realized that his face was wet again. He wondered if he'd been crying in front of his employees, and decided that he didn't care. Fuck them and their pity. It was an accusation, even if they didn't know it. It was an accusation because he knew. He knew what they didn't. He hadn't asked for their pity or consolations. Consolation was like a judgment, and though they didn't know, that didn't stop them from judging him just the same.

They didn't know that he'd killed his family.

Or that he'd killed Cecelia, too.

Beneath his skin, Harold's tumors began to throb.

He stopped off at The Coliseum for a drink, and ended up having several. He slammed his fifth shot of Maker's Mark, tried to concentrate on watching the Ravens get their asses handed to them, and found that he couldn't. Those same looks, those knowing stares of pity, followed him here. He saw it reflected in the eyes of the bartender and of the regulars.

He'd never brought Cecelia here, thank God for that. There was nobody to add two plus two, nobody who could say they saw them together. His only tie to the slim dancer was her signature on the receipt for the thirty-two inch Panasonic and matching DVD player he'd sold her, and that was over a year and a half ago.

"Want another one, Harold?" The bartender nodded at his empty shot glass.

He held up his hand, shaking his head. "No, I'm not feeling so good. Think I'm gonna head home."

"You don't look so good, if you don't mind me saying so."

"It's the flu, probably." Harold pulled out his wallet and placed a pile of bills on the bar. His family stared back at him and he snapped the wallet closed. "One of the guys at work had it, and I think he spread it to the whole damn store."

The bartender leaned toward him, his expression that of a conspirator. "That's not what I mean, Harold."

"Well, what then?"

The big man fumbled for the words. "You look—lost. I dunno. Like you're feeling guilty or something."

Harold jumped.

"It's okay, man," the bartender continued, "I know how it must be, going through this, all by yourself."

"You do?" Harold's voice was a whisper.

"Sure I do, man. I mean, how longs it been? Year and a half? Two years almost? You're lonely and you miss your wife, but you don't want to hook up with anybody again because you'd feel guilty. You'd feel like you were cheating on Marcy. But look man, what happened to your family wasn't your fault. You need to—"

Harold didn't hear the rest. The blood pounding in his ears sounded like an onrushing freight train.

He turned and ran out of the bar.

The tumors hurt the whole way home. Stuck in traffic on Interstate 83, the car next to him blasted rap music with the bass cranked to a thunderous level. Wave after wave of sound crashed over Harold and his tumors throbbed with each beat. He reached into the glove compartment, grabbed the aspirin, and downed two of them, grimacing at the taste. With each beat of his heart, there was a twinge in his chest. It hurt to breathe. Then the pain faded, replaced by the ache in his hand. Groaning, he flexed his fingers.

As the traffic crawled along, he shifted his weight, trying to get comfortable. The pain in his hand and chest had shifted to his back and groin, and each movement was agony.

The rap song in the car next to his was over. Now, a pop princess was mangling Elvis Presley's 'Are You Lonesome Tonight'.

"Is your heart filled with pain? Shall I come back again..."
The traffic started to move, and Harold gripped the wheel. He turned his own stereo on in retaliation, searching for escape.
"I used to love her, but I had to kill her..."
Cursing, Harold stabbed the eject button and flung the CD out the window.

He coughed, tasted blood, and reached for two more aspirin. He considered it for a moment, pondering the dangers of consuming aspirin along with the drinks he'd had at the bar, and then swallowed them anyway. What was the worst thing that could happen? He'd die? He was dying anyway, according to the doctor.

By the time he arrived home, Harold could barely stand. He felt the bile rising, and just made it to the toilet when the aspirin, the whiskey, and something that looked like part of his guts came spewing out. When it was over, he wiped his mouth with the back of his hand. It came away red.

He collapsed onto the bed and curled into a ball. He lay there moaning.

Eventually, he slept.

At first, the dreams were nothing more than memories.

It had all been Thom's fault.

Thom Fox had applied for a salesperson's job that October. Harold was short-handed (Branson had been transferred to another store, and the god-damned Nock kid had quit) and the Christmas season was right around the corner. Christmas was their busiest time—a time when all of the salesmen would be working long hours, and when Harold himself would be working seven days a week, open to close. Fortunately, they would also make a lot of money. The salesmen earned commission off of every item they sold, and Harold's managerial bonus was based on their sales volume. Between Thanksgiving and Christmas, they could easily make seventy-five percent of their yearly commission. After the holidays, things would slow down again until air conditioner season.

Despite the fact that Thom Fox had no previous home electronics experience, and even though he looked disheveled and spoke slower than turtle shit, Harold hired him. He had no choice. He needed cannon fodder—somebody to fill in the gaps while the rest of his staff hustled and bustled and glad-handed and asked "How can I help you folks today" or said "Yes, this is the top of the line." Maybe the kid would get lucky, and sell a few microwaves and car stereos. Except the kid couldn't sell, and to help the store's performance (and his own paycheck) Harold began closing Thom's deals.

That was how he'd met Cecelia Ramirez. She'd had her eye on a TV (a Christmas present to herself, she'd said) but was still hesitant. Thom asked Harold to get involved and close the sale.

She was beautiful—a Cuban immigrant with skin the color of light coffee. She had long, raven-black hair that flowed with her every movement. She was slender, graceful, and Harold learned that she was a dancer at the Foxy Lady downtown. Her low-cut jeans hugged her hips in just the right places, and her belly ring gleamed like a diamond.

Harold talked up the television, demonstrating the twin tuner picture-in-picture technology, the black screen for better picture quality, and the benefits of the universal remote. As he did, he felt himself hardening. He was embarrassed, and tried to turn away, but she brushed up lightly against him, smiling as she did.

"It look's awfully hard to hook up," she purred, and her accent almost sent him over the edge right there in the store. He chuckled nervously and backed away.

Her eyes dropped to his crotch and then rose back to his face. "Do you have someone who can hook it up for me?"

"Normally, our salespeople are glad to come to your home and do the installation. You pay them directly for the service. But I'm the manager, and since you're buying the DVD player too, I guess I could do it this evening—no charge."

It had been that easy. He'd read about it (in those phony letters to Penthouse) and seen it in the movies, but he'd never expected it to happen to him. Harold was thirty-nine, and middle-age had begun to settle upon him. His six-pack abs were lost beneath a small pot belly, and his thinning hair had just begun to sprout some strands of gray. Despite that, this beautiful creature wanted him.

He'd shown up that night, hooked up the television and DVD player, and then accepted her offer of a drink. Half an hour later, they were undressing each other on her couch. They made love in the bedroom, and when Harold awoke at four in the morning, his heart pounded with apprehension.

When he arrived home, Marcy and the kids were sleeping soundly. He hadn't been missed. They never missed him. Things hadn't been good with Marcy for a long time.

"You have my heart." That's what Harold had told her through their first few years of their marriage, holding her at night when she worried about the bills or having children or affording to buy a home.

You have my heart...

By the time he slept with Cecilia, Marcy no longer held that position, and hadn't for quite some time. In the years before the affair, he'd thought often of leaving her, but then Harold Jr. came along, followed a few years later by Danielle. He'd tried to make it all right—to enjoy what he had. Playing baseball in the backyard with Harry and giving horsy rides to Danielle until his back ached. But thirty came and went, and Harold grew resentful. The three of them were like anchors, weighing him down. Marcy was distant, and their lovemaking was nothing more than a ghost—murdered by valiums and antidepressants. Harry Jr. grew into a sullen pre-teen, a stranger, and Danielle decided that she much preferred her mother's company.

His father had died at sixty, his grandfather at sixty-two. The odds didn't look good for him either. That meant his life was half over. At times, Harold could feel his mortality approaching, as surely as the hands ticking on a clock. Cecilia changed that. That first month with her, he felt alive again. He hadn't felt that way since college. She told him she loved him during the second month, murmured it into his neck as he thrust into her. He'd reciprocated the words in the dark, and meant them. She said she wanted him for herself, and made promises in the dark.

Now the dream shifted, as if on fast-forward.

"Don't sweat it," Tony assured him. "We'll make it look like she took off with the kids. The cops will never suspect a thing, as long as you've got your alibi—and as long as you keep your mouth shut."

"Of course I will." Harold was sweating. "Come on, Tony! How long have you guys known me? I've sold Mr. Marano every piece of equipment he's got in his house. You know I wouldn't do that."

"You got the money?" Vince asked around a mouthful of pasta.

Harold handed it to them, and as the envelope exchanged hands he thought, *There's no turning back now. Good. That's good. I'm doing this for Cecelia.*

"How will you—" he began to ask, and then realized he didn't want to know.

Tony took the envelope from Vince and placed it inside his jacket. "We don't ask you why a four-head VCR is better than a two-head. You don't ask us how we do our job. Keep your mouth shut."

But Harold hadn't kept his mouth shut. When his family vanished, Cecelia had been properly sympathetic at first, but Harold could see the relief and sheer glee beneath the surface. Two months later, after an especially frenetic bout of lovemaking, he had told her the truth.

Her reaction was not what he expected, but watching it now through the lens of a dream, Harold didn't know what he had expected. Certainly not for her to slap him, or to reach for the phone, threatening to call the police, which was what she had done.

It replayed in his mind—the struggle, his hands around her throat, her nightgown open beneath him, and as she thrashed, he was both horrified and excited to find that he was aroused again.

After, he'd called Tony, frantic and almost speechless from exertion and shock.

"Don't sweat it," Tony had told him again. "We've got a guy down on Roosevelt Avenue that can take care of these things. But it'll cost you. From now on, when Mr. Marano wants a new piece of equipment, we'll expect it for more than the standard manager's discount. And we'll want to help ourselves to your warehouse from time to time."

Now the dream shifted from memory to the surreal, because as the gangsters were rolling the trash bags over her, Cecelia opened her eyes and spoke to him.

"I'll be back, lover."

Harold screamed, and was still screaming when the phone awoke him. He sat up, bolts of pain going off behind his eyes. He felt funny. Weighted. He fumbled for the phone in the dark.

"Hello?"

"Harold? It's Will."

"What time is it?"

"Umm...nine o'clock. Did I wake you?"

"It's okay. What's up?"

"Well, there're two guys down here. I've seen them in the store before—customers of yours. They say they want a fifty-six inch Magnavox and to put it on the Marano account, but I can't find any record of financing or—"

Harold cut him off. "Give them what they want. Set up delivery. I'll take care of it when I come back."

Will said something in reply, but Harold didn't hear it, because the words were drowned out by a voice in his ear.

"Horsy ride, Daddy. Give me a horsy ride."

Harold gasped.

"Harold, what's wrong?"

"I'm alright, Will. Sorry. A spider ran across the bed."

Another voice whispered in the dark. "I have your heart, Harold. Isn't that what you used to tell me?"

"Is there someone else there, Harold? I didn't mean to interrupt."

"Will, I've gotta go."

He hung up, cutting Will off in mid-sentence, and turned on the light.

His wife's face stared back at him from his chest.

"I have your heart," the face on the tumor repeated. The voice was squeaky, but undeniably Marcy's. The tumor had grown to the size of an apple, and now protruded from the area directly above his heart.

Harold grabbed the sheets, noticing again how heavy his hand felt. He glanced down, and his son smiled back at him. The tumor on his hand wore his son's face, and a second one, the size of a toothpick, had begun to sprout from between his fingers. It looked remarkably like a miniature arm. It's tiny fingers waved at him.

"Want to toss the ball around in the backyard, Dad?"

Harold swung his feet to the floor and tried to get out of bed. The pressing weight on his back almost bore him to the floor, and he heard Danielle's voice again, pleading insistently in his ear "Horsy ride, Daddy. Giddy up!"

He crawled on all fours, while his family chattered at him in their cartoon voices. His wife shook her head back and forth, and seemed to stretch. The tumor grew bigger, now covering his breast.

With a sudden terrible clarity, Harold paused, and with his good hand, lifted the waistband of his boxer shorts and peeked inside.

Cecelia grinned back at him from the head of his penis.

*　　*　　*

"How may I help you?"

The man on the other end of the line was shouting above the clamoring voices in the background.

"My name is Harold Newton! I need to speak to Doctor Rahn!"

"I'm sorry sir, this is Doctor Rahn's answering service. He's unavailable for the evening. Is this an emergency?"

In the background, a child laughed, and the caller screamed in pain.

"Yes, this is a fucking emergency! Tell him we have to cut the tumors out! We've got to remove them!"

"Please calm down, Mr. Newton. What seems to be the trouble?"

The only answer was a long, anguished howl, and more laughter.

"Please hold the line, Mr. Newton. I'll get an emergency operator on the line for you and send help to your location."

"No time! I'll have to do it myself! Please hurry! Tell them—"

The line went dead.

When the paramedics and police arrived, they found Marcy Newton and her children watching television in the living room, along with a woman they identified as a friend of the family, a woman named Cecelia Ramirez. There was no sign of Harold, and when the police returned the next day for further questioning, the family and the Ramirez woman had vanished as well.

———

STORY NOTE: I wrote this for an anthology about murderous families. The editor requested a story in which one family member killed another. The characters of Tony and Vince, their mysterious boss Mr. Marano, and the "guy down on Roosevelt Avenue" have only a small walk-on roll in this tale, but they've had much bigger parts in several of my other works, particularly the novels Clickers 2, Clickers 3, and Clickers vs. Zombies (all co-written with J.F. Gonzalez), and the short stories "The Siqqusim Who Stole Christmas" and "Crazy For You" (the latter of which was co-written with Mike Oliveri).

Golden Boy

I shit gold.

It started around the time I hit puberty. I thought there was something wrong with me. Cancer or parasites or something like that, because when I looked down into the bowl, a golden turd was sitting on the bottom. When I wiped, there were gold stains on the toilet paper. Then I flushed and went back to watching cartoons. Ten minutes later, I'd forgotten all about it.

You know how kids are.

But it wasn't just my shit. I pissed gold. (No golden showers jokes, please. I've heard them all before). I started sweating gold. It oozed out of my pores in little droplets, drying on my skin in flakes. It peeled off easily enough. Just like dead skin after a bad case of sunburn. Then my spit and mucous started turning into gold. I'd hock gold nuggets onto the sidewalk. One day, I was picking mulberries from a tree in a pasture. There was a barbed-wire fence beneath the tree, and to reach the higher branches, I stood on the fence. I lost my balance and the barbed-wire took three big chunks out of the back of my thigh. My blood was liquid gold. And like I said, this was around puberty, so you can only imagine what my wet dreams were like. Many nights, instead of waking up wet and sticky, I woke up with a hard, metallic mess on my sheets and in my pajamas.

Understand, my bodily fluids weren't just gold colored. If they had been, things might have turned out differently. But they were actual gold—that precious metal coveted all over the world. Gold—the source of wars and peace, the rise of empires and their eventual collapse, murders and robberies, wealth and poverty, love and hate.

My parents figured it out soon enough. So did the first doctor they took me to. Oh, yeah. That doctor was very interested. He wanted to keep me for observation. Wanted to conduct some more tests. He said all this with his doctor voice but you could see the greed in his eyes.

And he was just the first.

Mom and Dad weren't having any of that. They took me home and told me this was going to be our little secret. I was special. I had a gift from God. A wonderful, magnificent talent—but one that might be misunderstood by others. They wanted to help me avoid that, they said. Didn't want me to be made fun of or taken advantage of. Even now, I honestly think they meant it at the time. They believed that their intentions were for the best. But you know what they say about good intentions. The road to hell is paved with them. That's bullshit, of course.

The road to hell is paved with fucking gold.

My parents started skimming my residue. Mom scraped gold dust from my clothes and the sheets when she did laundry and from the rim of my glass after dinner. One night, they told me I couldn't watch my favorite TV show because I wouldn't eat my broccoli. I cried gold tears. After that, it seemed like they made me cry a lot.

Everywhere I went, I left a trail of gold behind me. My parents collected it, invested it, and soon, we moved to a bigger house in a nicer neighborhood with a better school. Our family of three grew. We had a maid and a cook and groundskeepers.

I hated it, at first. The new house was too big. We'd been a blue-collar family. Now, Mom and Dad didn't work anymore and I suddenly found myself thrown into classrooms with a bunch of snobby rich kids—all because of my gift. I had nothing in common with my classmates. They talked about books and music that I'd never heard of, and argued politics and civic responsibilities and French Impressionism. They idolized Che Guevara and Ayn Rand and Ernest Hemingway. I read comic books and listened to hip-hop and liked Spider-Man.

So I tried to fit in. Nobody wants to be hated. It's human nature—wanting to be liked by your peers. Soon enough, I found a way. I let them in on my little secret. Within a week, I was the most popular kid in school. I had more friends than I knew what to do with. Everybody wanted to be friends with the golden boy. But here's the thing. They didn't want to be friends with me because of who I was. They wanted to be friends with me because of *who* I was. There's a big difference between those two things.

So I had friends. Girlfriends, too.

I remember the first girl I ever loved. She was beautiful. There's nothing as powerful or pure or unstable as first love. I thought about her constantly. Stared at her in class. Dreamed of her at night. And when she returned my interest, my body felt like a coiled spring. It was the happiest day of my life. But she didn't love me for who I was. Like everyone else, she loved me for *who* I was.

So have all the rest. Both ex-wives and the string of long-term girlfriends between them. My happiest relationships are one night stands. The only women I'm truly comfortable with are the ones I only know for a few brief hours. I never tell them who I am or what I can do. And before you ask, yes, I always wear a condom and no, I can't have children. There are no little golden boys in my future. I don't shoot blanks. I shoot bullets.

I've no shortage of job opportunities. Banks, financial groups, precious metals dealers, jewelers, even several governments. Of course, I don't need to work. I can live off my talent for the rest of my life. So can everyone else around me. But that doesn't stop the employment offers from coming. And they're so insincere and patronizing. So very fucking patronizing. They want to invest in my future. Just like my parents and my friends and my wives, they only want what's best for me. Or so they claim.

But I know what they really want.

And I can't take it anymore.

I'm spent. My gold is tarnished. It's lost its gleam. Its shine. I can see it, and I wonder if others are noticing, too.

Here's what's going to happen. I'm going to put this gun to my head and blow my brains out all over the room, leaving a golden spray pattern on the wall. The medical examiner will pick skull fragments and gold nuggets out of the plaster. The mortician can line his pockets before embalming me. You can sell my remains on eBay, and invest in them, and fight over what's left.

I want to fade away, but gold never fades. This is my gift. This is my legacy. This is my curse.

I have only one thing to leave behind.
You can spend me when I'm gone.

———

STORY NOTES: The first and last sentences of this story came to me one day, and I liked them so much that I wrote a story to tie them together. Author Kelli Owen read this story prior to its publication, and said it was a metaphor for my current place in the horror genre. But Kelli is quite possibly mentally ill, and she says that about all of my work. Plus, I'm fairly certain she was drunk when she read it. Take from "Golden Boy" what you will, but I just think it's a quirky and kind of fun fable. Not a metaphor, and (hopefully) not a prediction of the future.

BRIAN KEENE is the author of over twenty-five books, including *Darkness on the Edge of Town, Take The Long Way Home, Urban Gothic, Castaways, Kill Whitey, Dark Hollow, Dead Sea,* and *The Rising.* He's also written comic books such as *The Last Zombie, Doom Patrol* and *Dead of Night: Devil Slayer.* His work has been translated into German, Spanish, Polish, Italian, French and Taiwanese. Several of his novels and stories have been developed for film, including *Ghoul* and *The Ties That Bind.* In addition to writing, Keene also oversees Maelstrom, his own small press publishing imprint specializing in collectible limited editions, via Thunderstorm Books. Keene's work has been praised in such diverse places as *The New York Times,* The History Channel, The Howard Stern Show, CNN.com, *Publisher's Weekly,* Media Bistro, *Fangoria Magazine,* and *Rue Morgue Magazine.* Keene lives in Pennsylvania. You can communicate with him online at www.briankeene.

Made in the USA
San Bernardino, CA
19 September 2014